CROSS
& CROWN

A SIDEWINDER STORY

ABIGAIL
ROUX

RIPTIDE
PUBLISHING

Riptide Publishing
PO Box 6652
Hillsborough, NJ 08844
www.riptidepublishing.com

Cross & Crown (A Sidewinder Story)

Cover Art by L.C. Chase, http://lcchase.com/design.htm
Editor: Rachel Haimowitz
Layout: L.C. Chase, http://lcchase.com/design.htm

ISBN: 978-1-62649-132-8

First edition
June, 2014

Also available in ebook:
ISBN: 978-1-62649-133-5

CROSS & CROWN

A SIDEWINDER STORY

ABIGAIL ROUX

I wish to have no connection with any ship that does not sail fast, for I intend to go in harm's way.

—John Paul Jones, 1778

TABLE OF CONTENTS

CHAPTER 1

Detective Nick O'Flaherty climbed out of the unmarked car and took the opportunity to stretch his back as he looked around the chaotic downtown crime scene. Gawkers were lined up at a checkpoint near a narrow side-road intersection, even though it was barely sunup. An ambulance sat with its lights off near the storefront. Uniforms milled around, waiting for the coroner to show up.

"Hey, Tommy," Nick said as one of the uniforms approached him. "How're your girls?"

"Same as always, Detective, running the show. How's your first week back off desk duty?"

"Blissfully boring. What've we got?" Nick asked him.

"Looks like a smash and grab gone wrong. Old bookstore. Shop's all busted up. Two dead."

"IDs?" Nick asked as he pulled a pair of latex gloves from his coat pocket.

"One's the shop owner. We're still waiting on the ID for the other. But there's something else you got to see."

Nick's partner joined them, brushing against Nick's shoulder. "Something besides the dead bodies?"

The officer nodded. "Good morning, Detective Hagan. Yes, we got a witness."

"Hallefuckinlujah," Nick muttered as he followed.

"Don't thank your lucky stars just yet."

Nick repressed a groan as Tommy led them toward some evidence tags in the middle of the road.

"This is where they found him," Tommy said.

"In the road?" Nick asked.

"On the ground?" Hagan added.

"Yes, sirs. Thought he was another body at first."

"Where is he?" Nick asked.

"Hospital."

Hagan smacked Nick on the arm. "That's why they gave us this one. So you could go question him and not fuck up a crime scene."

"Hey," Nick grunted.

"You're the people person who donated half his liver to his dad," Hagan said. "You take the easy part, I'll go get coffee."

Nick grunted as his stocky partner trundled off toward one of the trucks. Hagan and his love affair with coffee were a bane of Nick's existence.

Nick glanced around the scene again. The front windows of the store had been busted out, probably shattered by the gunfire. Two bodies were sprawled on the sidewalk in front. Shelves of books inside had been toppled, the interior a mess of old tomes. Dust motes floated in the floodlights. Standing behind the barricades was a mass of onlookers.

Nick sighed heavily and scanned the crowd. He didn't see anyone who looked like they might be trying to offer information, just a bunch of people with nothing better to do than gawk as the sun rose. Then his eyes landed on someone who looked familiar. Tall, broad shoulders, dark hair. He was wearing sunglasses, and his turned-up coat collar hid some of his face.

But Nick thought he recognized him. He started toward the barriers. "Garrett?"

The man ducked his head and disappeared into the crowd. Nick trailed to a stop. Zane Garrett would not have ignored Nick's greeting. Nick had obviously been mistaken.

When Hagan returned with two steaming cups of coffee, they climbed back into their unmarked, and Nick dumped his coffee into the street before closing the door and heading off for the hospital to check on their witness.

Hagan's coffee, and apparently his patience along with it, were reaching the dregs when they finally found the room their witness had been moved to after his MRI and CT scans and whatever else they'd put the poor guy through. An officer was on the door, and a nurse was in the room checking the man's vitals.

He was sitting on the edge of his bed, a blanket around his shoulders. He had his head down. His hair was light and wavy, and he had a day's worth of stubble. There was a bandage on his neck that seemed to stretch up into his hairline. He was wearing jeans and a blue cardigan, and his shoulder was covered in blood. He certainly wasn't dressed for midnight acrobatics like a robbery, and though his current state spoke of more than just one bad night in a row, he didn't ping Nick as an addict.

Nick slid his suit jacket aside to show his badge before approaching the witness. "Morning, sir," he said.

The man looked up. He was haggard, with circles under his eyes. But he was handsome regardless, with eyes that were an unnervingly clear blue. And he seemed confused and scared. Nick couldn't really blame him.

"I'm Detective O'Flaherty. This is Detective Hagan. Were you hurt this morning, sir?"

The man stared at Nick for a few seconds, his eyes glazing over. He blinked and focused his attention back on Nick. When he spoke, his accent wasn't local. It was so far from local that Nick couldn't begin to place it, other than he sounded a little Southern and a little British. It might have even been fake. "They said I was shot in the head."

Nick could think of nothing to say to that. He glanced at the nurse for confirmation.

"He took a glancing blow. It knocked him unconscious, but didn't penetrate the skull. And I told you to stay in bed," she said, forcing the witness to recline and covering him with a sheet.

Nick gaped at her. "Jesus."

The witness cleared his throat and fiddled with the sheet, obviously uncomfortable.

"What's your name, sir?" Nick asked him.

"I don't know." He looked back at Nick, his expression sincerely distressed.

Nick sniffed and scratched at his chin, not sure whether to be annoyed or concerned. Either the man was exceptionally good at stonewalling, or he had a serious case of traumatic amnesia. "All right. Can you tell me what happened this morning?"

"No, I'm sorry. I don't remember. I don't know."

"What *do* you know?"

"I know I got shot in the head."

"You don't remember anything?"

The witness winced. "No."

"You don't remember your name."

"No, Detective. I'm sorry."

Nick nodded and carefully patted the man on the shoulder. He turned to his partner, who stood near the doorway. Hagan had both eyebrows raised, his jaw working back and forth. Nick excused himself, and he and Hagan moved into the hallway, leaning their heads close to talk.

The officer on the door offered what little he knew. "He's got no ID on him. Nothing; looks like whoever shot him thought he was dead and picked him clean."

Hagan huffed. "So not only do we got a witness who's got no idea what happened, he's got no idea who he is?" He barely restrained an incredulous laugh. "That's not a witness, it's another motherfucking crime."

Nick glanced over his shoulder through the door, to the man on the hospital bed. "No ID, no memory, shot in the head in the middle of a gunfight outside a robbery of a used bookstore. What. The. Fuck."

"This ain't a robbery," Hagan said with a grunt. "You don't shoot three people for an old book, I don't care if it's the Gutenberg Bible."

Nick nodded. "You realize this guy could be the doer."

"You think he's faking?"

"He's either a very lucky witness who lived through this, a perp who legit can't remember, or he's faking." Nick shrugged.

"You were spec ops. You were trained to lie and shit. Can you tell if he's lying?"

"Yeah, but if he's faking, he's damn good at it, 'cause I'm leaning toward believing him."

They both turned to the witness again. He was once again sitting in bed with his head hanging and his eyes closed. His hands were trembling as they clenched at the blanket in his lap. The nurse had left him.

"What do we do?" Hagan asked.

Nick was at a loss. Did they treat the man as a witness or a suspect? "Either way, if he's a perp or he's a witness, he'll need someone on him," he finally said.

Hagan patted Nick's shoulder. "Great. You go break the news to him, I'm going to get some coffee."

Nick glared after his partner as the man lumbered off toward the nurses' station. He took a deep breath to steady himself. It wasn't his first case back since his surgery, but it was his first case back from behind a desk. He hadn't been dealing with people lately so much as paperwork.

The witness looked up when Nick approached, and tried to straighten his shoulders, but they slumped again, probably under the weight of his injury and exhaustion.

Nick's heart went out to him, and he had to fight to keep his attitude professional. "I'm going to have this officer stay with you in the hospital until they release you. Keep an eye on you. Then he's going to bring you the station to talk with us a little more. That sound okay?"

The man nodded, then winced and brought his hand up to his bandage. "You think I'm in danger?"

Nick chewed on his lip for a second. "It's a real possibility, I won't lie."

"It's also a possibility I shot those people, isn't it?"

Nick stared at him, shocked again by the man's strange mix of perception and vulnerability. "That is also a possibility, yes."

The witness rubbed a trembling hand over his face. Nick placed a hand on his shoulder in an attempt to offer comfort. The man reached up and gripped his fingers hard. He didn't raise his head or say anything. He just seemed to need the contact.

"It'll be okay," Nick whispered. "We'll figure this out."

"So, we got the shopkeeper's daughter coming in to try to ID the body," Hagan told Nick, returning from the station break room with two cups of coffee. They'd been partners for almost three years and Hagan still couldn't remember that Nick didn't drink coffee.

Hagan set the cup down in front of him, steaming and giving off a sickeningly strong smell.

"Throw that away," Nick ordered.

"Whatever. You're welcome." Hagan sat and chucked his feet up on the desk opposite Nick's. They were set up facing each other. Nick glared at the coffee cup, then his partner. Hagan gave him a toothy smile. "What else we got working?"

"Prints are going through the system for the other victim, and the amnesiac witness." Nick held up a photograph from the crime scene. "Aside from the fact that the perps apparently riffled the bookshelves and made a damn mess of everything, the only things that seem to be missing were in this display cabinet." He set it down and slid it across to Hagan. "Don't get your coffee near that."

"Yes, Mother." Hagan picked it up, sipping his coffee as he studied the photo of the display case. The glass doors were intact, the wood unscathed. Whatever had been inside hadn't been under lock and key. "I mean, what else does a bookstore display besides books?"

Nick shrugged. "I've seen some where they have antiques on show. They're usually just for atmosphere, though, nothing worth a motherfucking *heist*."

Hagan raised an eyebrow from behind the rim of his coffee cup.

"Yeah. Heist. Everything we have here is looking like a pro job. The security was disabled, there's no sign of forced entry, and since the shopkeeper bled out where he fell on the sidewalk, it's probable he wasn't supposed to be there and the robbers literally ran into him on their way out and panicked."

"That's a lot to infer from what little we have."

Nick shrugged. He'd always had a knack for seeing crime scenes lay out. He never denied that he could be wrong, but he usually wasn't.

"One more odd job for this one, one of the dead guys had a bag under him. They found it when they moved the body. It had four books in it."

"From the shop?" Hagan asked.

"We can only assume until the daughter gets here to ID them. They're all old, too."

"Just old? Or old as balls?"

Nick barked a laugh before he could stop himself. "The latter, I assume. Three early nineteenth century, one dating to the Revolutionary War. We can probably assume they were in that display case along with whatever objects were taken because everything else was just trashed, not stolen."

"So, you're a bookshop owner and you have this display case set up with rare books," Hagan mused.

"Uh huh?"

"The objects you'd put in there for atmosphere would be related to the books, right? Somehow?"

"In my world they would be," Nick agreed. He pondered it briefly, then nodded and called over one of the uniformed officers working nearby. "Do me a favor, bud, put out some feelers to city pawnshops and dealers, stay on the lookout for artifacts dating from 1750 to 1820. They might be stolen."

The officer nodded and headed off.

Hagan scowled at the photo again. "Was the case wiped clean? Why would they wipe it down if they were wearing gloves?"

"They didn't. Get this. Best the Crime Lab can tell, they wiped the motherfucking dust off the case to ruin the outline of whatever objects were there."

"Covering their tracks, or . . .?"

"I guess. At least slowing us down. Shouldn't be hard to find out what was in there, though," Nick said, still staring at the photos of the crime scene. He absently reached for the cup on his desk, taking a sip before remembering it was coffee.

He turned his head and spit it out into the trash can, coughing and gagging as Hagan laughed at him.

"Motherfucker," Nick grumbled. He tossed the coffee cup into the trash and glared at his partner again.

"Detective O'Flaherty!" Captain Branson called from his office door. Nick turned in his chair and glanced over his shoulder. The captain waved him over.

"What's up, sir?" he asked when he got closer.

"The witness from the bookshop?"

"Yes, sir?"

"He's here. You need to get in on this one."

"Sure thing."

Branson handed him a file. It was labeled John Doe. Nick shook his head; all it contained was the report from the hospital. He made his way to one of the interview rooms and greeted the officer on the door with a pat on the shoulder. When he entered the room, the blond man met his eyes.

"Hello, Detective."

"How you doing?" Nick asked as he sat opposite him.

"I would say I've been better, but . . . I don't really know if that's true," the man said with a wry laugh.

Nick snorted. "Still got your sense of humor at least. That's something." He opened the file again. It was paltry at best. Useless. "They been calling you John Doe?"

"Yeah, it's . . . it's a name, I guess."

"Yeah, I can see that getting old fast. Listen, all the John Does I ever knew were already dead, so how about I call you JD? That work for you?"

He nodded and gave Nick a tired smile. "Yeah. Yeah, that works."

Nick was silent for a moment, studying the man. He looked even more worn than he had at the crime scene yesterday. Under that, Nick could see the fear. "Has anyone offered you coffee? Something to eat?"

"I had a bagel. Don't have much appetite."

"Okay." Nick put both elbows on the table. "You remember anything new? Anything at all?"

"No, Detective, I'm sorry. The doctors said I have amnesia caused by the trauma. Physical or mental, they couldn't say. They also couldn't say when or if my memory would return. They said amnesia was a very case-by-case type of thing, so . . . it might all come rushing back, or it might come back in pieces. Or it might not at all. Ever."

"Wow. That's rough."

JD laughed bitterly. He twisted his fingers and nodded.

Nick was having a hard time reading him, something he was usually pretty good at. JD's exhaustion was masking everything else. Nick gave it a minute or so of silence, waiting to see if the man would begin to fidget or talk. But JD merely sat there, watching his hands, occasionally glancing up to meet Nick's eyes.

Nick finally gave up on that tactic. He tapped the file in front of him. "Even though you don't remember anything, we're going to treat you as a witness and put you under protection. Ballistics are telling us there were at least two shooters. One was standing behind you, clipped you in the head." Nick tapped his own head in the area where JD was bandaged. "Killed at least one of those two victims."

"Just one?"

"The other bullet hasn't been recovered yet. We'll know more soon. But until we get to the bottom of this, you need to be safe. Whoever did this won't know you can't ID them when they find out you aren't dead."

JD nodded. He glanced up at Nick, his blue eyes piercing. "You don't have to dance around it, Detective."

"Pardon?"

"I know I'm a suspect. It's okay. You don't have to mince words."

Nick met his eyes for several seconds, letting JD see what suspects usually saw: a hardened, intelligent cop who would put them behind bars if they made even the tiniest of slips. "All right then. You *are* a suspect. Our only suspect, right now."

Despite his show of bravado, JD blanched. Nick couldn't help but feel sorry for the guy. Not knowing who he was or what kind of man he was, it had to be terrifying. Add to that the fact that he was facing a potential murder charge? He had to be reeling.

Nick took his notepad and a pen from his pocket and placed it on the table, then slid it toward JD. "I'm going to go arrange for somewhere for you to stay tonight. While I'm gone, try to write down anything about yourself you can think of."

JD frowned. "Like what? I already told you I don't remember anything."

Nick shrugged. "Anything. Anything you've noticed. Your feelings, your thoughts, tattoos or scars, your shoe size, do you have contacts, are you wearing underwear? Anything."

JD laughed and reached for Nick's notepad. "Okay."

Nick smiled and left him there, hoping the exercise would at least keep JD's mind off his troubles while Nick tried to find somewhere to stick him for the night.

It took him nearly half an hour to arrange for a hotel and an officer for the door. He and Hagan played a quick three out of five roshambo to decide who had to stay with him, and Nick won. Which was good, because he had plans this weekend.

When he returned to the interview room, Captain Branson was standing at the window, watching JD.

"Sir," Nick said as he approached.

The captain turned. "You're good with him, O'Flaherty. That's the most he's responded all night."

"He's just scared, sir. Anyone would be."

"Stay on him. Babysit him. Play the good cop. He's the biggest break we have in this case right now. If he's comfortable, he's more likely to remember. And if he's faking, you're more likely to figure it out."

Nick cleared his throat and nodded. "Does that mean you want me to stick with him at the safe house?" he asked, unable to conceal the dread in his voice.

Branson smirked at him and raised an eyebrow. "Isn't your boyfriend coming to town tonight?"

"Yes, sir."

"Even I'm not that cruel. Take the weekend. Let Hagan bad cop him for a few days. After that, it's O'Flaherty to the rescue, understand?"

"Of course, sir."

Branson slapped him on the back. Nick watched him walk away, breathing out a sigh of relief, then glanced at the officer on the door.

"Do you even know how to play good cop, Detective?" the man drawled.

"I don't know, no one's ever let me do it." Nick put his shoulder against the door and pushed into the room. JD's head shot up. He'd been dozing. Nick smiled gently for him. "Doing okay?"

"I guess so." He pushed the notepad across the table. "I wrote down everything I could think of."

Nick took the notepad and flipped it over. JD had written bullet points in a neat block print. Nick snorted. It was the type of handwriting that was hard as hell to analyze. The kind that people who worked black ops often had a habit of using. Nick wrote in the same neat block print. "You always write like that?" he asked JD.

"I guess. Why?"

Nick shrugged one shoulder and stuck the notepad back in his pocket. "Muscle memory. It can be interesting. I'll look over this in a bit. Right now I'm going to take you to get something to eat, then to a hotel so you can get some rest."

JD stood hesitantly. "*You're* taking me?"

"Yeah, my partner has some things to tie up before he can meet us there. Is that a problem?"

"No. No, I just assumed it'd be someone . . . lower on the rung."

"I'm going to take you out there and get you settled, but Detective Hagan and a uniform are going to stay with you tonight," Nick answered as he led JD out of the room.

"Is this going to be your case, Detective? I mean . . . you're the one who'll be working it?"

"That's right, me and my partner." Nick stopped and turned to face JD. They were almost the same height, but JD was thinner and more compact. He took a tiny step back when Nick faced him, like he was intimidated. Nick tried to give him a reassuring smile, but he knew himself well enough to know that when he smiled, it rarely reassured anyone. "I'll figure this out, man. I promise."

JD sat with his hands on the table, folded over each other. He played with his fingers as he took in his surroundings. Nick got the feeling that he was used to having something on or in his hands to mess with. A ring, maybe. There was no mark, though, no calluses to give evidence of anything being worn there recently.

JD's eyes strayed to the memorabilia along the brick walls of the pub as he continued to fidget. Nick tried not to watch him too closely. He knew the scrutiny would make him nervous, and JD already had enough nervous energy to power a small appliance.

Nick supposed he couldn't blame the guy, though. He looked away, trying to find something else to focus on for a while.

His eyes followed a waitress as she walked by, and his gaze landed right back on JD once she was gone. He had stopped moving, and his narrowed eyes were raking over the wall next to him. The lines around his mouth had relaxed.

Nick straightened. JD had the look of a man who might have recognized something. Nick glanced up at the reproduction plaque on the wall. He had sat under it many times, gazing at it idly as he waited for his food, reading the words when his dinner mate went to the bathroom, staring at it listlessly as he ordered for that last drink that would send him into taxi territory.

It was a common fake wood plaque, roughly two feet tall and one wide, featuring a frieze of a nameless baseball player in pinstripes—something many people had defaced over the years because those pinstripes looked far too much like Yankee pinstripes and this was Boston, baby. It was also covered in Red Sox stickers and graffiti.

Nick looked up at it dubiously, then back at JD. "Are you remembering something?"

JD was still scowling. He shook his head minutely, still examining the plaque. "I just . . . looking at that gives me a feeling I think is familiar."

"Have you seen it before?"

"I don't know. I think . . . I think maybe I hate the Yankees," JD answered with a shrug.

Nick snorted and couldn't help but smile as he took a drink.

"I guess that's nothing spectacular, huh?"

"Well. It's not going to help narrow you down from the crowd any."

The amusement faded from JD's eyes and he returned his attention to his hands, twisting his fingers together and shifting uneasily in the chair. Nick watched him in sympathy. He couldn't begin to imagine what was going through his mind.

"Are you okay?"

JD was already shaking his head. He turned his head toward the bar as he leaned back in his seat. "I remember that Greg Maddux is the greatest pitcher ever to play the game and that Stan Musial had 3,630 hits in his career. I remember that Darth Vader is a bad guy and that vampires are suddenly good guys who sparkle. I remember that I like spinach and artichoke dip, but not when it comes with tortillas. I know that tequila will make me sick and just the thought of a worm at the bottom of a bottle will make me want to hurl. I know that the tattoo on your forearm means you were a Recon Marine and that makes you a Grade A badass, even if you kind of try to hide it. Probably because you like to go under the radar so you can have the advantage in a fight. But I don't know my own name. I don't know where I come from, how old I am."

He lowered his head. His eyes were misting over, whether from frustration, sorrow, or merely exhaustion was anyone's guess. Nick was shocked by how observant the man was even in the midst of this ordeal, though, and the realization made him uneasy. Only one person had ever called him out for trying to appear less dangerous than he was, and Ty Grady was the most observant man Nick knew.

Then there was the tattoo. Nick had a lot of tattoos, including the Celtic cross that traced his spine from the nape of his neck to the small of his back; and the eagle, globe, and anchor that dominated his left shoulder. He also had one on each forearm, and while he usually hid them with dress shirts and suits, he'd rolled his sleeves up when he'd sat down at the pub.

On the right was an ornate Celtic knotwork gauntlet that covered his entire forearm from just below his wrist to an inch or so from his elbow. On the inside of his other forearm was the Force Recon Jack, one that usually got lost amidst the flashier work he had. It was a skull with breathing gear, with a spade and knife crossed behind it, and wings fluttering out from either side. The skull had thirteen bullet holes in it.

The knotwork gauntlet was far more impressive, but JD had zeroed in on the Jack in particular—the one with special meaning. Nick hadn't met many people who actually knew what a Recon Jack even was, so the fact that JD did meant he might be associated with the military somehow. Closely associated.

"I can't even tell you if I'm a good person or not," JD said. His eyes betrayed the frustration and stark fear he'd been hiding so well up to this point. "I mean, what was I doing there in the middle of the night, stone-cold sober at a bookstore? I could be some sort of criminal and not even know it! I could be a cold-blooded killer, and you're sitting here eating floppy chips with me!"

"Listen to me," Nick said harshly. He leaned forward on the table, seeing the turmoil of his own past reflected in JD's eyes. "We will find out who you are."

"You can't promise that, Detective."

"The hell I can't. And I'll tell you one more thing. I've dealt with a lot of bad people before. None of them are ever torn up wondering if they're a good person."

JD swallowed, but the words seemed to mollify him. He calmed, his shoulders losing their tension. He sighed and gave Nick a weak smile. "When you put it that way . . ."

"Damn straight," Nick said.

JD smiled softly. "You're awfully optimistic for a cop."

"What's that supposed to mean?"

"I mean, I thought all you police-type guys were these brooding, stoic, 'drink yourself blind to drown out the ugliness of the world' types."

Nick barked a laugh. "You're thinking of Vice."

JD just shook his head. "This happy exterior is hiding some deep, dark secret in your past, isn't it?"

Nick shook his head in amusement as he reached for his drink.

"You're an alcoholic. You're closeted. You obliterated an innocent town while you were in the Marines. You're a macho cop who likes to shoot a pearl-handle .22."

"I drink in moderation unless I'm pregaming, I've quite openly liked dick for the past couple of years, I obliterated a lot of things in the Marines, and the pearl-handle is a .38 Special with a pink tint to it," Nick answered with a sly grin before taking a sip of his water.

JD laughed, his eyes sparkling. "You're not mysterious at all. You should try amnesia."

"I'll leave that to you," Nick offered with a mockingly humble shrug.

JD rolled his eyes. Nick took the opportunity to study him for a moment. He seemed better than he had, but that wasn't saying a lot. He still had dark rings under his eyes, and prominent worry lines around his mouth and on his forehead. He probably wasn't as old as he looked right now, maybe younger than Nick. He'd spent a lot of time in the sun, judging by the difference in his blond hair versus the scruff of darker beard growing in. He had no visible scars or tattoos, nothing to identify him with. And his strange blue eyes were truly haunting.

"So," JD said on a sigh. "A hotel with an armed police guard?"

Nick stared at him thoughtfully. "Until we get all this straightened out, yeah."

JD smiled weakly. "Sounds lovely. I don't guess I can count on you being there at all, huh?"

"Not until the first of the week, but hopefully we'll have this all figured out by then. You'll be safe. And I'll find out who you are. I promise."

JD nodded, chewing on his lip. "You always keep your promises, Detective?"

Nick was silent for several tense seconds before smiling. "Yes, I do."

"Then I believe you."

"Good." Nick grabbed his coat and slid from the booth, gesturing for JD to stand with him. "And right now I have to get you to your room, because I promised someone else I'd pick them up at the airport tonight."

Kelly Abbott's flight from Colorado had taken nearly four hours longer than it should have, including a lengthy layover in Charlotte where he'd played with every gadget in the Brookstone store and then made good use of the bar. He was tired, a little wobbly, and had a cramp in his neck because he'd fallen asleep with his head against the window instead of drooling on the guy next to him on the plane.

When he hit the escalators that would take him down to the baggage claim at Logan, he bent to scan the crowd below for Nick. It was June in Massachusetts, so it wasn't like people were all bundled up, but it was busy as hell, so it was hard to tell if Nick was down there.

Before Kelly had left his house for the Denver airport this morning, Nick had warned him that he might have to send a car to pick him up if his new case warranted it. Kelly didn't mind; in fact, he was the reason Nick had gone back to work at all.

Nick had been ready to quit. He'd been a cop for almost as many years as he'd been a Marine, but when the Corps had called him back for a last tour of duty, something inside Nick had snapped. He'd come home and declared he was done with carrying a gun. Kelly had given it a few weeks to let the boredom set in before convincing Nick he was acting rashly.

Nick never acted rashly; that was Kelly's job. Besides, he'd been bored as hell without his badge, so he'd gone back to the department for a test run. The first few months had gone off without a hitch.

Kelly was halfway down the escalator when he caught sight of Nick, and his heart skipped a beat. Nick was dressed in a suit and tie, with a tan trench coat that made him look like a private eye from the '50s. He was wearing his badge on his belt, and Kelly's trained eyes could see the telltale outline of a gun at his hip. He had his phone out, frowning at the screen.

Kelly's feet hit the end of the escalator as he stared, and he nearly fell all over himself.

He stumbled out into the baggage claim area, and Nick obviously saw the motion out of the side of his eye because he looked up quickly, flinching like he might be going for his gun. A smile graced his handsome face when he saw Kelly, though, and he moved toward him, meeting him halfway and wrapping him up in a hug.

"Have a nice trip?" he asked, laughing softly.

"Shut up. Jesus, you look good."

Nick kissed his cheek, then his lips. He didn't linger over it, though. "I barely got here, didn't have time to change. You look rough, babe."

"I feel rough. Let's get the hell out of here."

Nick grabbed his hand to halt him as Kelly marched toward the door. "Don't you have a suitcase?"

Kelly glanced at the crowd around the baggage conveyors. His shoulders slumped. All he wanted to do was get Nick somewhere private. Now. "Oh yeah."

Nick pulled him closer, sliding his hands under Kelly's jacket to rest on the small of his back. He kissed him gently, with the crowds bustling around them. Kelly realized this might be their first official PDA, and neither of them cared.

Nick rested his temple against Kelly's and smiled against his neck. "I missed you."

"Me too." Kelly wrapped his arm around Nick's neck and dropped his carry-on bag to the floor to get another kiss, but Nick raised his head instead.

"Is that your bag? With all the patches on it?"

Kelly grunted and turned to the conveyor. His rucksack had patches from almost every destination he'd traveled, so it was hard to miss. "Yeah. Fucking cockblock."

Nick burst out laughing. It was a sound Kelly had sorely missed. It sent a shiver through him, making the scar of the bullet wound on his chest throb. He rubbed at it as Nick kissed him again before letting him go and then striding over to catch his rucksack for him. The coat made him look even wider at the shoulders than he already was. Kelly flashed back to all the many mornings he'd seen Nick stalking across whatever camp, base, or ship they'd been stationed on, barking orders.

He wondered sometimes how he'd gone five years in Recon without molesting his friend. He'd either been absolutely blind to the attraction or he was rewriting the memories in his head, because *damn*.

Nick returned, Kelly's bag thrown over his shoulder and a smile on his face. "Ready to go home?"

"You're not even going to feed me first?" Kelly teased. "Just going to take me to your boat and fuck me?"

"That's SOP, yeah. Come on." He led Kelly out into the brisk evening.

His Range Rover was parked in a no loading zone right beside the taxi lane, and airport security was standing beside it, writing out a ticket. Nick handed Kelly his bag and gestured for him to load it in the car. Kelly watched him as he slid his overcoat and suit jacket aside and tapped the badge on his belt with one long finger.

The rent-a-cop gave him a wave and moved away, and Kelly climbed into the passenger side. Nick got into the car a moment later, grinning crookedly.

"You just abused your authority," Kelly told him.

Nick nodded and started the car.

"You enjoyed it, didn't you?"

Nick side-eyed him. "So did you."

"So much."

CHAPTER 2

The choppy water lapped at the hull of Nick's yacht, the sound rhythmic and deep, like Kelly could feel it in his chest as he lay awake in the main cabin. Nick was curled beside him, his breathing uneven, his body tense.

He was dreaming, and his restlessness made it impossible for Kelly to sleep. Nick tossed his head and murmured something, and as he moved, his fingers grazed Kelly's arm. Kelly flinched, wincing in anticipation of Nick waking. The last time Nick had rolled into him during a dream, he'd startled awake and pinned Kelly to the mattress, his hand around Kelly's throat, before Kelly could say anything to calm him.

Not that Kelly minded, because not only could he defend himself with ease, but also the way Nick apologized was pretty fantastically sweaty and naked.

That had been weeks ago, of course, in Kelly's cabin in Colorado where Nick wasn't quite as familiar with his surroundings. Nick usually slept easy, especially on his boat, and the more time that passed since his last deployment, the fewer issues he had. But on stormy nights, when the seas tossed the boat beneath them, when thunder crashed above them and the sounds of the sea infiltrated the hull, Nick was restless and quick to strike out when his nightmares were interrupted.

Nick murmured something in his sleep again, and Kelly finally gave up on trying to get to sleep himself and pushed the blanket off. He slipped out of bed carefully, not wanting to wake Nick as he headed for the salon upstairs.

Photos were scattered on the walls there, and the occasional knickknack sat around, but other than that the décor of the yacht was pretty sparse. It wasn't Spartan or empty, though.

Kelly had spent plenty of time aboard the yacht since Nick had purchased it. He'd thought nothing on board was foreign to him, but when Nick had shown him the drawer full of sex toys beneath his bed, Kelly had been both shocked and incredibly turned on. He kind of wondered what else Nick had managed to hide away in spaces Kelly didn't know were there.

The clouds hid the moon in the sky, and only the skyline of Boston provided light. Kelly closed the shades against it and threw the yacht into almost pitch darkness. He didn't like the press of a big city so close to him.

He flopped onto the couch in the salon, letting his eyes adjust to the darkness and glancing around at the nooks and crannies where Nick stored all his personal belongings. Hardback books were piled everywhere, most of them on history, archaeology, or lost treasures and mysteries. That had always been Nick's thing, though. Nick was one of the only jarheads Kelly had ever met who didn't have a single gun magazine subscription or hang knives on his walls. Kelly wasn't even sure where Nick kept his medals, because he sure as hell didn't have them sitting out or displayed.

The coffee table was covered with files Nick had brought home from work. He'd intended to take vacation days, but Kelly had convinced him not to. He'd used enough of his vacation last year for emergencies; Kelly didn't want him wasting more to stay home. He wanted him to take *real* vacations this year. Preferably somewhere warm. Preferably with him.

Over dinner Nick had mentioned a few details of the case he was working on, a robbery gone wrong that had ended up in murder. Then he'd apologized for bringing work home when Kelly was there to spend time with him, and he'd shoved the files away in favor of resting his head in Kelly's lap as they watched a movie on Netflix.

Kelly smiled softly with the memory. Nick had swiftly drifted off to sleep, and Kelly had ignored the movie in favor of twisting his fingers through Nick's curly hair.

The memory made the silent boat feel that much lonelier. Kelly fought past the tumbling feeling in his gut. He had two more weeks here. He wasn't going to start getting melancholy about leaving yet, Jesus.

He stretched to flip on a lamp beside the couch so he wasn't sitting in the dark like a creeper, and then absently flipped through the pages of Nick's files on the table. Was it illegal for him to be seeing this information? He shrugged and scanned Nick's handwritten notes. He loved the way Nick wrote; block print, no discernible quirks, only the slightest hint of a lefty slant. But the faster he wrote, or the more agitated he grew, the more beautiful the scrawl became. He lost the blocking and it took on a personality all its own, a hybrid of print and cursive with precise curves and flourishes. It was so telling of Nick's personality, the hidden part of him only a few people got to see.

He must have written the notes in shorthand or some sort of code, though, because it read like nonsense. Kelly placed the notepad back where he'd found it and sighed deeply, then hunted for the remote. He might sleep if the television was going.

He found the remote resting on top of a book beside the lamp: *Mysteries of the Golden and Rosy Cross.*

Kelly frowned at the title. Nick liked adventure books, especially the ones that added a little historical mystery to the story. Maybe Kelly could read himself to sleep and he wouldn't risk waking Nick with the sound of the TV.

When he opened the book, though, a sheet of paper fell out. Kelly scrambled for it before it could flutter to the floor or disappear into the couch cushions. It was the same kind of paper as in the Moleskine notepad Nick carried around. It had obviously been torn away, and on it were two grids, like tic-tac-toe boards, and two Xs, all with symbols in each empty space. A pigpen cipher: a simple substitution cipher that usually used dots instead of symbols. Kelly had taught the kids at the camp he worked at in Colorado how to do these, trying to get them interested in linguistics.

Kelly had his thumb in the pages the note had been stuck between, and on them he found the same sort of cipher, this time with the correct series of dots, and notes explaining how it was used. Not that Nick needed to look up a pigpen cipher; he was the one who'd taught Kelly how to do them.

Kelly flipped through the rest of the book. It wasn't a novel after all, but a book about secret societies, specifically one called the Rosicrucians. Kelly had never heard of them. "What are you up to, Nicko?"

After a few more minutes of contemplating the cipher, which he couldn't figure out because the symbols were foreign to him, it occurred to him that this might have to do with a case Nick was working on. He slipped the paper into the book and set it back where he'd found it.

A yawn caught him off guard, and he clicked the lamp off and made his way carefully below to the main cabin. Nick was still and silent, his nightmares no longer plaguing him. It was a relief to slide under the covers beside him and have him curl almost immediately around Kelly.

Nick's hand was warm on Kelly's bare stomach, his fingers curling against Kelly's abs. Kelly carefully placed his hand over Nick's, Nick's eyelashes fluttered and his nose curled in his sleep. Kelly closed his eyes and rolled in Nick's embrace until he had cuddled closer and Nick's arms enveloped him.

Nick woke with a gasp.

"It's me, babe," Kelly whispered against Nick's chest. "It's Doc, you're safe."

Nick tightened his grip and pulled Kelly closer. "Hey," he said, his deep voice even gruffer with sleep. "You okay?"

Kelly pushed his head back so he could see Nick's face. Nick was still half-asleep, his eyes washed of their usual green in the darkness. His brow was furrowed. It wasn't unusual for him to be concerned when he woke with Kelly in his arms like this; he could be cuddling, or he could be choking Kelly unconscious.

Kelly kissed his chin, then scooted up so he could reach Nick's lips. Nick hummed into the kiss.

"I'm fine," Kelly said. "Couldn't sleep."

Kelly rolled onto his back, pulling Nick with him. Nick curled around him in a way that still surprised Kelly, resting his head on Kelly's chest and throwing a leg over Kelly's hips. Nick was about as alpha top as a man could get, but when it came to cuddling, he had no compunctions about being held. Kelly wrapped his arm around Nick's shoulder and squeezed him tight.

"Boat still throws you off, huh?" Nick mumbled against Kelly's chest.

Kelly nodded as he ran his fingers through Nick's hair. When they'd been discharged from the armed services, Kelly had gone home to Colorado and stayed there in a cabin he'd built with his own two hands and a very dedicated earthmover. He'd grown accustomed to the smells of pine and snow and earth, the sounds of the wind whispering through branches and animals skittering through the underbrush coming from his open windows.

The waves lapping at the hull near his head were a sound from the past he hadn't thought he'd sleep to again. The hustle and bustle of Boston in the distance was completely foreign to him. All the times he'd visited Nick before, he'd always been too drunk by nightfall to care.

He stuffed his nose into Nick's curls and inhaled deeply. Nick smelled of the sea, salty and cool. He always had, even in the middle of the desert with the hot sun pounding down on their backs or climbing the freezing shale mountains of Afghanistan. Or maybe the sea had always smelled of Nick. Kelly had a hard time deciphering which came first in his mind.

"We can get a hotel, if you want," Nick offered. He was waking up, his voice becoming clear and strong even as he rested his head against Kelly's chest. "You're here for another two weeks, no point in you not sleeping the whole time."

Kelly's lips twitched on a sigh. "I'd rather be here."

Nick rested his chin against Kelly's chest, rolling over to his stomach and gazing up at him. Kelly stroked his hair, then let his fingers travel down his back, tracing hard muscles under bare skin. Nick shivered when Kelly's fingers trailed over one of the long scars on his back.

"I need to get used to it anyway, right?" Kelly asked, but the question caused a flurry of butterflies in his stomach. He and Nick hadn't talked much about their future. In fact, they'd only gotten as far as telling each other they were in it for the long haul, but they still didn't have details worked out. Where would they go, what would they do? Would they compromise and move somewhere new, would one of them quit his job, or would they share time between both homes like they'd been doing? They hadn't even begun to think of any of that stuff.

Nick had asked Kelly to marry him not long ago, but he'd been fresh out of surgery to donate a piece of his liver to his dying father, and so drugged that Kelly wondered if Nick remembered anything that had happened that day. He'd been told after Nick's surgery that the surgeons had been forced to give Nick ketamine, which explained why Nick had hallucinated for a solid week after he'd gotten out of the hospital. He'd spent most of it rambling about killing an old colleague of theirs named Liam Bell and telling Kelly he was beautiful.

He'd never brought up being engaged, never even panicked about it. That was what really gave it away, actually. Nick was notoriously twitchy about commitment. He'd probably disappear into a puff of smoke that spelled out "nope" in the air if Kelly told him he'd proposed while drugged.

Kelly hadn't brought it up again. Just knowing Nick was thinking permanently while high on Dilaudid and ketamine was sufficient to make him giddy, and he was willing to wait until Nick was comfortable enough to bring it up again. While sober. But hell, they were still living in two different states, thousands of miles apart. They had bigger issues than forgotten proposals.

Nick interrupted Kelly's musings by pushing himself up, leaning his elbow on the mattress at Kelly's side and placing his hand over the bullet scar on Kelly's chest. "We both know you'd go nuts living on a boat all the time, Kels."

Kelly swallowed hard, nerves swamping him. Nick really was going to talk about this, about them living together. "And you'd go stir-crazy in a cabin in the woods where you couldn't see the ocean or meet new people every day," he said with false cheer. "I'm Navy, baby, I was born for boats."

Nick's smile was genuine, but melancholy at best. "Liar. You need trees and grass."

"So get me a bonsai tree and I'll grow my weed on the flybridge."

"Wrong kind of grass," Nick said as he pulled himself closer and gave Kelly a slow, teasing kiss. He slid his fingers over Kelly's cheek before clutching at his hair and resting his weight on Kelly.

Desire tore through Kelly like a wildfire. It always did when Nick touched him. This was his first relationship with another man, but the excitement and adventure had yet to wear off. He was certain that with Nick, it would never fade.

"I guess we need to talk about it, huh?" Nick murmured between kisses.

"Unless you want to keep going like we have," Kelly said. "A week here, two there. A month apart. It sucks, babe."

Nick nodded fervently and dove in for another kiss.

"But I know you and I know me," Kelly managed to say through Nick's kisses. "We'll work it out. I'm good with it for now."

"Well, I'm not." Nick said before a long, tense silence. He flopped onto his back with a huff. "So let's figure it out."

"Now?" Kelly practically squeaked. "It's the middle of the night."

"We're both up."

Kelly gestured to himself emphatically. "*Up* is the appropriate word, yes."

Nick laughed, the sound warming the cool cabin as it drowned out the waves beating at the hull.

Kelly huffed and rolled to straddle Nick, placing both hands on Nick's chest and settling onto Nick's groin, grinning over the fact that Nick was half-hard. Nick shifted beneath him, gripping his thighs. Kelly leaned far to his left to switch on the lamp beside the bed. They both winced away from its dim light, but Kelly was finally able to meet Nick's incredible green eyes. Nick was gazing at him, indulgent and ... smitten.

"I love you," Kelly blurted, unsure of why he felt inclined to say it just then.

"Yeah, you do," Nick drawled, grinning wider. His expression softened quickly. "I love you too."

"Fuck first or talk first?" Kelly asked.

Nick pursed his lips, scowling in thought. "What if we go at it first, then fall asleep and forget to talk? Then it's still a problem in the morning."

"Valid. But what if we wind up fighting about it? We'll miss out on the fucking."

"There's always makeup sex."

Kelly pointed at him. "Ooh, and *angry* sex."

Nick's eyebrows rose higher, and he was obviously fighting a smile. "We've never had either. Might be fun."

Kelly couldn't keep from laughing any longer. He ran his hands over Nick's chest. "Should I pick a fight?"

Nick's hands rose higher, settling on Kelly's waist. "Not just yet," he murmured, giving Kelly a tug.

Nick sat up to meet him as Kelly leaned over him, and he wrapped his arms around Kelly as they kissed. He crossed his legs, getting more comfortable as Kelly settled into his lap.

"Thought you voted talk before fuck," Kelly grumbled.

Nick kissed him again, nodding. His hands dragged down Kelly's back. "I did. We're talking."

Kelly laughed. He put both hands on Nick's shoulders and shimmied his hips, rubbing Nick's hardening cock against his. "No, we're not."

"Good, then shut up," Nick growled. The next kiss was a consuming one, clearly meant to silence Kelly's habit of rambling when Nick was trying to seduce him.

Nick's grip tightened, and before Kelly knew what was happening, Nick had wrapped him up and rolled them, pinning Kelly to the mattress with his head at the foot of the bed and his legs wrapped around Nick's waist.

"Okay, that was fun," Kelly gasped.

Nick shushed him, then kissed him and rolled his hips. They'd already taken care of these needs once tonight; almost as soon as their feet had hit the deck of the yacht, Nick'd had Kelly pressed against the hull, kissing him silly. But it had been almost a month since they'd seen each other, and Nick was finally fully healed from his surgery. Kelly had expected nothing less. In fact, he'd be a little pissed if Nick didn't maul him a few times a day in the first week of his visit.

Nick's cell phone began to ring as they kissed. The sound was muffled, like it was coming from inside something. Nick pushed up with an aggrieved curse. "I'm not answering that."

"Aren't you technically on duty?" Kelly asked.

Nick muttered something unintelligible and rolled toward the head of the bed. He fumbled under his pillow and came out with the phone.

"You keep your phone under your pillow?" Kelly asked with a laugh. This was the first time they'd shared a bed while Nick was on duty. "How does it fit beside your gun and your knife and the lube?"

"Shhh. This is O'Flaherty," Nick practically growled when he answered. His eyes narrowed and he started toward Kelly as if he intended to continue what they'd started, but then his expression changed from predatory to alarm, his face softening, his eyebrows rising, his motion halting. "When? What happened? Were they attacked?"

Kelly sat up, scowling. He hoped this was work and not another distress call from one of their friends. The men of their former Recon team, Sidewinder, seemed to have a knack for getting into trouble. And no matter which one of them needed help or what kind of help they needed, Nick was always the first one *any* of them called.

"I'll be right there," Nick spat, then ended the call and tossed the phone aside. He clambered out of the bed and to the closet, talking over his shoulder as he pulled a shirt on. "I have to go. Come with me?"

"Of course." Kelly scrambled to put more clothes on, but he took his cues from Nick, who didn't even take the time to put real pants on. He just stayed in his sweatpants and slid his bare feet into a pair of plastic flip-flops as he headed for the steps. Kelly was still struggling to get a shirt on as he followed.

Nick broke a record number of traffic laws on the way to wherever they were going, but the small, portable flashing light on his dash seemed to make it okay. Was that legit? He'd been in a car with Nick a thousand times, though, and he wasn't even compelled to hold on to the handle when they weaved through traffic or took a sharp turn. Nick was possibly the best driver Kelly had ever known. Sometimes it seemed ill-advised, but Kelly trusted him implicitly. In the driver's seat, that was. The one time Nick had flown a helicopter was a different story. Their buddy Owen still refused to get into a helicopter after that trip.

When they arrived at a nondescript hotel, there wasn't any hustle or bustle like Kelly had expected. No uniformed cops on the streets, no flashing lights, no panicking guests in the almost empty lobby.

Nothing but a single man in uniform as they stepped off the elevator. Nick held up the badge on a chain around his neck as he walked by.

"He's with me, he's okay," he said in passing, pointing at Kelly. Kelly nodded to the man, trying not to feel awkward. He had been special operations in the military and was extremely capable both in the field and in any situation stateside. He had medical training that could save a life under enemy fire, and he could break a man's neck before they knew he was there.

But he wasn't a cop. He didn't know the first thing about investigating or the law. The only reason he was here was because he was trailing after his boyfriend. He didn't like the feeling.

Nick headed for room 319, where another officer stood guard, a plastic chair near him against the wall. Nick showed his badge again, even though each man they'd passed obviously knew him by sight. When they entered the hotel room, a stocky man with silvering hair stood near the bathroom door, shaking his head at Nick.

"What the hell happened?" Nick demanded.

"He freaked. I don't know. He won't talk to me. I figured you have the rapport with him, he might respond."

Nick nodded, frowning at the bathroom door, then glancing over his shoulder at Kelly. "Uh, Kels, this is Detective Alan Hagan, my partner. He's useless when I'm supposed to have the night off."

Kelly shook the man's hand, introducing himself. He didn't offer his relationship to Nick, though. That was Nick's job, and frankly, Kelly didn't know how sensitive the subject was for him. He knew Nick had come out as bi to basically everyone in his life not long after he'd come out to Kelly. How everyone had handled it, Nick had never said.

"You're the boyfriend?" Hagan asked as he shook Kelly's hand. "O talks about you all the damn time."

Kelly flushed, clearing his throat and smiling uncontrollably. He glanced at Nick again. He wasn't sure why he kept being surprised by how open Nick was about their relationship. He knew Nick hated secrets, hated having them especially. He should have known Nick wouldn't hide him. Hide them.

Nick had his ear against the bathroom door. He knocked gently. "Hey, bud, it's Detective O'Flaherty," he called, keeping his voice low and soothing. "You okay in there?"

The response was muffled, but from the way Hagan raised an eyebrow and cocked his head, it was more response than he'd been receiving.

"Come closer to the door, we can't hear you," Nick called. He waited, holding his breath. There was a thump against the door and he moved away a little like he hoped the man was opening it.

"I'm sorry," the voice said from the other side. "I'm sorry I freaked out. I just . . ."

Nick leaned his shoulder into the doorjamb. "Hey, it's okay. You got every right to be freaking out, we all know that. If you feel safer in there, you go ahead and stay, okay? That's all we want is for you to feel safe right now."

Nick paused, and his eyes met Kelly's. He smiled gently and winked. Kelly bit his lip to keep from smiling at such an inappropriate time. He'd seen Nick talk dozens of frightened young Marines down from panicking. He could be soothing, if he chose to be.

"I would like to know what scared you, though," Nick continued. "Do you feel like telling me?"

"Do you have kids, Detective?" the man in the bathroom asked.

Nick frowned in confusion. "No."

"I figured you might have toddlers or something. You're talking to me like one right now."

Nick's eyes narrowed, and he gave the door an insulted frown. "Fine! So how about you get your ass out of the bathroom and we'll talk like adults."

Hagan inhaled sharply, and the guard on the door tensed. The man in the bathroom was silent. Kelly winced when it seemed like Nick's tactic had backfired, but then they heard soft laughter through the door.

The lock clicked and the door edged open. Kelly had sort of expected a neurotic-looking little bald guy in glasses or something, but the man who peered out was maybe six feet tall, just an inch or two shorter than Nick. He was wiry and fit, with a healthy tan and shaggy blond hair that had obviously been bleached by time in the sun. His eyes were a blue that seemed Photoshopped. Fuck, he was kind of Nick's type.

Nick was still leaning against the doorjamb, one eyebrow raised at the man. "Touché, Detective," the blond man said.

Nick nodded, crossing his arms smugly.

The guy glanced at Hagan. "Sorry."

"Hey, I get it. Don't hurt my feelings any. People always like him better."

The guy's eyes landed on Kelly, and Kelly tried to offer him a comforting smile even though he still had no clue what was going on.

"JD, this is my partner, Kelly Abbott," Nick said as he waved his hand in Kelly's direction. "Kels, this is our witness who doesn't know who he is."

"Seriously?" Kelly whispered.

"I thought . . . I thought Detective Hagan was your partner," JD said, frowning and looking between them.

"Partner," Nick said gently, pointing at Hagan. Then he transferred the finger to Kelly. "Boyfriend. You want to sit down and tell me what happened?"

JD cleared his throat and nodded, glancing again at Kelly and Hagan as a flush rose to his cheeks.

"Guys, give us a minute, huh?" Nick said as JD headed for the beds in the hotel room. Nick stopped and took Kelly's arm, giving him a quick kiss on the cheek. "I'm sorry, this'll be a couple minutes."

"It's okay." Kelly's heart was still fluttering from the fact that Nick had so readily claimed him in front of anyone and everyone, from the possessive glint in Nick's eyes. He would have sat out in the hall waiting all night just to see that glint in Nick's eyes again.

He headed out of the room with Hagan, glancing back to see JD sitting on the end of one of the beds and Nick settling onto the dresser opposite him so they could talk. He looked very professional about it, if you discounted the sweatpants that were drenched at the bottom and the plastic flip-flops he was wearing.

The door fell closed and Kelly was left with the two cops in the hallway. He stuffed his hands into his pockets and bounced up onto his toes. "So!" he said cheerfully. "This is fun."

"This guy's a fucking basket case," Hagan grunted. "Might be here awhile. Want some coffee?"

Kelly shook his head and leaned his back against the wall. He slid down to sit, propping his arms against his knees. If there was one thing spec ops knew how to do, it was sleep sitting up.

Nick kept crossing his arms and then forcing himself to stop, resting his hands in his lap instead. He didn't want to give off body language that said he was irritated, impatient, or closed off. It was hard, though, when he was going on a few hours' sleep and had been interrupted during what was supposed to have been an entire weekend alone with Kelly.

"What happened?"

"I had a dream," JD said with a helpless shrug. "I woke up in a panic, bolted for the bathroom, and sat in the tub until I could breathe."

Nick nodded, his expression carefully neutral. "You remember the dream?"

JD shook his head, wincing. He was wringing his hands, rocking a little. "I feel stupid. I'm so sorry. I'm sorry they called you down here."

"Hey." Nick leaned closer, lowering his voice. "People aren't built for this kind of stress, all right? You handle it however you can, no shame in that."

JD sniffed and laughed ruefully. "Have you ever woken up in a bathtub, Detective?"

Nick opened his mouth and then closed it fast, looking over JD's head as the memory flashed through his mind. "Yes. But I was hungover and . . . not alone. My point, though, is that waking up and bolting for safety is nothing to be ashamed of. I wake up swinging all the time. I tried to kill my boyfriend with a TV remote one time, so . . . I get where you're coming from. There's no shame in fear."

JD took in a shaky breath and rubbed a hand over his face.

"You still can't remember anything?"

"I think I dreamed about the bookstore. I was there." JD shook his head. "But then we knew that already, huh? All I remember is something about a book, I don't know."

Nick had his Moleskine pad out, jotting down notes. He nodded for JD to continue talking as he wrote.

"I think ... I felt like I wasn't in the right place, you know? Like I knew I wasn't supposed to be there. I couldn't get away though."

Nick made an asterisk and wrote out the possibility that JD had been forced to accompany someone to the robbery. He glanced up to find JD rocking faster. It was a habit he was familiar with, and it usually signified it was time to switch topics. "Okay. Tell you what, bud, why don't you try to get some rest tonight. Monday morning I'm hoping I'll have some pictures to show you; we'll see if they jog anything else loose."

JD nodded.

"I've also got someone running down your prints, going through missing persons reports. By morning, those results should be back."

JD tensed, glancing up to meet Nick's eyes.

"What's wrong?"

"What if they come in and tell you I'm someone horrible?"

A pang of sympathy hit a little too close to home. It was one thing to struggle with your humanity. It must have been torturous to do so without the benefit of past actions or even past thoughts to back up your conclusions.

"I can't imagine it will," he offered gently. He leaned forward and patted JD on the knee. "Try to get some rest, okay? I'm going to call Hagan back in and—"

"You can't stay, can you?" JD blurted. When Nick raised an eyebrow at him, he paled, looking shocked that he'd spoken at all. "I mean ... he's nice and all, but you're the only person I've felt comfortable with. I ..."

Nick had to fight hard not to groan. He always managed to pick up the strays somehow. He shook his head, feeling guilty for blowing off such a sincere request because he wanted to go home and fuck his boyfriend. "I'm sorry, we can't just switch things up without reporting it and giving a compelling reason to do it."

JD lowered his head, looking crestfallen. He nodded, though, and took a deep breath. "Okay."

"You good for tonight?"

JD nodded again, more confidently this time. "I'm good."

Nick sat with him for a few more minutes, letting him know he was merely a call away, that he'd be right back on the case on Monday, and there was nothing to worry about as long as he stuck with Hagan or one of the officers assigned to their door.

"I'm sorry I brought you out so late. Tell your boyfriend I'm sorry too; this must be weird for him."

"We met in Recon," Nick said. "He's used to weird."

He stood and gave JD's shoulder a last pat before heading for the door. When he stepped into the hall, Hagan was leaning against the wall, his head back and his mouth open as he snored. Kelly had fallen asleep sitting ramrod straight against the wall right beside the door.

Nick snorted and glanced at the uniformed officer, who was sitting in his chair with a cup of coffee and giving Nick a smirk. "Are you guys the cavalry?"

Hagan jerked and snorted, shaking his head as he woke. "I'm awake."

Nick chuckled and nodded, stepping aside so Hagan could get back into the room. "I told him you'd call me if anything came up."

"You got it, brother. You deal with this shit better than me," Hagan said, and then stumbled toward his bed and flopped into it.

Kelly was still sitting with his back against the wall, blinking up blearily at Nick.

"You can fall asleep in under five minutes sitting in the hallway of a hotel, but you can't sleep in my nice soft bed on my boat."

Kelly licked his lips and reached up for Nick to help him to his feet. "Maybe we should sleep on the flybridge again," he said as they headed for the elevators. "I slept like a baby up there on that pool float with Ty that one time."

Nick snorted and jabbed at the elevator button. "We're getting a hotel."

"So, tell me about this case. The witness has amnesia?" Kelly asked in the car on the way back to the Boston Harbor Marina. He'd tried as long as he could to keep out of it, but he was just too curious.

"Yeah, he took a bullet to the back of the head. Doctors said it's either physical damage or shock of some kind."

"Kind of like that time I got kicked in the head by that goat."

Nick burst out laughing. "Yeah, kind of like that."

Kelly glanced at him, admiring his profile. He still owed Nick for that. They'd been on a mission when they'd taken cover in a gully that just happened to be sheltering several goats, including one territorial billy goat who'd taken a shot at Kelly's head. He'd woken up as they'd been carting him back to camp, and Nick had convinced him he was a Bible salesman from Oklahoma who'd gotten fresh with the livestock and paid for it with a hoof. Kelly'd believed it for two whole hours before his memory came back. He still had trouble looking at goats without flashes of completely unwarranted guilt.

"Asshole," Kelly muttered.

Nick very nearly giggled before he got himself under control. He cleared his throat. "Anyway. We don't know if he has any solid information or not, we don't even know who he is."

"Could he be one of the robbers? Got knocked out at the scene and just pulled something out of his ass when he woke up rather than going to jail?"

"It's a real possibility, yeah. That's the other reason we've got him under protection."

"Oh. Smart."

"Indeed," Nick drawled, throwing Kelly a sly smirk before he turned his eyes back to the road.

"I don't think I've ever seen you in detective mode. It's kind of . . . sexy."

Nick merely smiled. Kelly watched him, pondering the silence that fell between them. It wasn't uncomfortable. It never had been, not from the first moment they'd met. It could sometimes be heavy, though, especially during the months after Nick had returned from his POW experience in Afghanistan.

This silence was something different. It was easy and light, devoid of expectation. Kelly liked it. But he could sense that Nick had more on his mind than the next few weeks with him.

"Hey babe, do you want me to go back home until you get this case wrapped?" Kelly asked. "I don't want to be in the way."

Nick glanced at him, eyes widened in alarm. "No. No, you're not in the way. I never said that."

"I know you never said it, but I also know how your brain works. You're not going to stop mulling over the mystery, but whenever you do think about it and you think you should be spending time with me instead, you're going to feel guilty for working."

"Not true."

"You are the shittiest liar in the history of lying liars."

Nick laughed softly, reached over the console, and grasped Kelly's hand. "Fine, you're probably right. But I don't want you to leave. Please?"

"Okay. So tell me more about the case. Can you?"

"Technically, no. But hell, I've told you national security shit you shouldn't know either so what the hell."

Kelly gestured to himself, tracing a circle in the air around his face. "It's this beautiful mug right here. Like a puppy. Does this look like the face of a spy?"

Nick glanced sideways at him. "Yes."

"Fair enough. But tell me anyway."

"The robbery was in an antiquarian bookstore."

"Antiquarian? That's specialty stuff, not just used paperbacks, right?"

"Right. Rare books, expensive stuff." Nick had to release Kelly's hand to flip the turn signal on, which apparently pissed off the car behind them because it honked at them as it passed. Nick ignored it. "Shop was busted up like they were looking for something. Security system would have been easy to bypass even for a rudimentary cat burglar, but they took it out without leaving a trace."

"So you think it was a professional team?"

"Probably." There were more honks behind Nick and he peered into the rearview mirror. He muttered under his breath. "What are these fuckers doing?"

Kelly glanced behind them. "Isn't that just how Massholes drive?"

Nick flicked on the police light on the dash. The honking stopped and the offending car slowed until more space was between them and Nick's Range Rover.

Kelly turned back around in his seat. "I'm really enjoying the power trip that comes with fucking a cop."

"That's what they all say. Anyway. Pro crew hits rare bookstore. They take four books and two objects out of a display case, all possibly linked to the Revolutionary War."

"What objects?"

"We don't know yet."

"Why not?"

"Because we're not psychic, dude."

"What about the shop owner?" Kelly asked.

"Dead. Killed on the sidewalk in front of the store along with one of the robbers. Reports say there were shots fired, witnesses are saying anywhere from five to a dozen. We haven't recovered all the bullets or casings yet, but there were at least four. One of which clipped JD."

"God. Who would kill for a handful of old books?"

"No clue." Nick rolled his window down and slid his security key into the marina's gate controls.

"What're your off-the-wall theories you're afraid to tell your partner 'cause he laughs at you?"

Nick grinned crookedly as he pulled into the marina parking lot. "You want my off-the-wall theories?"

"Give it to me."

"You sure?"

"I want it hard, babe, come on." Kelly offered him a cheeky leer.

Nick snorted. He threw the car in park, then turned it off and sat back, his hands on the wheel. "Intergalactic tea-loving time travelers trying to help the British win the Revolutionary War. Pissed-off historians in an attempt to liberate artifacts from their cages. Or treasure hunters out to find the missing Knights Templar library."

Kelly laughed and leaned his head against the cool glass of the window, pointing a mocking finger at Nick. "Where do you get this shit?"

Nick smacked him in the chest. Kelly grabbed his hand and refused to let it go. "Can I play devil's advocate for your theories?"

"No," Nick grunted. He unbuckled Kelly and reached for him with the other hand, dragging him across the console. Kelly began to protest, but Nick kissed him almost brutally, his fingers tightening in Kelly's hair, his other hand bunched in Kelly's shirt.

"What happened?" Kelly panted. Nick had a habit of being turned on at the oddest times by the most random things. Kelly never knew when Nick was going to grope him. It made things interesting.

"We started something, I was thinking we'd finish it," Nick growled, still tugging Kelly across the console.

The tone of his voice hit Kelly deep in the gut. "Not in the boat?"

"I won't be able to walk to the boat, babe." Kelly climbed the rest of the way over the console and into Nick's lap. His elbow hit the horn as they kissed, and the Range Rover sat there screaming about how its occupants were making out until Nick reclined the seat. He shoved it all the way back, taking Kelly with him, and Kelly straddled him, laughing again.

"You're fucking insane," he gasped. He stroked his hand across Nick's cheek to lighten the blow of the words. "What the hell turned you on this time?"

Nick reached for his neck, gripping it hard and pulling him down into another demanding kiss. He kept his hand on the back of Kelly's head, refusing to let him sit up, refusing to let him break the press of their bodies. "Just you. Moonlight on your smile."

"Romantic, but are you sure this isn't just a history nerdgasm you're having right now?" Nick smiled against his lips. "Revolutionary War, you've probably been hard since you heard those words."

"So help me out with that."

"I did earlier."

"Then fucking do it again."

Kelly shifted in his lap until his hardening cock rubbed against Nick's through the sweats they both wore. Nick groaned and spread his legs further until he was able to prop his bare foot up on the dash beside the steering wheel. He raised his hips, shoving his cock against Kelly's, and they both moaned between their kiss.

"Shrapnel in your thigh, bad knee. How are you this flexible still?"

"Motivation," Nick said, and he was just breathless enough that it sent another jolt through Kelly's body. He loved when Nick got so turned on he didn't try to wait for a bed. Or privacy. God, he loved it.

He ducked to kiss Nick again, delving into his mouth, licking at his teeth, and finally sucking on the tip of his tongue as Nick's hands tightened on him. The kiss went on and on, and Nick's hand found its way under Kelly's sweatpants to grab his ass. He dug his fingernails in. Kelly had never experienced this kind of possessiveness before he'd started fucking Nick, but now everything Nick did seemed to claim him.

There was a loud banging on the window right beside Kelly's head. They both startled, but when Kelly tried to lift up, to react, Nick held him right where he was, trapped against the steering wheel, not breaking the kiss.

"Hey, you can't do that out here!" their intruder shouted. Nick fumbled between their chests and found his badge, then slammed it against the glass, holding it there as the chain tapped against the window.

"Sorry, Detective," the disgruntled security guard said. "Didn't recognize you."

Nick snickered as he dropped the badge to resume his hold on Kelly's hair.

"That was fucking hot, man."

"So are you," Nick grunted. He raised his hips, his hard cock sliding along Kelly's, the head jutting against the inside of Kelly's thigh. He pulled at Kelly's ass, ready to recommence as if they'd never been interrupted.

Kelly groaned and lowered his head, gritting his teeth. "Nick."

Nick merely chased Kelly's mouth with his own, kissing him fiercely, pulling his hair as the kiss consumed them both. Kelly's hips started moving again of their own accord. Nick held him as if Kelly might try to get away from him.

"Let's get to the boat," Kelly gritted out. "I want you inside me."

"Too fucking late, don't stop moving," Nick gasped against Kelly's lips. He took in a deep breath as he writhed under Kelly. Kelly grunted his name again when he realized Nick was coming. Nick's grip hardened. "Kels," he whispered almost reverently. The way he gazed up at Kelly, the love and utter devotion in his eyes, was something Kelly saw every time they touched, every time they made love. He'd never seen Nick look at anyone or anything else that way.

Kelly nuzzled against his face, then bit his neck as he gave in to his own orgasm, gritting his teeth around Nick's skin to keep from shouting out for mercy. Nick shouted for him, though.

"I love you." The breathy gasp in Kelly's ear sent shivers through his body.

Kelly kissed him as they both came down from the post-orgasm high. "Love you too," he whispered. "Even if you do like hunting intergalactic librarians."

Nick rolled his eyes, valiantly fighting not to smile. He popped the handle on the door, and Kelly went tumbling out of the Range Rover to the ground.

"It was intergalactic *historians*. Damn, son, get it right."

The shower in the master berth wasn't what one would call spacious, but Nick had still convinced Kelly to join him in it. They couldn't move without touching each other, and that was just fine with Nick.

They had actually shared a lot of showers before they'd become romantically involved. Sometimes in the places they were sent with Sidewinder, water was scarce and sharing was practical. Sometimes it'd been time that was scarce, and sharing had been practical. Nick had worked hard not to make that practice even remotely sexual, no matter which teammate or random strange Marine he was sharing with. It had always been hardest with Kelly because the man had no sense of personal space and no hint of self-consciousness. But now Nick was completely at liberty to run his hands down Kelly's sides, to press him against the tile and kiss his neck, to steal the water because he was a few inches taller.

Okay, that last one he'd always done.

When they were both clean, they crawled into bed. The sun would be coming up soon. He'd have to go back to work in twenty-four hours. Until then, however, he and Kelly could wrap up together under the covers and close out the world.

Nick was almost asleep, curled on his side with Kelly wrapped around him from behind. It didn't matter how they started; Kelly always wound up the big spoon.

"What books were they?"

Nick startled back to full consciousness, inhaling noisily and blinking the sleep away. "What?"

"I'm sorry, I thought you were still awake."

"What indicated that? Was it the snoring?"

"Shut up. What books were they?"

"Uh . . ." Nick rolled to his back and rubbed his face. "One was a firsthand account of the Battles of Lexington and Concord. Diary. Really rare. Another was something about English royalty. The last one was a book of maps."

"You said there were four. What was the last one?"

"I . . . have no idea. Why?"

"Well, if they took the books, they're obviously important."

It wasn't exactly a new concept to Nick, but he'd been concentrating more on the missing objects and assuming they were *valuable*. Not necessarily that they were *important*. He pushed up onto his elbows and looked at Kelly through the darkness. "Explain."

"Okay, going with your treasure hunters theory."

"Kels, I was joking about that. Intergalactic time travelers? Come on."

"I know, but listen. They went for *books*, dude. Your average dead guy in the street can't sell rare books on the black market, and pawnshops don't deal with shit like that. Where are you going to get money for a rare book?"

"An antiquarian bookshop."

"Right, and you just fucking robbed it. So you're not trying to make money off your haul. What are books good for?"

"Hitting intruders?" Nick mumbled. He rubbed his eyes again. "Doorstops. Insomnia. Special interrogation techniques. Silencing bedmates in the middle of the night."

"All totally valid. But I'm talking about information. Books are good for information."

Nick continued to rub the heel of his palm against his eye, ruminating on that. He finally looked up, seeing stars briefly before Kelly's face swam back into focus. "You're saying they weren't after things to sell, but they're looking for something in particular."

Kelly shrugged. "Makes as much sense as robbing a bookstore, dude. How'd you know which books were stolen, anyway?"

"We recovered them at the scene." Nick sat up, staring at the mirror that lined the closet across the cabin. "Huh."

Kelly's hand drifted over Nick's bare back, tracing the lines of his tattoo and making him shiver. "What?"

"I saw someone that morning; I'd forgotten about it. I thought it was Garrett, even called out to him. But . . ."

"You thought you saw Zane? Do I need to be worried about this little zombie bromance you two have struck up?"

Nick huffed, too tired to offer Kelly a real smile. "Yeah, I'm fucking Ty's fiancé on the side, Kels. Sorry."

"I'm good with it," Kelly said with a shrug. His fingers continued to trace the lines of Nick's back. "So who was it you saw?"

"Do you remember me telling you about Ty and Zane and the CIA chasing them a few years back? Ty called from the road begging for me to pick them up in Philly?"

"Yeah, you fired at CIA agents and then got arrested to give Ty and them time to get away. That's why there's holes in your boat."

"It still floats. Anyway, the dude they were trying to keep safe, his name was Julian Cross. He was an operator trying to make a break from the Company."

"Yeah?"

"He looked a whole lot like Garrett. Maybe it was him I saw."

Kelly laughed softly, his fingers gentle against Nick's skin. "Was he nice? Did he say hi with a super-secret decoder ring?"

"I'm serious."

"You always are," Kelly drawled. He sat up, and the sheets pooled in their laps. "You think this Cross guy is behind the robbery?"

"First instinct is no. He really did seem like he was trying to break when he was on the run with Ty and Zane. He had his boyfriend with him, scared rabbit type."

"Wow, that's . . . judgey."

Nick laughed weakly. "Well, he was. And Cross was a hitter. He didn't do jobs like this."

Kelly rested his chin on Nick's shoulder, face so close that Nick couldn't even turn his head to meet his eyes. Instead, they looked at each other in the mirror. It made Nick smile, and he tried to hide it by pressing his lips together hard.

"So, why bring him up?" Kelly asked before kissing Nick's bare skin.

Nick shivered and closed his eyes. "He was there when he should be in hiding. He might know something. Might be involved."

"How do you find him?" Kelly kissed him again, moving down Nick's arm.

Nick grunted. "I don't know. I'll give Ty a call later, see if he has any advice. Actually . . . I'll call Garrett; Cross and Ty didn't get along very well."

"Surprise," Kelly sang, and he kissed the back of Nick's shoulder a last time and then flopped to the mattress. "Okay, I'm sorry I woke you. Come here and keep me warm."

Nick lay back down, sliding his body against Kelly's and finally settling with his head on Kelly's shoulder. Kelly's fingers drifted through his hair, trying to soothe him to sleep. But Nick's mind was whirring now. He kissed Kelly's chest, humming.

"You want to go in right now and start working on this, don't you?" Kelly asked, deadpan.

Nick raised his head. "Sort of. Do you mind?"

Kelly chuckled and shook his head. "My fault for waking the sleeping dog. Go on."

Nick kissed him quickly and rolled out of bed to get dressed. "Call me when you wake up, I'll come get you."

"Get me for what?"

"I'm going to see if I can get the captain to hire you as a consultant on the case." He hopped as he pulled his pants up and fastened them.

"What? Why?"

Nick grinned mischievously and crawled back into bed, his belt still in his hand. He kissed Kelly soundly. "Because I'm running with your treasure hunter theory and I'll need you to back me up."

"What?" Kelly sounded breathless and a little panicked. Nick headed for the steps, buttoning his dress shirt as he went. "That's not my theory, it's *your* theory!"

"Not according to the report I'll be submitting!" Nick called back.

"Don't you dare put my name to a time-traveling Knights Templar librarian, you crackpot!"

Nick laughed as he slid his feet into his shoes and headed for the door.

CHAPTER 3

"What are you doing here on a Saturday? How the fuck long have you been here?" Hagan asked Nick as he tossed his coat onto his desk chair.

Nick looked up from the files he was studying.

"Oh my God," Hagan said as he saw Nick's face. "You look like a feral cat in an alleyway. What have you done to yourself?"

"Found a case of energy drinks in the break room," Nick answered, his words clipped and precise. "I think I got something on this case, man."

"Is it contagious? 'Cause I'd rather not do . . . this," Hagan said as he waved his hand at Nick.

"No. Okay so, we have the books they went after in the shop, right? But why take books you can't hope to sell? Discounting the highly unlikely scenario that they had a buyer for those specific rare books, which could be true I guess—"

"O."

"I mean they could just be front men for someone with money, but still, it had to be the books themselves they were after and those books specifically."

"Dude, can you feel your tongue?"

Nick picked up the book he'd been examining and turned it so Hagan could see it. "Look. This one has a complete surveyor's map of Boston from 1819, and a copy of an earlier reproduction from 1779."

Hagan raised an eyebrow. "What happened in 1819?"

"Nothing. I don't know. But that's what all four have in common."

"1819?"

"No. They're all contemporary reports from Boston in the years after the Revolution."

"Vive la révolution. So . . . a crew of highly trained thieves broke into a rare bookstore, stole four books and two as yet unknown objects, and then *killed* a man, all because they're planning a heist of Revolutionary War era Boston?"

Nick glanced up at his partner, nodding.

"Where are they hitting next to get their time machine parts? We should put a few unis on that shit."

Nick glared at him for several seconds, then his eyes darted over Hagan's hands. "Where's my coffee?"

"Oh, fuck no." Hagan threw both cups of coffee in the trash can, shaking his head. "No more caffeine for you."

Nick stared at them, seriously thinking about reaching in after one of them, when Captain Branson paced over to their desks. Nick and Hagan both watched him expectantly. He stood over them with his hands behind his back. Nick was pretty sure he and Hagan hadn't done anything to draw their captain's ire, but you never knew.

Branson pursed his lips and peered into the trash can, then back at Nick. "Correct me if I'm misreading you, Detective O'Flaherty, but were you about to go after that cup of coffee in the trash bin?"

Nick's eyes darted to the trash can, then back to his captain's again. "Yes, sir."

Branson nodded sagely. "How long have you been here?"

"I'm not sure, sir."

Hagan cleared his throat. "Please don't ask him to explain his current theory."

Nick pressed his lips tightly together, self-aware enough to know when *not* to speak. He avoided Branson's eyes for all of two seconds before he gave in, though. "I have a consultant I'd like to bring in on the case."

"For?"

"Hunting treasure."

Branson frowned, gave Hagan one last sideways glance, then cocked his head at Nick. "Okay. Make sure he signs the waivers."

Nick and Hagan watched him walk away, aiming for his office with a steaming mug of coffee in hand.

"What just happened?" Hagan finally asked.

Nick shook his head, still frowning at his captain. Then he turned back Hagan and straightened up. "Where's the witness?"

"I left him in the break room with a uni."

"How'd he do last night?"

"After you left, he was fine. You got the Midas touch, my friend." Hagan reached to his desk like he was grasping for a cup. He looked confused for a moment before seeming to realize he'd tossed his own coffee in the trash as well. He and Nick both leaned over the edge of the desk to eye their trash can.

"I won't tell if you don't," Nick offered.

Hagan gave a single nod, then stood up and coughed, making a show of fixing his tie and smiling around the squad room as Nick fished the cups out of the trash.

Kelly had to get directions to Nick's desk, and it was like trying to find his way through a rabbit warren as he navigated the department. When he finally saw someone he recognized, Nick's partner Hagan, Kelly could have hugged the man.

"Hey, Doc, how they hanging?" Hagan asked as soon as he saw Kelly.

"Um . . . they can't complain with the current situation."

Hagan laughed. "Sorry, O always calls you Doc. I don't remember your real name," he admitted. He gestured toward the desk opposite him. "Have a seat. Want some coffee?"

"No, I'm good, thanks." Kelly eased into the chair, Nick's chair, watching Hagan suspiciously. He actually reminded Kelly a little of Nick; he was so deadpan you could never tell when he was joking.

Hagan was alternately tapping at his computer and reading a notepad on his desk, probably filling out a report or transferring notes. Kelly glanced around the room. There were more pods of desks like this one, in various degrees of organization. Nick's desk, in comparison to the others, was very clean. It was almost empty, in fact. There was a large doodling pad in the center with notes and rough sketches all over it. There was the regular desktop fare, such as a stapler and a cup of pens and a computer. Nick had been back at work for several months, but most of that time had been spent doing desk work. Kelly could imagine him sitting here, bored to tears, organizing everything again and again.

A single photograph adorned the desk, in a simple black frame. Kelly reached for it, letting a finger run across the faces of his brothers-in-arms. It was a photo of the six men of Sidewinder, all of them ten years younger, all of them grinning at the camera, dressed in their combat gear. They'd taken a picture before every mission, just in case no one came back. This had been their last mission before being decommissioned.

Nick stood in the middle of the back row, a smile on his grease-painted face. Ty had his arm around Nick's neck, and Nick was resting his elbow on Kelly's shoulder. The other three members of the team, Owen Johns, Elias Sanchez, and the Cajun they'd called Digger, were kneeling in front of them.

Kelly glanced at the desktop again. No pictures of family. None of Nick's sisters, whom Kelly knew he loved dearly. None of any of his coworkers here in Boston, past or present. Just Sidewinder.

Kelly's chest twisted and tightened, and he rubbed at the scar near his heart as it throbbed. He replaced the frame carefully.

When he looked up, Hagan was watching him. "You boys must have been some kind of special."

"We were."

A hand clapped his shoulder, and he jerked in the seat. It was difficult sometimes for Kelly to resist the urge to defend himself when something surprised him, even a decade after seeing his last combat. Of course, almost being killed on vacation in New Orleans a year or so ago, and then again on vacation in Scotland several months back, had reinforced the instinct a little.

Nick leaned over and kissed him on the cheek. Kelly turned his head and caught a real kiss from him before he straightened. He was shocked by the public display, but then, he kept having to remind himself that Nick had been out for a few years now.

"You got here okay?" Nick asked him. He sat on the edge of the desk, grinning down at Kelly.

"Yeah, no problem. Why do you look like you just ate a canary?"

Nick reached across his desk and opened a manila file folder. He tapped the paper and handed Kelly a pen. "Congratulations, you're our newest special consultant."

Kelly grunted. "Are you serious?"

"You have to promise the city you won't sue if you die."

"How could I sue if I died?"

"A paralegal," Hagan said without looking up from his computer.

Nick barked a laugh. Kelly rolled his eyes and yanked the pen from his hand, signing the consent form before either of them could make another joke.

"What am I supposed to be specializing in?" Kelly asked.

"Treasure hunting," Nick answered, still grinning widely.

"You're insane. Seriously. Did you get checked out when they let you out of the Corps this time?"

"No." Nick put a hand on Kelly's head as he slid off his desk. "Come with me."

"Are you . . . high?" Kelly muttered as he followed.

"There may have been a little too much caffeine consumption this morning, but it's evened out."

"You sure about that, bud?"

Nick laughed and ushered Kelly into what appeared to be a break room. The man from last night, JD, was sitting on one of the sofas. He stood when they entered, shuffling nervously.

Kelly went over to shake his hand. "How are you feeling?"

"I'm good, thanks."

"Still no memory, though," Nick added. He had his hand on the small of Kelly's back, his fingers sliding beneath the belt. Kelly was almost positive he didn't realize he was doing it. "We're going to work on maybe trying to jog something loose. I was hoping you'd sit in with us."

Kelly took a seat beside Nick. He knew what Nick wanted him to do without Nick having to ask him: he was using Kelly as a lie detector test without letting JD in on the fact that they were testing him.

Nick flopped a folder on the break room table and gestured for JD to sit with them. "Okay, I'm going to show you some pictures— just hold them up and then set them down. You don't say anything, just let them sink in, okay?"

JD nodded, glancing between them uneasily.

Nick opened the folder and took the top photo. He held it for a few seconds, then laid it on the side of the pile. He went through several more, and Kelly focused on JD's eyes. Whenever he thought he saw a glimmer of recognition or a reaction of any sort, he would tap Nick's thigh beneath the table and Nick would lay that photo sideways.

When they got through the whole pile, Nick separated them, taking only the photos he'd set down sideways. "Okay," he said to JD, still smiling warmly. "This time if you get anything, let us know. Okay?"

"Okay."

Nick held up the first few photos. Kelly couldn't see what they were, but as he watched JD's face, he could see the man struggling to remember. He'd figured out what they were doing. He knew the photos in this second round were somehow more important than the first. Kelly's heart went out to him. He looked so lost and frustrated.

On the fifth photo, JD held his hand out. "Stop," he said urgently.

Nick froze, holding the photo up as JD stared at it.

"I've seen that," JD whispered. He plucked the photo from Nick's fingers and scowled at it. "This feels familiar to me. I know I've seen this before. What is this?"

Nick glanced at Kelly, and suddenly he looked grim. He rested both elbows on the table and frowned at JD. "It's one of the items that was stolen from the bookstore. We got the IDs an hour ago."

JD's head shot up, his eyes widening.

"It's a brooch worn by a Revolutionary War soldier during the Battle of Bunker Hill. The owner's daughter said it'd been in their family for over two-hundred years."

JD's mouth worked silently, and he looked from the photo to Nick and back. "So since I recognize it . . . does this mean I stole it?"

Kelly glanced at Nick, holding his breath when Nick met his eyes. Nick looked truly regretful. He joked about being the bad cop and how everyone here considered him a hard-ass, but Kelly knew better. Nick had the purest heart of anyone he'd ever known.

"All it means is that you've seen this before," Nick assured JD. "You could have been a regular customer at the shop. You could have seen this photo somewhere, say . . . an insurance company or a museum. The only thing it proves is that you weren't there by chance. You are connected to this robbery somehow, that's all we can say with any certainty."

JD took a deep, shaky breath. "Okay."

Nick tapped his stack of photos, straightening them, then he set them on the table as he stood. "We'll be right back. You need anything? Food, drink?"

JD answered with a dejected shake of his head.

Nick and Kelly left him sitting there. Kelly noticed a uniform lurking near the door as they exited, and Nick gave him a nod as they passed. Whether JD knew it or not, he was being held prisoner.

"You were blowing smoke up his ass, right?" Kelly said under his breath. "He's your main suspect, isn't he?"

"Pretty much," Nick admitted. "He's looking damn guilty."

"That sucks. To commit a crime and not even remember why you did it?"

"Like Tijuana that one time."

Nick and Kelly both shuddered with the shared memory. Nick sat at his desk and turned his chair to glance back at the break room.

"Dude," Hagan said. "I know in your mind he's a puppy in a cardboard box with a 'take me home' sign around his neck, but you can't fight the evidence building up here."

"Did the prints come back yet?" Nick asked, sounding frustrated.

"Yeah. John Doe Number Alive didn't hit anywhere. But John Doe Number Dead came up with a prior." Hagan turned his computer screen around so Nick and Kelly could see it.

"Darragh O'Doyle," Nick read under his breath.

"That sounds made up," Kelly said. "Is that real?"

"He's not local," Hagan told them.

"Irish national?" Nick asked. Hagan nodded. "Known associates?"

"None listed. He got pinched last year but he never turned on his crew. Did six months, got out on good behavior, last record of him was that he'd headed back to Ireland."

"Well he's back now. So we have an Irish connection." Nick sat back in his chair, making a clicking sound with his teeth and tongue as he stared at the screen. "Let's expand the fingerprints to international databases, see if we get a hit."

Kelly cleared his throat, waiting until Hagan got up and left before leaning toward Nick. "Isn't Julian Cross Irish?"

Nick nodded and pulled his phone from his back pocket. "We need to talk to him." He hit the speaker button and set his phone on the desk between them.

"Special Agent in Charge Garrett here."

"Well, aren't we fancy," Kelly teased.

Nick shook his head. "Hey, Garrett, it's O'Flaherty. And the Doc, obviously."

"Oh God, what now? Are you in jail? Being held by the IRA? Stuck on a reef in the Caribbean?"

"Wow," Kelly said. "That's uncalled for."

Zane laughed. "I thought being engaged to Ty gave me some extra snark privileges."

"Hey!" Nick shouted. "Do I come running when you need help? Did I get shoved off the edge of a cliff for your ungrateful ass? Does my boat still have bullet holes in it?"

"It still floats," Zane countered, a smirk obvious in his voice.

Nick grunted.

"Haven't heard from you two in a while, what's going on?" Zane said, voice casual. Kelly had grown familiar enough with Zane to know he was taking care with his words, though. "You need to come to Baltimore, come see us."

Kelly gave Nick a sideways glance to see how he'd react to that, but Nick was expressionless. "Sorry, babe, this isn't a social call. I need to know how to get in touch with Julian Cross."

"Cross. Why?"

Nick made another clicking sound, refusing to answer.

"Never mind, I didn't ask," Zane said quickly. "I don't know how to get in touch with him. I assume he just shows up when he smells blood."

"How about Grady? You think he'd know?"

"Hell no. Ty spits nails when you mention Cross's name. He says Cross stole his kitties."

"That's what I figured," Nick said with a sigh. "That's why I called you."

"Is it?" Zane asked pointedly.

Kelly tensed and couldn't stop himself from glancing toward the framed photo of their team, Ty's arm around Nick's shoulders as they smiled. The state of Nick and Ty's fracturing friendship was a topic only the bravest of men would touch on. Zane had balls of brass to do it.

Kelly cleared his throat and leaned closer to the phone. "We figured with your Bureau contacts, you'd be the better source. Since Ty is all . . . wild card now."

"Right," Zane said wryly.

"You got a lead on Cross, or no?" Nick asked, his words more clipped than they had been.

"No. Want me to put out some feelers? Or get Ty on it? Please God, let me put Ty on it, he needs something to do besides remodeling that damn building."

"No. Fuck no. I don't want Cross to know I'm coming."

"If you're looking for him, he already knows."

"Right. Hey, thanks Garrett. We'll talk to you later." Nick ended the call and slammed his hand onto the desk. "Damn it!"

"That mean Cross is a dead end?" Kelly asked gently.

"For now. Next thread." Nick tapped the evidence photos of the books that had been recovered at the scene. "We follow your books."

"My books? No. No, you're not pinning those on me for when they go bust." Nick smirked. Kelly snorted. "You're enjoying this too much."

"Come on, babe, it's a treasure hunt," Nick teased.

"You *hope* it's a treasure hunt, or you're going to look stupid."

"You're the special consultant."

"You're the detective who called in the special consultant."

Nick glanced over Kelly's shoulder, then stood and stole a quick kiss. "Come on. Let's get some lunch before Hagan gets back and I have to buy his food."

They didn't even make it to the stairs before Hagan caught them trying to sneak out. "Fuck no, I get to interrogate the boyfriend, damn you," Hagan called to them. He grabbed his coat off his chair, making it spin around and bang into the desk.

They stopped to wait for him. Nick was chuckling softly.

"I like your partner," Kelly said quietly.

"Yeah, don't tell him that though."

Kelly nodded, but Nick's eyes were straying to the break room, where the uniformed officer was still standing guard. Kelly's brow furrowed as he thought about JD sitting in there alone, his mind turning over everything he couldn't remember. He knew Nick was thinking the same thing.

"Hey," he murmured. "Is it legal and shit to take your witness with us? Maybe new surroundings will get him remembering faster."

Nick chewed on his bottom lip, frowning, his eyes lingering on the break room door. He took a deep breath and then sighed before heading over there.

Hagan was fighting with his coat when he joined Kelly. "He bringing the stray to lunch?"

"Did you expect anything less from him?" Kelly asked fondly.

Hagan grunted. "You should see the last stray he convinced me to keep around. Teeny tiny little puppy he found in a storm drain, half-dead and starving in the middle of the night. All the local shelters were closed up so we had to take it in for the night. Bastard told me he couldn't have it on his boat 'cause it'd fall off and drown. Fucking thing was too weak to walk and he convinced me it'd take a header off the side of a boat!"

Kelly couldn't stop his grin.

Hagan appeared almost sheepish. "I still got that damn mutt. Weighs a hundred pounds. Best friend I ever had."

Kelly laughed. "Well he can't keep this stray either. You have room for an amnesiac with great bone structure?"

"Not if he pisses on the carpet like the last one," Hagan grumbled as he headed for the elevators.

They sat at a booth in a local pub near the precinct house that obviously catered to cops. In fact, after staring around at the pictures on the walls long enough, Kelly found Nick up there. He gazed up at the photo, smirking. Most of the photos were official, full uniform and regalia, with stone-faced men and women staring at the camera like they could cause it to burst into flame. It reminded Kelly of the military photos they'd taken.

Nick didn't exactly smile in photos, but he didn't keep a straight face either. The look he usually gave was more of a challenge, with a half smirk that basically said "come at me, bro" and a glint that said Nick would enjoy the fight. He'd made the same expression in his police portrait that sat high on one of the walls, and Kelly couldn't take his eyes off that face.

"So," JD finally said, clearing his throat and glancing around uncomfortably. "Is this like a last meal or something?"

"You're awful fatalistic for a dude who lived through being shot in the head," Hagan observed.

"Maybe if I remembered it, I'd be more likely to look on the bright side," JD grumbled.

"Innocent until proven guilty, babe." Nick's voice was low and sent a shiver up Kelly's spine. "Look, we haven't had any hits, but we have eliminated some things, and frankly, that's as good as we could hope for."

"Right." Hagan pointed his fork at Nick. "We put you through all the systems and got nothing."

"That . . . sounds awesome," JD said, voice flat and sarcastic.

"What that means is you don't have a record," Nick offered.

"Meaning I'm a smart felon and I've never been caught. You're right, that is good news."

Kelly coughed to cover a laugh.

Nick pursed his lips, narrowing his eyes. "It also means you're not military, and you've never worked government or municipal. You're not part of any education systems, and so on. Rules out everything you would have been printed for."

JD nodded and looked down at his hands, turning them over to run a finger across his tips. His nails were still stained from the ink they'd printed him with.

Nick was watching him too, frowning harder the longer he looked at him. He reached to the cuff of his shirt, unbuttoning and rolling it up. He showed JD the inside of his arm and tapped the tattoo with his finger. "You know what this is?"

JD nodded. "I told you yesterday, I recognized it. It's the Recon Jack."

Nick glanced at Kelly, one eyebrow raised. Kelly couldn't school his features fast enough to hide the surprise. Nick looked around the pub. It was early for lunch, so there weren't many people there. He began to unbutton his shirt.

"Dude," Hagan said through a mouthful of food. "That's your *other* job. Got to stop confusing them. Tired of suspects stuffing your pants with dollar bills during interrogation."

Nick shoved his sleeve aside, then pulled up the sleeve of his undershirt to reveal a well-defined biceps and shoulder. Kelly leaned away from him to get a better view. Nick glanced sideways at him, giving him a dirty look.

"Yeah, I'm perving on you. What then?" Kelly asked.

They all laughed at him, and Hagan whistled and pointed his fork at the bite mark Nick had exposed on his neck. "Good Lord," he said. "Do you even call it sex, or is it more like sparring with you two?"

Nick rolled his eyes. He tapped the oversized tattoo on his shoulder. It covered his entire shoulder, running from the center of his collarbone to his biceps and covering both the front and back sides of his arm. It was a work of art, pure and simple, following the defined lines of Nick's muscles. "You know what this is?"

"Eagle, globe, and anchor," JD answered immediately. "Marines."

Hagan's eyebrows had shot higher, but he remained silent.

Nick began to button up his shirt again, and he jerked his chin toward Kelly. "Show him yours."

Kelly nodded. The one on his arm was partially visible under the sleeve of his T-shirt, so he just pulled the sleeve up and turned so JD could get a good look. It was a simple anchor, but with snakes encircling it and wings at the top to form a caduceus. The word NAVY was written on a scroll at the bottom.

JD studied it for a moment, then glanced between Nick and Kelly. "Well, it's a Navy tattoo, that much is obvious. I don't recognize it, but I know it means you were a corpsman. Probably a SARC, since you two served together and he's a Marine."

"Goddamn, he knows more about this shit than I do," Hagan said.

Kelly glanced between them. He wasn't sure what this meant since he didn't have the whole picture, but Nick looked troubled. Kelly didn't blame him. This guy hadn't printed as military, but he knew what Nick's Recon Jack was, and that was a pretty specialized symbol. People might recognize it as being military, but they didn't know what it meant, not really.

JD did. People who knew military but weren't military were usually mercs.

"What?" JD asked, beginning to fidget again. "Is this bad? I see the look on your faces; this is bad."

Nick ran his fingers across his lower lip, not responding. Kelly watched him, wondering if he'd come to the same conclusion, and if he'd be honest with his suspect when he did.

"Okay," Nick finally said. "You've obviously been exposed to some military culture at some point because your knowledge is above average."

"So . . . what, I'm some sort of gun for hire then? Like Blackwater, or . . ." JD trailed off, staring at the tabletop. "How'd I know that name? How do I know what that is?"

"Hey, yesterday you were telling me you knew all kinds of things, sparkly vampires and whatever," Nick said, his voice sliding back into that soothing honey tone he used so often. "Blackwater is a well-known company, it's not weird you'd know it. Just stay calm about it. This is stuff any military brat would know, okay?"

Hagan gave JD a pat on the shoulder and an almost reassuring smile. "We'll figure this shit out. My boy here is a dog with a bone; we got you."

Kelly stayed quiet. He did wonder, however, if Hagan's words were a warning for JD to heed when his memory did start coming back.

We got you.

CHAPTER 4

Nick led the way out of the pub, holding the door for the others and giving the street a cursory glance out of habit. Movement out of the corner of his eye drew his attention, and standing on the other side of the street was Julian Cross. His hands were in his pockets, his head cocked as he watched them.

Nick let the door fall away from his hand, and it closed in Kelly's face. Nick heard the impact and the cussing that accompanied it, but he took a step toward the road anyway.

"Hey!" he shouted.

Cross merely shook his head, then turned and melted into the lunchtime crowd. Glass shattered behind Nick, accompanied by the pops of gunfire. Nick lunged for a nearby car, glancing back at the others. They were still inside the restaurant. Kelly had gotten them to cover as soon as he'd sensed that Nick had seen something.

Nick drew his gun and crouched behind the car, trying to decide where the shots had originated. Was it Cross? No one was that fast, the shots were coming from an entirely different location. If the shooter had been aiming for Nick, they'd have hit him. The shots sprayed the door to the pub instead, ruining the entryway, gouging holes in the brick and mortar.

"Doc!" Nick shouted above the din. He couldn't see any of them, and he prayed they'd gotten to cover.

Just as quickly as it had begun, it was over. An otherworldly silence fell on the normally bustling street. Nick waited a few breaths before peering over the top of the car. All he saw were people flattened on the sidewalks, covering their heads. No one was running. No one was trying to conceal a weapon.

Glass tinkled behind him, and Nick saw Kelly crouching against the doorframe, gaze raking the street.

"You okay?" he called to Nick.

Nick nodded. He gestured for Kelly to retreat back into the restaurant, and Kelly immediately backed into the dim interior. Nick peered over the car again. People were cautiously raising their heads, crying, looking around like frightened animals in an earthquake.

Then one man rose calmly to his feet, brushed off his black overcoat, and began walking down the sidewalk as if nothing had happened.

Nick stood. "Cross!"

Julian didn't hesitate or look back. He broke into a sprint. Nick lunged to his feet and gave chase.

Kelly shoved away from the doorway and onto the sidewalk as soon as Nick bolted. He put a hand on his head, cursing under his breath. His eyes scanned the building tops and the people who were slowly getting to their feet. He didn't see any threats. Whoever had opened fire on them had retreated by now.

"Did he get eyes on the shooter?" Hagan shouted as he jogged out to join Kelly. He stood on his tiptoes to catch sight of Nick and the man he was chasing.

They could see both men dodging passersby, veering out into the road as the chase carried them toward the massive intersection that Kelly was pretty sure bordered Boston Commons.

"He's gaining on him," JD said. He had joined them without Kelly realizing it.

Kelly glanced around, then put a hand on JD's shoulder. "You need to get back inside, come on."

Several cops had been eating at the pub, both on and off duty, and they streamed out to help contain the scene. Hagan stood in the doorway, calling in the incident and requesting backup for his partner, who was in pursuit of a suspect.

Kelly finally gave in and climbed on top of the ruined car Nick had taken cover behind. He stretched to see down the narrow street, trying to find either man. He finally caught sight of Nick, trudging back down the sidewalk, alone.

"Oh, he's going to be so pissed," Hagan grumbled as soon as Kelly relayed the information.

When Nick got closer, he was indeed fuming.

"What happened?" Kelly demanded.

"I lost him!" Nick snapped.

"Was it the shooter?" Hagan asked.

"I don't think so."

"Then why'd you chase him down?" Hagan asked.

Nick sighed heavily and shrugged at Kelly. "You know the holes in my boat?" he asked Hagan.

"Yeah, but it still floats."

"Right. That was the guy. Cross. I've seen him twice now, once at the murder scene, and just now. He's up to something."

Hagan flopped his arms dramatically. "Why is the CIA robbing a bookstore in Boston?"

"Are . . . are you saying I might be CIA?" JD asked incredulously.

"No," Nick and Hagan both said at the same time.

"I thought Cross got out of the game," Kelly said. "Why's he back in it?"

Nick shook his head and lowered it a little, like a bull preparing to charge. His jaw tightened and his nostrils flared. Kelly tensed, like he might need to talk Nick down from something. He rarely needed to, because Nick's control of his temper was near legendary. But when he did . . . Kelly had put him on his back a few times to keep him from hurting someone.

"Cross wasn't the one taking shots at our witness, so let's worry about him later and get JD somewhere safe," Nick finally said through gritted teeth.

"This place have a back door?" Kelly asked.

Hagan indicated for them to follow him. Nick shrugged out of his suit coat and put it around JD's shoulders, and he stole a Red Sox hat from the coat rack as they passed by it and placed it on JD's head.

"Eyes on the ground," Nick murmured close to his ear.

JD pulled the hat lower and hunched his shoulders, shrugging into Nick's coat as they stepped into the narrow alleyway behind the pub. He and Hagan started off toward the end of the alley, but Nick stopped and pulled Kelly aside.

"If the words 'I want you to go home until it's safe' come out of your mouth, I'm going to break one of your ribs," Kelly told him before Nick could speak.

Nick finally tore his eyes away from JD's retreating form and met Kelly's with a small smile. "You know me better than that." He bent and took his spare gun from a holster at his ankle, then pressed it into Kelly's hands. "I do want you do go back to the *Fiddler*, though, and get two spares for us. You know where I keep them?"

"In every nook and cranny you can find." Kelly automatically checked the gun, even though he knew Nick would have it loaded and ready.

"Good. Ammo's in a galley drawer. If you're going to be shot at, you might as well be able to shoot back."

Kelly nodded silently. "What's the plan? With the witness, I mean?"

"We'll have to find him a new safe house. Make sure we're not tailed. They knew he was at the precinct; we have to assume the hotel is blown." Nick chewed on the inside of his cheek, his eyes focused on something over Kelly's shoulder. "I'm thinking about putting him on the *Fiddler*."

Kelly glanced up at him, eyes widening. "You're going to hide a witness on your boat?"

"The marina has security. We'd both be there; we'll pull Hagan too. We can put her out in the harbor each night, make it a job to get to him."

"Nick."

Nick met his eyes again, and they were hard as jade. The stunning color almost made Kelly stutter.

He took a deep breath. "Look, I know you've got a soft spot for this guy, but you've got to remember he might not be what he says he is."

"Soft spot?"

"Please," Kelly said with weak laugh. "If we weren't a thing, you'd be all over him."

Nick opened his mouth to protest, then shut it with a snap of his teeth. "You're probably right," he admitted. A sly smile came over him and he hooked his finger through Kelly's belt loop. "But we *are* a thing."

Kelly allowed him a brief kiss, just enough time for him to get back in Kelly's good graces, then he playfully shoved Nick away and turned to follow after Hagan and JD.

"Making out in back alleys!" Hagan called to Nick. "Old habits die hard, huh buddy?"

"Shut up!"

"You want me to sleep on a boat?" Hagan asked. "You remember I get seasick, right?"

"When you give me a better idea, I'll run with it," Nick challenged. He knew it wasn't a perfect plan, and it wouldn't hold up for long, but until they had a safe house they could be confident in, he would rather keep JD close.

JD sat in the hard plastic chair beside their desks, frowning as he listened. "I wonder if I get seasick," he mused. "I guess we'll find out."

Nick glanced at him, then back at his partner. "Why does the guy with amnesia who's been shot at twice in two days complain *less* than you do?"

Hagan grumbled and stood, tossing his tie over his shoulder in a huff. He grabbed his empty coffee cup to go off in search of a refill.

Nick sat back, lacing his fingers behind his head and closing his eyes with a sigh.

"Detective?" JD whispered. He waited until Nick had opened his eyes again to continue. "When the shooting started today, I remembered something."

Nick sat forward. "Yeah? What was it?"

"A face. It like . . . flashed through my mind. I think it might be the guy who shot at me before."

"Can you describe him?"

"Yeah, dark hair, blue eyes—"

"Not to me, to an artist. Hold on." Nick reached for the phone. "This is Detective O'Flaherty, Robbery/Homicide. I need an artist up here to work with my witness."

The woman gave him confirmation and he hung up, turning his chair so he could face JD. "Okay. So far I've got these little threads to this case, and I can't seem to tie any of them together. I need your help."

Fear settled in JD's eyes in a way Nick felt almost guilty for. He'd been coddling the man, wanting him to feel safe, but someone had tried to put a second bullet in him today. It was time to take off the gloves.

JD's jaw hardened, though, and he nodded. "Whatever you need from me."

"I'm going to give you three subjects, okay, and you tell me off the top of your head what they have to do with each other."

JD's brow furrowed, but he nodded anyway.

Nick held up his hand and counted off. "American Revolution. Ireland. Stolen goods."

JD opened his mouth like he was going to respond, then shut it again, staring off over Nick's shoulder with a scowl. He opened his mouth again, leaning forward, then sat back and frowned harder. "The Continental payroll gold."

"What?"

"Yeah. Yeah. The Continental payroll! There was a redcoat lieutenant during the war. The legend is that he and his men intercepted a Continental Army payroll delivery somewhere. Took off with a wagon full of gold bars as it sat at a roadside inn."

Nick ran a finger over one eyebrow, trying not to look skeptical, or worse, annoyed. He was writing all of it down anyway. "Okay. Go on."

"That's . . . that's all I know. The gold was never recovered."

Nick stared at him for a few seconds, and Hagan returned and flopped into his seat, looking between them silently.

"Okay," Nick said patiently. "What does a missing Continental Army payroll have to do with Ireland?"

"The lieutenant was later revealed to be a supporter of Ireland. He was involved in the Irish Rebellion of 1798."

"What are we talking about now?" Hagan asked.

Nick sighed heavily. "I told him to give me a connection between all our threads. Revolutionary War objects, Irish thugs, and stealing shit."

Hagan placed a fresh cup of coffee by Nick's elbow. He pointed at JD. "You can't remember your own name, but you can recite facts about the fucking Irish Rebellion of seventeen whatever it was?"

JD shrugged one shoulder, looking a little perturbed. "At least I can remember he doesn't like coffee," he said with a jab of his finger at Nick.

"Ha!" Nick barked.

"Friendly fire," Hagan said. He put on a fake Irish accent. "Jesus, Mary, and Joseph."

Nick fired up his computer. "We'll just Google this bitch." A few moments later he'd brought up a search page for the British lieutenant's name. Almost every result was about the lost Revolutionary War treasure. Nick clicked the first one.

JD moved his chair so he could see the screen too. It was a chat board for amateur treasure seekers, with each post offering theories on where the gold had gone, stories about the poster having gone searching for it somewhere, and the occasional person telling everyone else they were stupid.

"See?" JD said. He pointed at one of the posts. "Right here in Boston."

Nick looked sideways at him, studying his profile while JD's attention was elsewhere. It was hard to forget the many warnings that had popped up about JD's authenticity, including the one from Kelly, but Nick hadn't felt like he was being lied to once. The man struck him as genuine.

Kelly cleared his throat as he approached the desk. Nick looked up at him, still scowling thoughtfully.

"Everything okay?" Kelly asked carefully.

"You know our treasure hunter theory?" Nick asked, wincing at their private joke. Kelly nodded. "We might have been a little too on the nose."

"What are you talking about?" Kelly craned his neck to see the computer. Nick watched his changeable eyes as they darted over the screen, scanning the posts. "Stolen Continental payroll?"

"They were paid in gold bars and coins," JD provided.

"Meaning if it was hidden somewhere and left there, it's worth millions today," Kelly surmised. "Yeah okay, that's worth killing over."

"Before you guys go all Indiana O'Flaherty on me," Hagan drawled, "what does that lost treasure have to do with our case?"

Nick took a breath to answer, but he realized he didn't exactly know. They all looked to JD.

"I . . . I didn't say it had anything to do with the robbery," JD reminded them, his blue eyes going wider. "You gave me three things to associate, I associated them."

Kelly sat on the edge of Nick's desk, turned sideways so he could still see Hagan and the computer screen. "What was the other thing stolen from the place? One was the brooch, what was the other?"

Nick tapped Kelly's knee to get him to scoot over, and he unlocked the desk drawer beneath him and reached in for the file. He set it on the desk and opened it up to find the photos. "It was a bundle of letters."

"Bundle of letters," Kelly echoed. "What the hell?"

"Yeah, the brooch I get, it had a few precious gems on it," Hagan said. "But the letters are . . . parchment. Tied with twine. No value whatsoever."

"The value of words is measured by those who read them," JD told him. He stopped short, scowling hard. "Is that a quote? What is that from? Did I come up with that?"

Nick almost laughed at him. He bit his lip to keep a straight face instead, and held up the photo the bookstore owner's daughter had provided of the stolen items. Kelly took it from him, looking it over in silence.

"These are Revolutionary War era?" he finally asked. Nick nodded. "Do we know what they said?"

"The daughter said her father had them transcribed once, because the handwriting was hard to decipher. She's trying to hunt up the file, said she'd email it when she found it. Why, what are you thinking?"

"I mean, if we go on the theory these people are hunting this lost payroll treasure, this makes sense," Kelly said with a tap of the photo. "These are contemporary accounts. And you said one of the books they stole was a soldier's diary, right?"

"Yeah, he was at the Battles of Lexington and Concord, and later Bunker Hill."

"Concord?" JD asked. "After their defeat, several British columns broke off and scattered across the countryside as they retreated along Battle Road to Boston. One of those could easily have intercepted a payroll delivery."

"Why hide it instead of making off with it?" Hagan asked.

"And desert the British Imperial Army?" JD shook his head, grinning widely. "Might as well take a knife to the eye, you'd live longer. The theory is they hid it somewhere, intending to come back for it when the war was won."

"Only they didn't win the war," Nick said.

JD clucked his tongue. He looked pleased with himself for the first time since they'd met him, but the expression faded quickly. He glanced down at his hands, twisting his fingers together.

"You okay, bud?" Kelly asked him.

JD gave them a weak attempt at a smile. "I know more about this than I do about myself."

"You do know a lot more about this than most," Kelly agreed. "At least you can remember it; that's a good sign."

Nick raised his head as an idea hit him. "Do they fingerprint college professors?" he asked Hagan.

Hagan pursed his lips. "Not to my knowledge. Some universities are starting to, but only for new hires."

"School's out, right? What if he's a professor at a local college? If he lived alone, no one might know he was gone until classes start back."

"No missing persons report would be filed yet," Hagan said with a nod.

"Send his photo out to every institution in a fifty mile radius. See if we can get a hit."

"On it," Hagan said, and he lurched out of his chair.

"College professor, huh?" JD said quietly. "Not international treasure thief. You're awfully optimistic, Detective."

"That's what we love about him," Kelly said, and when Nick raised his head, Kelly's eyes were on him, a gentle smile gracing his lips. Nick squeezed his knee, keeping his hand there.

"What's the next move?" JD asked. If he was uncomfortable with Nick and Kelly's small shows of affection, he didn't let on.

"After you work with the sketch artist, we'll get you somewhere safe. The *Fiddler's Green* should do the trick, just need to get the captain to sign off on it."

JD scowled, biting his lip instead of saying anything.

"What?"

"I just . . . if these people are trying to kill me, the only way I'll really be safe is if they're caught. We should try to find the treasure they're after."

Nick laughed and scratched at his chin. "Find the treasure."

"Right?" JD asked eagerly. "We find the treasure, we find them, and I don't have to duck in alleyways anymore."

"I get you, I do," Nick offered. "But I'm a cop, man, not a treasure hunter. I told you I'd keep you safe, that I'd find out who you are, and that's what I intend to do."

JD sat back in his plastic chair, nodding dejectedly. A few moments later the sketch artist arrived, and she took JD into one of the interrogation pods where they could work.

Kelly slid into the chair, his knee knocking against Nick's thigh as he slouched. "Why did you play dumb with him?" Kelly asked quietly.

"What are you talking about?"

"The Battle of Bunker Hill. Lexington and Concord. Missing treasure right here under your nose in Boston. Look me in the eye and tell me you didn't know anything about any of that, you goddamn history nerd."

Nick's lips twitched, and he sighed heavily. "I knew I'd regret fucking someone who's known me for over a decade."

Kelly snickered quietly, waiting for an answer.

"I wanted him to give us the information," Nick explained. "I wanted to see if he'd be right, for one, if he'd omit anything important. Or lie."

Kelly remained silent, watching him. Nick slid his hand over Kelly's knee. "You're dying to go digging into that treasure story, aren't you?"

Nick nodded fervently, not even trying to deny it.

Kelly laughed, throwing his head back. He slumped further in the chair, and his knee slid along Nick's thigh. Nick cleared his throat and glanced around the room, shifting uncomfortably.

"So what's our *real* next move?"

"Julian Cross." Nick leaned forward, his hand squeezing Kelly's knee. "He's out there for a reason, showing himself; we just need to bring him in. How do you feel about a little bait and switch?"

Kelly licked his lips, then grinned slowly. "Sounds about as fun as you bending me over one of those interrogation desks."

Nick groaned and pushed his chair back so they were no longer in contact. "Don't fucking tempt me, okay? Those rooms have video feeds."

"Really? Do they record?"

Nick had to get up and walk away as Kelly laughed merrily at his desk. "You're killing me, Kels," he called over his shoulder. "*Killing* me!"

Kelly left before Hagan came back, and before JD was done with the sketch artist. He headed out of the front of the building, taking his time as he strolled toward the parking lot where Nick's Range Rover was parked. He removed his black leather jacket and tossed it into the car, then rummaged in the backseat for Nick's green canvas jacket instead. It was too big at the chest, but it didn't envelop him. He gave his shoulders a shake and pulled the coat tighter around him as he meandered out of the parking lot. He wandered along the quaint little side streets of Boston, enjoying the architecture, window-shopping until he was near the station again. He leaned against the side of a building, standing near a pillar and watching.

They had put JD in Nick's suit coat again, covering his shaggy blond hair with the pilfered Red Sox hat and walking him down the back alley behind the police station toward Nick's Range Rover.

Nick walked alongside him, his hand loose on JD's elbow. Kelly knew himself well enough to know he was a little jealous of the chemistry Nick and JD seemed to have. But he also knew Nick well enough to know he didn't need to be worried.

He reminded himself what he was supposed to be doing, and he glanced around the area, watching the shadows, watching the narrows. Nick was supposed to lead JD into a bottleneck, where a fence jutted out near a big blue dumpster and would force them to veer toward the entrance to a side alley, and that was where Kelly headed.

He was almost too late. As soon as Nick and JD neared the alley, Nick shoved JD to the side and pulled his gun, obviously seeing something coming out of the corner of his eye.

Kelly moved with lightning speed, hitting the big man from the side and wrapping him up as they fell. He rolled with him, then let him loose, sending him into an uncontrolled tumble as Kelly hopped to his feet. Before Julian Cross could right himself, Kelly was on him again. He kicked at his chest, and Julian blocked the blow, but he wasn't fast enough to block the next one when Kelly came up with a roundhouse kick that caught him in the side of the head and sent him sprawling.

Julian was on his hands and knees, pushing himself to his feet, and Kelly went at him again. Julian was at least four inches taller than he was, but Kelly didn't care. Size had never fazed him before. He aimed high this time, landing a few blows around the ribs and kidneys, missing a few as Julian blocked them. Then Kelly went in for the kill, leaping at Julian with a kick to the chest that should've leveled him. Julian brought up both hands, though, catching Kelly's foot. Kelly went with the momentum, kicking off the ground and using Julian's hold on him for leverage. He caught Julian under the chin as he flipped himself backward, and he landed in a crouch several feet from his opponent.

He was breathing hard, body tense in expectation of Julian getting up again. He heard Nick's footsteps behind him and he stood slowly. Nick patted him on the shoulder as they both stood over Julian, who was holding his face and lying on his back, cursing in an Irish accent.

"That's a lot more fun to watch when it's not me you're doing it to," Nick told Kelly, his voice warm with pride and possibly a little lust.

Kelly smirked at him.

Nick grabbed Julian by his elbow and hefted him off the ground, then jerked his arms behind him and shoved him against the wall of the nearest building. He patted him down from head to toe, taking special care around his wrists. Kelly wound up holding an armful of weaponry and other . . . implements. Then Nick slapped a pair of handcuffs on Julian and hissed in his ear. "Welcome to Boston."

CHAPTER 5

Kelly sat in the backseat with Julian, watching him like a hawk. Nick could see them in his rearview mirror as he guided the car toward the marina. Any other collar, and he'd have taken him right back inside to the precinct, but Nick had dealt with Julian Cross before. He wasn't the type you paraded into a police department without expecting trouble—and probably the CIA—to follow close behind.

"I thought you were some sort of camp counselor," Julian finally said to Kelly. "Work with troubled kids and all that."

Kelly pursed his lips. "Yeah. It's called Camp Asskicker. I'll give you a 'you tried' badge next time I see you."

Julian snorted and actually smiled before meeting Nick's eyes in the mirror. "The handcuffs aren't really necessary, Detective."

"Humor me," Nick said. "You're lucky you're not in a cell. Why are you in Boston? Who's your mark?"

"I don't have a mark. I'm retired, didn't Grady tell you?"

"Seeing is believing, babe. And I've seen you at not one but two crime scenes in the past two days. So I'll ask you again, why are you in Boston?"

Julian sighed, and his eyes darted to JD. "I'd rather speak in private, if it's all the same to you."

"Fine," Nick growled.

They pulled into the marina parking lot and Nick swiped his security card to open the gates. He could feel the tension pouring off everyone in the car, including himself. It was days like this he sort of wished he'd pulled anchor on his yacht and just sailed into the Atlantic when he'd gotten home.

They got several double takes and glares from Nick's neighbors as he led Julian, still handcuffed, toward his boat slip. The *Fiddler's Green* was the largest vessel in the marina, and it sat on the very end of the very last dock. They had to walk past basically every other boat in the marina. Nick didn't care, though. Whenever any of these fuckers had a problem, they came to Detective O'Flaherty to fix it. They could deal with dangerous international criminals being led by in handcuffs every couple of years.

They boarded the yacht, and Nick shoved Julian toward one of the sofas in the salon. "You here to talk?"

Julian nodded. "I still owe you for your previous assistance, Detective. I intend to keep this civil."

"Attacking them in an alleyway, that's civil?" Kelly asked.

"I believe *I* was the one who was attacked," Julian corrected. "You'll notice I didn't take a single swing at you. I was waiting until the detective was away from his partner to approach him."

Nick stared at him for several more seconds, then handed Kelly the keys to the handcuffs. "Let him loose. I'll be right back."

Kelly nodded silently, and Julian stood up to give him access to the handcuffs. Nick gestured for JD to follow him toward the lower deck. They both had to duck going down the steps. It was second nature for Nick, but JD bumped his head and cursed quietly, rubbing the spot as he followed Nick to the VIP cabin.

Nick gestured toward the bed and the bathroom. "Make yourself at home, okay? But stay here until one of us comes to get you."

"Right," JD said with a nervous nod. "Is he the one trying to kill me? Are you sure it's okay to let him go?"

"No," Nick answered. "And no. But we'll trust him until he proves me wrong."

JD met his eyes, and it was obvious from the look on his face that he caught Nick's meaning. "Just like you're trusting me. Right?"

"Exactly," Nick said. "Stay here."

He left JD, closing the door behind him, and headed back up to join Julian and Kelly in the salon. They were sitting opposite each other, both of them unblinking, both of them smirking slightly.

Nick put his hands on his hips and took a deep breath to get control of his temper. "Okay," he said finally. "Julian Cross, this is Kelly Abbott. He kicked your ass once and he'll do it again."

"Again. I wasn't fighting back," Julian reminded. He looked Kelly up and down. "Although he does seem quite formidable for his stature."

"Whatever," Nick said, knowing that nothing Julian could say would ruffle Kelly's feathers. He sat in the chair beside Kelly and leaned both elbows on his knees, waiting for Julian to begin talking.

"Do you know who you have in that cabin downstairs?" Julian finally asked.

"No. Do you?"

"No, unfortunately."

Disappointment spiked hard before Nick could get control of it. He had been resting a lot of hope on Julian being able to shed some light on this. "Okay," he said through gritted teeth. "So what do you know?"

Julian clucked his tongue. "I know what they're after."

Nick and Kelly waited, staring at Julian as he grinned at them.

"Well, what are you waiting for here, dude, dramatic music?" Kelly finally blurted. "What the hell are they after?"

Julian looked a little annoyed that they hadn't enjoyed the theatrics. He sat back and pulled his coat away, showing the inside to Nick before he reached in and extracted a folded piece of paper. He unfolded it carefully, then turned it so they could see the photocopied object. "The crown jewels of Ireland."

"Crown jewels of Ireland?" Kelly said. "Is that real? That doesn't sound real."

Nick lowered his head, rubbing his face with both hands. "The crown jewels of Ireland disappeared in the early 1900s. Why are they stealing documents from the Revolutionary War if that's what they're after?"

"Wait, is this real?" Kelly asked again.

Nick nodded. "They were pieces made for the Order of St. Patrick in seventeen . . . something. I don't remember. They disappeared in 1908. After they were stolen, the papers started calling them the Irish Crown Jewels."

"Jesus." Kelly gaped at Nick. "Is there any obscure piece of history that you don't know off the top of your head? Seriously!"

"Actually, it was 1907," Julian said. "But I had to look up the information, so I'm impressed with your knowledge, Detective."

Nick rolled his fingers through the air. "Get to the important part."

"The order was created in 1783. You'll notice the proximity to the end of your country's Revolution."

Nick closed his eyes and nodded impatiently. He was still waiting for any of this to connect to anything they'd found.

"The jewels, however, were not made until 1831 to replace the original rather plain ones worn by the Order."

"How about you skip to the end, huh?" Nick demanded.

Julian glared for a moment, then he shook himself and nodded. "Fine. There is a theory that the payroll supposedly stolen from the Continentals at the beginning of the American Revolution was actually not a payroll at all, but rather a small trove of Masonic belongings, including one golden cross."

"Masons," Nick said, gritting his teeth. "You're coming at us with Masons?"

"No."

"Wait, what does this cross have to do with the Irish family jewels?" Kelly asked.

"*Crown* jewels," Nick grunted.

"If you would let me finish before you get your knickers in a twist, this would be easier."

Nick held up both hands and sat with a huff, gesturing for Julian to go on.

"The Masons were actually an offshoot of a much older society called the Rosicrucians," Julian continued. Nick felt Kelly's eyes on him, and he glanced at his lover questioningly. Julian continued, oblivious to their silent communication. "They inspired the Masonic Order of the Golden and Rosy Cross. It's part of the Scottish Rites, extremely secretive stuff. Many believe there was an *actual* golden and rosy cross created by the Rosicrucians in the early part of the seventeenth century that was handed down into Masonic hands."

"And people believe it was part of the Continental treasure?" Nick asked.

"Some, yes."

"What's so important about this cross?" Kelly asked. "Besides being really old?"

"It was quite large, purported to have been wrapped in hundreds of layers of gold foil, and encrusted in rare pink diamonds. It would literally be priceless."

Nick found himself nodding. He could understand even the rumor of a treasure like that inspiring a certain type of individual. "Okay. I follow. But what does that have to do with the Irish Crown Jewels? Why are they after those instead of this cross?"

"The main piece in the Irish collection was the Diamond Star of the Grand Master," Julian said. He laid his paper out and pointed to one of the pieces. "Four square inches of pure white diamond, with a ruby cross and an emerald trefoil in the forefront. Itself worth millions in today's market, but nothing compared to the value of the golden and rosy cross, if it exists."

"Right. But the Irish Crown Jewels were stolen a hundred years ago, and the Continental treasure and this pink cross disappeared over a hundred years before that. So I say again, where's the connection?" Nick asked.

Julian tapped the photo of the Irish Crown Jewels. "This is a map."

"The brooch?" Kelly asked.

"Star. Technically."

"Yeah, well I say 'star' and it gets all confusing."

Julian scoffed. "Are you trying to say you're not confused already?"

"This is a map to the missing Continental treasure?" Nick asked, tapping the grainy picture.

"I mean are we talking about the Big Dipper or are we talking about jewelry?" Kelly asked. "It's a fucking brooch."

"Your entire Recon team must be insufferable," Julian muttered to Nick.

Nick just nodded. "Okay, so the star thingy is a map."

"A star map!" Kelly said, grinning widely at Nick. "You were right, interstellar librarians."

"What in the bloody hell . . . no," Julian growled. "No interstellar . . . what? No. Whatever you want to call this piece of jewelry, people think it can lead to the Continental treasure, and with it, the actual golden and rosy cross."

"That's great, but the star is gone too," Nick pointed out.

"Not entirely," Julian countered. "By all accounts, it's here. In Boston."

"What accounts?" Nick demanded.

"I don't know, I'm only being fed information I can use to track it."

"By?"

"I don't know," Julian snarled.

"So you're hunting this treasure for someone else?"

"Yes."

"Why?"

Julian merely stared at Nick with black eyes that gave away nothing. His jaw was tight. Nick didn't know him well enough to read him.

"Fine, you're retired, you need a payday, whatever," Kelly said with a wave of his hand. "Who hired you?"

"I keep telling you, I don't know. And if I did, they'd be dead."

"These are people willing to track down and fuck with an ex-CIA hit man for a *rumor* about a treasure. I'm going to need more than 'I don't know' from you," Nick snapped.

"That's all I have!" Julian practically shouted.

"Okay, okay. Where is the star thing?" Kelly asked.

"I don't know. The records that led us here have been lost or stolen. That's why I was following the men at the bookstore. I had hoped they'd gleaned some information I had yet to come across. And when I heard someone had witnessed the robbery, that's when I decided to contact you."

"Next time, how about just . . . saying hi," Nick huffed. "Maybe a nice text message. I'll give you my number."

"I'll remember that, Detective," Julian said between gritted teeth. He put both hands out like he was trying to keep everyone calm. "I am telling you all I have. I am here, in your city, asking for your help."

Nick narrowed his eyes.

Julian inhaled shakily. "Begging. I'm begging for it."

That brought Nick up short, his next question forgotten as he stared into Julian's black eyes.

"Why the fuck are you doing all this?" Kelly asked him again.

Julian lowered his gaze, struggling with his reply. "Let's just say I had no choice in the matter."

A sudden dread came over Nick and he leaned closer. "Cameron?" Julian didn't move.

"Who is Cameron?" Kelly asked.

"My . . ." Julian shook his head, pursing his lips.

"His boyfriend," Nick provided. "Civilian. Very civilian."

"He's not . . ." Julian nearly choked on the words he couldn't get out.

"Oh shit," Kelly whispered.

Julian took a deep breath and raised his head. "We weren't careful enough with our location. Cameron made . . . he made a phone call that . . . Anyway. If I don't find this fucking treasure before someone else does, they'll kill him."

Nick offered to cook for them, but they insisted he order out so he wouldn't have to bother with it. Kelly wanted to tell Julian and JD that cooking sometimes eased Nick's nerves, but he kept his mouth shut.

Hagan joined them just as the food was getting there, and Nick spent five minutes bitching about how Hagan had a citywide radar set out for free food but couldn't remember to get him a damn Gatorade instead of coffee in the morning.

They sat up on the flybridge, eating Thai food and watching the sun set, filling JD and Hagan in as they ate. Kelly kept close enough to Nick to maintain contact surreptitiously. He could feel Nick winding up, and Nick's peace of mind often fed off contact. Now and then Nick would seek out Kelly's hand and merely squeeze it, then go back to eating.

"Masons, Revolutionary treasure, Irish royalty," Hagan said through a mouthful of food. "I think you're all insane."

"I bet we get a shrink in here, he'd say you're right," Nick said. He stretched out, throwing his arm over the back of the bench seat behind Kelly. Kelly put his plate down and leaned into him, resting his feet on a stool off to the side.

"So, let me see if I have the timelines correct," JD said. He was looking down at his food, pushing it around his plate. He hadn't eaten much. "The Rosicrucians pop up in Germany in 1600. They're . . . esoteric, to say the least. They concentrate on learning, secrets of nature, and healing. But they gain enough steam to inspire the Masons two hundred years later, who become a far more prevailing organization. Based more in wealth and power."

"So far I'm following," Hagan commented.

"The Masons stretch across the sea to the Americas, they build themselves a country, and they amass a treasure," JD continued, wincing a little. "And then some dumb shit loses it to a British lieutenant and shrugs and says whoops?"

"We've all heard the theories about how the Masons inspired the American forefathers," Nick said, taking up the timeline. "Whether they're true or not . . . eh." He shrugged, wobbling his hand in the air. "But there are enough proven connections to make me believe in a Colonial treasure trove of Masonic origin. I buy that. But why in God's name would they pile all that treasure into a wagon, and then cart it into the middle of a war?"

"They had to have some purpose for it," Julian mused. "A hiding place. Hell, perhaps they really were using it to pay soldiers."

Nick shrugged.

"Maybe it was a payment for something else," Kelly suggested. "Something besides the soldiers."

Nick pursed his lips, humming thoughtfully. "They were looking for help from the French. They could have been taking it north as oil to grease the wheels of a treaty."

Kelly put a hand on Nick's thigh and let it rest there. "Okay, so the treasure is taken, the British soldiers hide it, intending to come back for it. But if the legends are true, they never do. A few years later, King Whoever the Something creates this Order of St. Patrick in Ireland." Kelly stopped, raising his hand. "See, that's where it loses me. Where's the connection between Colonial treasure, the British getting their asses handed to them, and Ireland?"

"Ireland is part of Britain?" Hagan tried.

"The lieutenant who took the treasure was Irish," JD reminded them. "He was a member of the Order of St. Patrick. And he fought in the Irish Rebellion of 1798. Oh God, that's so obscure."

Nick wrinkled his nose. "Let's . . . make some assumptions for the sake of argument, here. Dude goes home to Ireland, becomes a knight, and realizes he doesn't need to deal with the sea crossing again to get to that shit he left back there. He'd want to leave a mark, though. He'd want people to know he took it away from the Americans, right? He'd want to somehow let someone know where to find it. Leave clues."

"Perhaps that's where the theft comes in," Julian offered. He'd barely eaten any of his dinner.

Kelly couldn't imagine what the man was suffering through, knowing the love of his life was in the hands of ruthless men and still trying to figure out a centuries-old mystery.

Nick shrugged. "Makes as much sense as anything else."

Julian gave a distracted wave.

"You know what don't make sense to me?" Nick continued, his voice still casual but his body tensing against Kelly's. "Why they'd tap you for this shit."

Julian put his utensils down with care and met Nick's eyes.

Nick cocked his head. "Hey bud, you don't have to prep for a fight every time I ask a question. I get it, okay? But I told you I'd help you. I'm not attacking you, you feel me? Just trying to understand."

Julian glanced around at them all, then met Nick's eyes once more and nodded.

"You're not alone in this," Nick assured him.

Kelly found himself leaning closer to Nick the more gentle his voice went. Nick squeezed him close, probably not even aware that he was doing it.

"I don't trust anyone," Julian finally said. "Do understand it's not personal."

"Fair enough. Your cover was as an antiques dealer, right?"

"That's correct."

"Nazi Germany was notorious for archaeological digs in search of religious relics. Do you have anything in your background that would ping you for a job like this? Hunting . . . myths? CIA? IRA?"

"I've been assured by a close contact within the Company that the CIA has nothing to do with this, nor do any of the other alphabets I've ever crossed. It's . . . a private matter. That was as much as he was able to glean without putting himself in an awkward position."

Nick smiled, laughing silently. "That wasn't what I asked."

Julian snorted. "Fine. I was schooled in the art of relieving artworks of their cages."

"You were an art thief," Kelly summed up.

"Very briefly. And very badly, might I add. It was one of the few things I was caught doing. It would be on a record . . . somewhere."

"What concerns me is that it wasn't your shitty art theft abilities that caught someone's attention," Kelly said. "I think your purpose is to . . . kill things, pretty much."

"Deftly put," Julian said with a hint of a smile.

"Well, someone had the contacts and the information to sniff you out, and to hand you these leads you've been following," Hagan said. His mouth was half-full and he was hurrying through his food. "What the hell kind of private citizen has those resources?"

Nick and Kelly shared a glanced, and Kelly raised an eyebrow. "What about Johns? He's back with that security company, he might have some feelers to put out."

"He's worth a call," Nick said with a curt nod. "I'll do it after dinner."

"You know," Hagan said. "If they're following clues, or hunting for them like they were at the bookstore, they'd have left a trail."

"What do you mean?" Nick asked.

"If they're looking for contemporaneous papers that tell where this treasure is, this isn't their first robbery. You don't get from Dublin Castle in Ireland to a bookstore in Boston without a little hint about where to go, know what I mean?"

"That's where we'll start tomorrow," Nick declared, nodding at his partner.

"Start that search in Dublin," Julian suggested.

"Oh, and I got the printout of the sketch from the artist JD talked to," Hagan said, and he stood and patted his pockets down to extract a folded-up piece of paper. He handed it to Nick.

Nick unfolded it and smoothed it out. Kelly felt Nick's body tense as soon as he saw the drawing.

"What?" Kelly whispered.

"This might complicate things a bit." Nick turned to JD. "You sure this man shot at you?"

"No, no. It's just . . . I remembered him when the gunfire started. I have no idea who he is."

Nick nodded, eyes on the drawing again. "I do."

There was a general outburst of questions from the others, but Nick's mouth was set in a grim line. He met Julian's eyes as he turned the drawing around. "It's Cam."

Julian blanched and snatched the paper from Nick's hand. He stood, staring at it for several beats before turning to JD, his black eyes ablaze.

"Whoa, whoa!" Kelly shouted, and he and Nick both hopped up to intercept before a fight could break out.

Nick wrapped Julian up and dragged him toward the edge of the flybridge, his arms around Julian's massive shoulders, his bare feet digging in to fight the weight of Julian's struggles. Julian might have been one of the few men Kelly'd seen who made Nick look small. Kelly positioned himself in front of JD, who was watching with wide eyes, confusion written in every line of his face.

"He's seen Cam!" Julian shouted as he struggled against Nick's hold. "He's been with him, he knows more than he's saying!"

Nick finally got him turned around facing the sea, and he was speaking to Julian in a low, urgent voice. His arms went from restraining to comforting, and his voice got loud enough that they could make out his words. "I swear to God, Cross, we'll find him. I'll help you find him. But you got to stay calm for me, you got to keep your head."

"I . . . I don't understand. What did I do?" JD asked desperately.

"You described the face of his boyfriend," Kelly explained. "Who's been kidnapped by the people who are looking for this treasure. Which means you . . . are involved a little more heavily than we were hoping."

"Oh Jesus," JD gasped. He put a hand on Kelly's shoulder, trying to get past him to get closer to Julian and Nick. Kelly didn't let him. "I don't . . . I don't know what to say. I don't remember. I'm truly sorry, but I don't remember!"

Julian was hanging his head, his knuckles turning white as he grasped the railing. Nick was still murmuring to him, an arm draped over his shoulder.

Julian finally raised his head and took a deep breath. "Of course," he managed. He turned around, and Nick carefully stepped away from him, giving him space. "I apologize for my outburst. If you'll all excuse me, I'm going to bed."

"Cross," Nick said before Julian could retreat down the stairwell. Julian stopped. "I'll hunt them down like he was mine. I promise."

Julian locked eyes with Nick, his expression unreadable. He descended the steps without another word, leaving the rest of them in an awkward silence.

The sun had set on them, the flickering of several citronella lanterns and the soft glow of the quaint café bulbs Nick always strung along the flybridge in the summer the only remaining light.

It was incredibly romantic, bobbing out in the harbor, the city of Boston twinkling in the distance. Kelly just wished they were alone instead of sharing the yacht with three other men and breaking up fights and hunting treasure and this was bullshit. Hell, they might as well have called Sidewinder in and slept in puppy piles on pool floats like they used to.

JD seemed to be trying to catch his breath as Julian disappeared down the steps and closed the hatch behind him. "Oh God," he whispered. "Is it possible I'm the one who . . ."

Nick trudged back over to his seat and flopped down. "It's best not to linger on that just yet."

JD had a hand over his mouth, and he looked positively ill. He finally cleared his throat and asked, "How do you not linger on that? How?"

"I have some Valium," Nick offered.

Kelly winced. "Bad idea, very bad with the amnesia thing. Nope."

"I think I need to . . . try to sleep," JD practically croaked. "Good night."

Kelly let him pass by as they all murmured good-nights to him. Then he joined Nick on the seat and leaned back into Nick's arm, sighing heavily.

"What a fucking mess," he said quietly. Nick nodded beside him.

They turned their attention to Hagan, who was stretched out on the chaise across from them, finishing his beer. He grinned mischievously. "Well aren't we cozy," he drawled.

Kelly snorted. Nick rubbed his fingers across his eyes.

"You two go on. I can't take the sexual tension anymore," Hagan teased. He tapped the cooler next to him. "I'll keep first watch."

Nick stood and pulled Kelly to his feet. "You asked for it," Nick growled to Hagan.

"Be a good neighbor, O'Flaherty," Hagan called as Kelly and Nick made their way down the steps. "Muffle the screams!"

Nick sat and stared at the file before him. He'd tried going to bed, but after only a few minutes Kelly had told him to get out because he kept tossing and turning. So he'd headed back up to the salon and gotten into his notes. He'd promised JD he would find out who he was, he'd promised Julian he would find Cameron, and both pledges haunted him. His fingers trembled as he leafed through his papers, and he gritted his teeth. He'd mostly gotten the hand tremor under control, but when it returned, it meant he was wearing himself too thin. He'd been going over every little detail he'd managed to glean in the past two days, trying to piece them together, trying to make sense of them. It seemed like the more he tried to force his brain to work, the less he managed to come up with, and the more frustrated he got.

His cell phone began to sing, a raucous fiddle tune that belonged to only one person in his contacts. Definitely the only one who would call him this late at night. Nick glanced at the phone, Ty Grady's picture on the display. He let it go to voice mail, though the song grated on his mind because he'd always reached to answer that call before. He still hadn't forgiven Ty for the last two debacles they'd gotten themselves into, for the lies his friend had told him, and frankly he didn't really feel like talking to the man much lately. He almost immediately felt guilty for not answering, though, and he picked up the phone to check the message.

It was curt and to the point, just like Ty. "Hey, Irish. Haven't heard from you in a while. I'm starting to get worried, so give me a call."

Nick shook his head and hit the button to call back. He kept in touch with his Recon boys, usually sending at least a text or something every few days. But he couldn't remember the last time he'd been compelled to send Ty anything. The feeling of having lost something precious made his chest ache, but it was tempered with so much anger he tried not to touch it at all.

"You better be shacked up with something spectacular," Ty said in greeting.

Nick huffed before he could stop himself. He put the phone on speaker and set it on the table. "I am, actually. Doc is in town."

"Oh. I take the spectacular comment back, then. Gross," Ty nearly whined. "What have y'all been up to? Zane said you called him today."

"I did, needed some info."

"I know things too, Irish. You couldn't call me? Say a fucking hello or something?"

"I'm sorry, Ty, I'm working a case. It's a little off. Haven't had much time for small talk."

Ty cleared his throat, wordlessly acknowledging the dig. Nick had always had time for Ty before. "Fair enough. What kind of off?"

"Nothing like the crap you get up to, but weird enough for me."

"You want to tell me about it?"

"It's late, Ty."

"I got time."

Nick stared at the phone, wishing with all his heart that talking to his oldest and dearest friend didn't feel so hard. He took a deep breath and nodded. He told Ty about JD, about finding him at the scene and his memory loss. He told him about trying to decipher the bits and pieces of information he'd gathered and make sense of whether JD was friend or foe. He didn't mention Julian at all. Julian had asked him to keep it quiet, and Nick was nothing if not good on his word. Finally, he told him about the suspicions that the basis of the case came down to missing treasure. Ty perked up at that.

"Treasure sounds fun," he said, tone hopeful. Since Ty had resigned from his job at the Bureau, he was going a little stir-crazy. He'd probably love it if Nick asked him to come to Boston to hunt for missing treasure.

Nick stared at the phone, trying to find the urge to invite him, trying to find the genuine desire to want Ty here to help them. "Yeah," he finally said, voice a little choked. "You'd think, but it's not. Not when my only witness is a fucking John Doe."

Ty was silent, mulling it over. "You should get a shrink in to question him," he finally suggested, his voice losing a little of its buoyancy. "Try to trip him up if he's faking."

"Yeah, he's got an appointment with one in the morning. Guy I've been going to, I trust his judgment."

"You been seeing a shrink?" Ty asked.

"My hands don't shake as much anymore. Worth the hour a week," Nick said, voice going colder.

Ty was silent for a long, tense moment. "That's good," he finally said in a rush, sounding like he was trying to catch up to the conversation. "That's good, it's good. So your amnesia guy, what's your take on him?"

"I don't think he's faking. I mean, could you pull that off 24/7 and never once slip?"

"Never tried," Ty said in all seriousness. "And you have nothing on him? Is he at least local? Does he have an accent?"

"Yeah, about that. I never heard this accent before."

"Really."

"It's like . . . Southern with a curlicue."

"What?" Ty was laughing, but Nick didn't find his frustration all that amusing.

"I'm serious. It's like yours, but not. Like he came over from England and put the two accents together. I . . ."

"Can you mimic him?"

"No! I've tried, and my tongue does not make that sound with an R."

"Your tongue can't make any kind of an R!"

"Whatever, hillbilly."

"Well, if you want, send me a recording tomorrow or let me talk to him. Maybe I can pump my FBI contact for info."

"Jesus, Ty, we've talked about Garrett and the sex jokes."

Ty snickered. "I'm serious. If I don't recognize it, maybe Zane can get it to the linguistics people at the Bureau. They owe me a few favors."

"Can you listen to him now?"

"What, like right now? You have a recording of him sitting around?"

"No, but I have him."

Ty was silent for a few breaths. When he spoke again, all teasing was put aside. "You have your suspect on your boat with you?"

"He *might* be a suspect, there's a difference."

"Might and suspect are synonymous, Irish! They mean the same thing!"

"Ty—"

"The 'might' is implied in the 'suspect'!"

"He's also a witness and could possibly be a victim himself," Nick said calmly, trying to head off what he recognized would be a pretty impressive Grady rant. "We don't know. Someone took a shot at him today. Right outside a cop bar, Ty. We had to move him from his safe house, and my boat is the safest place in the fucking city. He's either a witness in need of protecting, or he's a doer in need of—"

"Being in jail."

"Shut up. We're trying to get his memory back, and he needs the right environment for it. Not to be sitting in some cell, alone, thinking he's a bad guy. He just needs to remember."

"Okay, so when he remembers that he kills people—"

"Ty, I had this conversation with my superiors today; shut up and be helpful."

"Fine. Go get him, I'll talk to him."

"Be right back." Nick got up and turned to head for the stairs. He stopped short and his hand immediately went to the gun in the holster on his hip when he found JD standing in the stairwell, his eyes just showing over the railing. Nick had been so caught up with his conversation, he'd allowed JD to get the drop on him. Goddamn.

"I . . . I couldn't sleep and I was feeling claustrophobic," JD explained as quickly as he could. "Hagan told me earlier he'd be keeping watch upstairs, that it'd be okay for me to . . . I heard you talking so I came to see who was with you, but I didn't . . . I didn't want to intrude." He seemed to be trying not to look at the gun Nick was still gripping, but his eyes strayed to Nick's hip anyway.

Nick breathed out a long, slow breath and nodded, letting his hand leave his weapon. "It's okay. Next time give me a little more noise, huh? Come here."

JD took the last few steps, looking worried. Nick knew the man must have heard the last part of his and Ty's conversation, but it wasn't anything he hadn't already been told or even said himself.

"This is my buddy Ty; Kelly and I were telling you about him earlier," Nick said as he pointed at the phone sitting on the table. "He's good with linguistics, he thinks maybe he can help us with your accent."

"What accent?" JD asked with a frown.

Nick laughed and put a hand on his shoulder, knowing the contact would calm him.

"JD, is it?" Ty's voice was small on the speaker, and they both sat and bent their heads toward it.

Ty asked JD to repeat a few sentences for him, ending with "The Boston Red Sox suck pavement, and the designated hitter was a sham."

JD was laughing as he said it, and he looked at Nick apologetically when he finished.

"Okay," Ty said, sounding pleased with himself. "I think I got what I needed."

Nick picked up the phone and switched the speaker off. He glanced at JD. "I've got a few more things to talk over with him."

JD nodded, getting up to head back down without saying a word.

Nick watched until his head disappeared below, then put the phone to his ear. "So?"

"That's Tidewater."

"What?"

"His accent. It's Tidewater."

"That's Virginia, right?"

"Yeah, near the coast. Maybe as far west as Richmond, but not by much."

"That's a pretty narrow field to put it down to. Thanks, babe, that's solid."

Ty hummed into the phone. "This getting us closer to even?"

"Don't start with this shit, Ty, not right now," Nick grunted.

"If not now, then when?"

"I got to go," Nick said. He pulled the phone away, but Ty's voice stopped him.

"Hey Nick?"

Nick took a steadying breath and closed his eyes, putting the phone to his ear again. "What?"

"I just . . . be careful, okay?"

Nick nodded, rolling his eyes. "Got it."

Nick hung up the phone before Ty could say more. He was tired of dealing with that heartache for tonight. He slid the phone into his pocket and glanced down the stairs with a frown. JD had obviously come up here for something, and Nick wasn't buying the "I need air" excuse. He looked over the railing into the lower deck of his boat. He knew Julian was in one of the bunks, with Hagan keeping an eye on things from up top until it was Nick's watch.

He headed down the steps, listening intently, expecting JD to have returned to the VIP cabin to sleep. He came up short when he reached the bottom of the stairs and almost bowled JD over.

"Sorry!" he whispered as he grabbed the man's arm to steady him. "What are you doing? Are you okay?"

JD nodded. "Yeah, I . . . I was just looking at your pictures."

Nick glanced at the frames that lined the wall.

"How long were you a Marine?"

"Ten years," Nick answered. JD was staring at the pictures, his sharp eyes taking them in, studying them. Nick knew every photo on the wall, but he rarely slowed to look at them anymore. Most were of him in uniform, and almost every one had Ty Grady in it. They had been best friends for so long, it was almost impossible to find a shot of Nick without him. Kelly was in many of them as well, and he and Nick had always gravitated toward each other. Nick often wondered if they'd just been completely blind to the attraction all those years, or if the connection they shared went beyond romance or attraction.

Nick stared at Kelly's smiling face for a long time before turning his attention back to JD, wondering at his intent interest. "Are you . . . remembering something? You think you were in service somehow? We could run your prints again, expand the search."

A blush crept over JD's face. "No. Me? God no. I mean, you saw how I reacted when the gunfire started."

"Well, ducking and covering is the smart move, so no judgment on my part."

They both laughed, albeit uncomfortably, and Nick ran a hand over his chin as he scanned the photos again. "Your accent is Tidewater," he told JD. "Means you spent at least most of your youth in Virginia, near the coast. That area is naval base central. These pictures might be attracting you because you were a Navy brat."

JD shook his head. He hesitated for a moment, then glanced at Nick and gave him an embarrassed smile. "I was just looking at you."

Nick's eyebrows jumped, and he grinned crookedly. "Well, we were all young and handsome at some point."

When Nick glanced at the array of pictures, he could feel JD's eyes still on him. Nick met his gaze with a growing sense of dread.

"I prefer you now," JD whispered.

Nick had no idea what to say. He couldn't turn away from the other man. He was drawn to him, to the mystery, to the distress, to those hypnotic blue eyes. Just like a puppy in a storm drain.

"I'm sorry," Nick said evenly as he lowered his head. "But that's a very bad idea."

"Yeah, you're right, I—I'm sorry, totally inappropriate," JD said in a rush. He put his hand over his mouth and took a step toward the VIP cabin, looking away and then back at Nick.

They stood staring at each other for a long moment.

"He's incredibly lucky, Detective," JD finally whispered.

"So am I," Nick said gently.

JD gave him a small smile before he retreated into his cabin. Nick stared at the doorway for a long moment before cursing under his breath and turning away.

Kelly sat in the salon, watching Nick move around the outside of the boat in the darkness. Reports of gale-force winds were coming in, and he probably didn't want to wake up to a sinking vessel, especially since parts were still riddled with buckshot.

Kelly had Nick's book in his lap, reading it in the light coming from beneath the galley cabinets.

When Julian had mentioned the Rosicrucians, Nick hadn't even flinched, although he'd obviously felt Kelly's eyes on him. What the hell was Nick up to? Kelly hated being out of the loop, and he hated even more feeling suspicious of his boyfriend.

He flipped through the pages until he came to the one bookmarked by the slip of paper he'd found the other night, the one with the pigpen cipher on it.

He still had it in his hand when Nick stepped into the salon and shuttered the doors and windows. Kelly watched him silently, waiting until Nick became aware of his presence. Nick finished the last lock and turned, taking a sip of water from a plastic Red Sox cup that was half-faded from so many washings. He stopped short when he found Kelly sitting on the love seat.

"Hey," he whispered. "What are you doing up, are you okay?"

"Couldn't sleep," Kelly admitted.

"Makes two of us." Nick came around the coffee table and thumped down beside Kelly on the sofa. He handed Kelly his water, and Kelly took a sip before giving it back.

"Are you reading in the dark?" Nick asked with a quiet laugh.

Kelly held the book up. "Why are you playing this so close to the vest?"

Nick frowned, the shadows casting lines across his face. "What are you talking about? What is that?" He tilted the book toward the light, trying to read the title.

"It's a book about secret societies." Kelly leaned across Nick and turned the lamp on. He set the book in Nick's lap. "You knew what Cross was talking about earlier. What are you up to?"

Nick picked it up, glancing at the paper in Kelly's hand. "Nothing," he said, sounding hurt.

"Nick."

"Kels. The department puts on a summer camp every year." Nick tossed Kelly a wounded look. "I was on desk duty for weeks until I was cleared by the liver docs, so they put me on it. I'm making up a scavenger hunt for them. I'm running out of ideas, so I was trying to think up new clues."

Kelly pointed at the cipher. "This is a clue for a kid?"

"Yeah. I got the book out because the example they have of that symbol there is kind of ornate," Nick said. He flipped to the right page and tapped the drawing in the book. "I traced it, then added symbols from the other clues in the scavenger hunt. It looks like gibberish to us, but the kids will know what the symbols mean by the time they find that one."

Kelly bit his bottom lip, trying to smile. He just nodded instead. Of course Nick wasn't up to anything nefarious. He was making a game for kids. Kids he claimed to not be fond of. Kelly finally huffed.

"What'd you think I was doing?" Nick asked with a teasing smirk.

Kelly shook his head, embarrassed to have brought it up. "I don't even know. I'm sorry."

Nick set his cup down, then leaned back, sinking into the soft couch. He put his feet up on the table and raised his arm for Kelly to lean against him. Kelly did so gladly, resting his feet next to Nick's and his head against Nick's shoulder. He covered them both with the blanket Nick kept on the sofa. Nick squeezed him, then buried his nose in Kelly's hair.

"I promise the next time I'm doing anything wicked, you'll be my partner in crime," he whispered.

Kelly snorted. "It's sad how true that is, dude."

They stayed that way for a long while, with Nick's arm wrapped around Kelly and Kelly's head on his chest. "I'm sorry about this," Nick finally said.

"What for?"

"This case. It's ruining our time together. I should have taken vacation days."

Kelly turned so he could see Nick. He rested his chin on Nick's chest, peering up at him. "I think we needed this," Kelly admitted.

"What?"

"I think we're based off murder and mayhem." Kelly pushed up, sitting cross-legged and facing Nick. "We've never known each other in times of peace."

"Sure we have," Nick argued. He tried to sit up, but Kelly put a hand on his chest and shoved him back down. For some reason it was easier to talk to Nick when he was lounging, wearing a pair of Red Sox pajama bottoms and little else.

"No we haven't," Kelly countered. "Even after being discharged, every time we got together, we got in trouble. Or we *made* trouble. It's in our nature, babe. And then New Orleans happened. It took me taking a bullet in the chest and almost dying to realize I was attracted to you. I just . . . I think our foundations are built on gunpowder and I'm just afraid they're going to . . ."

"Kels," Nick whispered. "Jesus Christ, are you breaking up with me right now? Because that's kind of what this feels like."

Kelly smiled gently. "Do you want me to?"

"Well, no!" Nick sat up again, and this time Kelly didn't stop him. "I swear to God, we'll go somewhere soon where it's not fucking possible for us to be shot at. Vacation in . . . Amish country or something. I'll prove we don't need it."

Kelly laughed and shook his head. Nick gripped the back of his neck, pulling their faces closer. "If our foundations are built on gunpowder, then so be it. They're foundations all the same."

Then his fingers loosened, and he dragged his thumb over Kelly's cheekbone, letting the backs of his fingers drift along Kelly's jaw and then trailing the tips down his neck.

"I love you," Nick whispered. "Has nothing to do with the circumstances, or our history, or how close to death we've come together. I would love you in any incarnation of yourself."

Kelly hadn't been expecting such a heartfelt declaration from his lover, who usually erred on the side of humor when something needed to be said. He found it hard to swallow, and he couldn't tear his eyes away from Nick's.

The longer Kelly's brain chugged for a response, the softer and more amused Nick's expression became. He finally ran his thumb across Kelly's lower lip, then pulled it down like he was making Kelly talk. "Love you too," he said in a poor imitation of Kelly's voice.

They both burst out laughing, quieting quickly so they wouldn't wake the others. Kelly wiped his lips and reached for Nick, pulling him in for a kiss. "You're fucking insane," he murmured.

Nick nodded, and he wound his arms around Kelly's waist and dragged him closer. He leaned back again, stretching out on the couch. Kelly lay out on top of him, kissing him for all he was worth. He had the presence of mind, though, to remember that he hadn't finished making his point yet. He'd been awake when Nick and JD had been outside the cabin door talking. He'd heard their conversation. He pushed up, frowning down at Nick.

"What?" Nick asked, voice full of dread. "Are you seriously going to try to break up with me twice in five minutes?"

Kelly chuckled and shook his head. "I just want . . . I want you to know if you wanted to try something else—"

"Kelly!" Nick sat up again, taking Kelly with him despite Kelly trying to shove him back down. He had his arm wrapped around Kelly's waist, and he rolled him into the back of the couch, pinning him against the cushions. Kelly didn't try to fight it, and soon enough Nick had him under him. Nick's face was shadowed, but Kelly could still see his almost desperate frown. "I'm not here with you because I don't have other options. You understand? This is not something I'm taking lightly, it's not a jaunt through the park for me."

Kelly licked his lips, trying to swallow. His mouth was too dry.

"Doc. There is no 'something else' for me. There's no second option. It's you. It's just you."

Nick rested on his elbow so he could glide a finger across Kelly's cheek. It brought their faces closer together. Kelly lifted his head and kissed him, almost exploratory, tentative and gentle. Nick returned it with the same tender attention, holding Kelly's chin between his thumb and forefinger.

"Okay," Kelly whispered after several long moments of the lingering kiss. "Okay. So let's go downstairs and you can prove it to me."

Nick hummed contentedly. "As you wish."

They had the presence of mind to finish battening down the hatches and for Nick to wake Hagan for the last shift before they headed down to their cabin, and they also had the presence of mind to be quiet when they reached the cabin. Barely. Nick pressed Kelly against the wall, holding him tightly with one arm, meeting his lips over and over as he closed the door with a quiet snick.

Kelly wrapped both arms around his neck and lifted one leg to hitch it over Nick's hip. He was still exploring all the ways that sex with a guy was new. Some things he loved, other things he missed. But one thing he would never get enough of was the size difference between him and Nick. He loved the fact that he had to reach up to kiss him, that Nick's muscles were bulkier than his own. He especially enjoyed that Nick could pick him up, and did so with great frequency during their foreplay. He'd once briefly fucked Kelly that way, holding him against a wall and entering him over and over until he'd wanted harder and faster and tossed Kelly onto a nearby couch instead.

Needless to say, Kelly had learned the little cues that Nick responded to, and he abused the hell out of them.

Nick grabbed the back of Kelly's thigh as soon as he raised his leg, and then he bent and hefted Kelly up, sliding his back against the wall and holding him there with his own weight. Kelly wrapped both legs around him, still kissing him.

He could feel Nick growing harder through his pajama pants, feel the tension in every muscle as he worked to support Kelly's weight.

"Babe," Kelly gasped. "What do I have to do to get you to fuck me like this?"

Nick chuckled darkly. "I'd be way too fucking loud doing that," he admitted, then bit at Kelly's lip and kissed him hungrily. He put his lips to Kelly's ear and hissed, "Come ride me."

Kelly groaned. "Yes, Staff Sergeant."

Nick released the viselike grip he'd had on Kelly and let him slide to the ground. As soon as his feet were on the floor, Kelly ran his hands under Nick's shirt. He'd probably seen Nick shirtless a thousand times before, but this never failed to be his favorite part of getting Nick undressed. The play of muscles on his shoulders and his back, the way the dark ink of his tattoos contrasted with his skin. It was fucking glorious.

Nick pulled the shirt off and tossed it aside, backing toward the bed with a smirk. He knew what he did to Kelly, but he wasn't afraid to return the favor and show Kelly he was turned on. He shoved his pants past his hard cock, leaving them when they hit his thighs.

"Goddamn it," Kelly hissed, and he yanked his own shirt over his head. He shoved his sweatpants down and kicked out of them.

Nick was watching him, his eyes predatory, licking his lips as he looked Kelly up and down. Kelly elbowed him to the bed, then climbed on top of him and pinned his hands.

Nick grinned evilly, lifting his hips so the head of his cock brushed against Kelly's balls.

Kelly shook his head. "You're going to have to work harder for it than that."

When Nick smiled, Kelly could see that he was biting his tongue. "You sure about that?" Nick asked slyly. "Last time you rode me, you came so hard I licked it off my lips."

Kelly groaned and hung his head. It was true, damn him. He released Nick's hands and reached for the pillows where they'd been stashing their lube. The drawer was just *so far* when they got to the stage where they needed it.

As he was reaching, Nick grabbed his hips, holding him in place. He licked at the tip of Kelly's cock, his fingers digging into Kelly's ass.

"Oh God, babe," Kelly grunted. He hung his head, gasping as his entire body pulsed with need.

Nick tugged at his hips, urging Kelly to crawl just a little closer to the headboard. He licked Kelly's balls, then went lower, lapping at Kelly's asshole. Kelly almost shouted. He brought his fist up and bit it to keep from making any noise. Nick licked all the way up to Kelly's balls again and sucked one into his mouth.

Kelly arched his back, reaching down to grab a handful of Nick's hair. His thighs were beginning to burn, but goddamn if he was going to worry about that when Nick was about to do what Kelly thought he was.

Nick's hands squeezed at Kelly's ass, pulling his cheeks apart before his tongue was there again, licking and massaging muscles that kept fighting back as Kelly tensed.

"Jesus Christ, you do tongue exercises when I'm not around, don't you?" Kelly said, the last word coming out a moan as Nick's tongue shoved past those muscles and inside him.

Nick hummed in response, and licked his way up to Kelly's balls again. His teeth scraped tender skin, and a small whimper escaped Kelly's lips before he could stop himself.

He squirted a liberal amount of lube into his palm, then reached blindly behind him. He grasped Nick's hard cock and squeezed, coating it with lubricant. Nick moaned loudly, but this time he had a mouthful of Kelly's balls and Kelly almost came right then and there. His cock was dripping as he contorted his body, trying to jack Nick while still giving Nick's tongue access. Nick licked at his asshole again, then dragged his tongue all the way up the shaft of Kelly's cock.

He sucked him between his lips, licking the pre-cum off the head before releasing him.

As soon as he was free, Kelly backed his ass into Nick, kissing him as he rubbed himself all over Nick's slick cock.

Nick's hand tangled in Kelly's hair and he shoved his hips toward Kelly with a groan. "Come on," he urged. His voice was as strained as his body was beneath Kelly.

Kelly grinned and lowered himself, rubbing his ass against the head of Nick's cock. "Like this?"

"Kels," Nick practically begged. He raised his hips, and the head of his cock slid along Kelly's ass with ease. Kelly pushed back, letting Nick almost enter him without even needing to guide him. Nick gasped and dug his fingers into the muscle of Kelly's ass. "Fuck, babe."

Kelly kissed him again, licking at his tongue, sucking on it, biting it. Nick whimpered into his mouth and shoved his hips up again when Kelly wouldn't release his tongue. He entered Kelly this time, and they both groaned wantonly. The head of his cock pushed at Kelly, spreading him apart. It inched into him, and the friction was enough to make anyone scream for more. Kelly sat down hard, and Nick shoved deep inside him.

Neither of them could cry out since they were still fighting over who got to keep Nick's tongue. Kelly kissed him one more time and sat up, shifting his hips as Nick sank balls deep inside him.

"Fuck, I remember why this was so fun now," Kelly moaned as he let his head fall back. Nick's hands were all over him, gliding up his ribs, smoothing across his chest, pulling him down by his shoulders as he tried to push deeper into him.

Kelly began a slow, rhythmic roll of his hips, and both of them writhed with pleasure. Nick brought his knees up, shoving into him as Kelly moved. It gave just one more dimension to the friction that was setting them both on fire.

Kelly dragged his nails down Nick's chest. "Don't stop," he ordered breathlessly.

Nick bit his lip and nodded. "Fuck!" he hissed. He gripped Kelly's hips tight. "Fuck, I knew we wouldn't be able to do this quiet."

"Fuck quiet," Kelly grunted. He fought against Nick's hold, moving his hips anyway. Nick grunted, sucking air through his teeth as he started the slow thrusts again.

There was nothing to cover the sound of their lovemaking. No white noise, no rough ocean, no music or city sounds in the distance. It was just Nick, Kelly, and the gasps and grunts each of them made as they drew closer and closer to release. There was no way the others wouldn't hear them if they were awake. And Kelly didn't care. In fact, he almost saw it as a chance to mark his territory.

Nick's nails dragged across Kelly's ribs, grasping at him desperately, blindly seeking out a handhold.

"You coming?" Kelly asked, barely able to say the words over the struggle against his own orgasm.

"Kelly," Nick gasped. The name sounded like a curse on his lips. He bucked his hips, pushing Kelly almost off the bed. Kelly laid a hand in the middle of Nick's chest, where he could feel the wild beating of Nick's heart as he came. He squeezed every muscle he could still control and Nick cried out, a hoarse, desperate plea of Kelly's name.

"That's right, babe," Kelly hissed.

Nick had his eyes closed, his head thrown back. He gritted his teeth so he wouldn't shout again. God, he was fucking beautiful when they fucked. Kelly could feel every straining muscle in Nick's powerful body, the possessiveness in his grasp, see the love and pleasure in his eyes when he met Kelly's, could feel his cock pulsing inside him. He gripped himself with his free hand, and all it took were a few strokes before he found his own release.

He knelt over Nick with his head hanging for long minutes, each of them trying to catch his breath, each of them slowly recommencing their gentle strokes and touches as their bodies calmed. Kelly finally managed to move, lifting himself off Nick and then collapsing beside him in bed.

Nick didn't move other than to rest his hand on Kelly's thigh and squeeze. Kelly took in his profile in the glaring light. He placed his hand over Nick's heart again, feeling it slow.

"I'm sorry I questioned this," Kelly said as he tapped Nick's chest.

Nick opened one eye, then turned his head to meet Kelly's eyes. "It's okay to question, Kels. But I promise I'll never give you a reason to."

Kelly kissed him gently, then rolled to his back again. "Who gets the light and the towel?" he asked after a few seconds. "I have spunk dripping out of my ass and it's your fault."

"Yeah, it is," Nick said, sounding pretty pleased with himself.

"Pretty sure you should have to get the towel."

"Roshambo," Nick said, and he held his fist up, waiting. Kelly made a fist and they counted off. Kelly threw scissors, and Nick chuckled. He'd thrown rock. He knocked his fist against Kelly's fingers. "Boom."

Kelly grunted as he rolled out of bed. "Fucker."

CHAPTER 6

"**S**o," Hagan drawled with a knowing look at Nick as soon as he appeared for breakfast. His hair was mussed and he was still wearing his T-shirt and jeans from last night.

Nick glanced at him, shaking his head as he tended to breakfast. He knew Hagan would give him hell.

"Where's your boy?" Hagan asked. He slid into the banquette on the other side of the kitchen counter so he could watch Nick cook.

"Still in bed." Nick glanced at him, glaring briefly. "Okay, go on."

"I didn't hear a thing," Hagan claimed, and he reached for the plate of food that was ready. "How long have you been up?"

"Not long. I got a search going for robberies where papers or historical documents were taken. It's worldwide, though, so might be a while."

"Solid. What are we going to do with your hit man?"

Nick shrugged, glancing at the stairs. "Help him, I guess. That's what I promised him I'd do."

"You ever make a promise and then think, ehhhh?"

Nick snickered, flipped a pancake in the air, and then dropped it back in the pan.

"Got any coffee?"

"I don't drink coffee. I've got tea."

Hagan shrugged, wrinkling his nose. "This city was founded on the concept of tossing tea into the harbor."

"That is . . . no. It was not."

There was a thump from below. A few moments later Kelly popped his head over the railing and sniffed the air like a dog. "Is that bacon?"

"And eggs, and pancakes. Come on," Nick said to him. He looked back to Hagan. "Appointment with the shrink at nine. Can you handle it, or should we get a few uniforms on it?"

"I got it covered," Hagan said as he tried to swallow a mouthful of eggs. "Damn, kid, this is good. I didn't know you could cook."

Kelly slipped behind Nick and grabbed a plate. He kept his hand on the small of Nick's back, ostensibly so Nick wouldn't back into him in the small galley. When he moved again, though, his hand stayed there. He gave Nick a sideways grin before dragging his fingers across Nick's hip and moving away.

Nick shivered violently. He was so intent on Kelly that he burned himself on the stove when he reached for the pan. He was still cursing and sucking on the end of his finger as he scrambled for his aloe plant when JD and Julian both joined them.

"Smooth, Detective," Julian commented. His voice was just as droll as Nick remembered it being from their first meeting.

Nick broke off a tip of one of the aloe leaves and rubbed it over his finger, casting a glare in Julian's direction. "I had an idea last night," Nick told him.

"Really? I can't imagine where you got the time," Julian drawled.

Nick narrowed his eyes, but he wasn't the type to be embarrassed about much of anything. "If that star is in Boston, I know someone who might be able to help us find it."

Julian perked up at that. He glanced at the others, who were all watching Nick with wide eyes. "And who might that be?"

"Well, it's stolen goods. Even in 1908, there were only so many people you could go to with stolen goods and keep it quiet for this long."

"That's a very bad idea," Hagan blurted.

Nick shrugged. "I'm open to better ones."

"I'm sorry, who are you talking about?" JD asked.

Kelly cleared his throat, rubbing his hand across the bridge of his nose. He had his eyes closed. "The Irish mob," he guessed. "He's talking about asking the Irish mob."

JD's mouth parted as he stared at Kelly, then looked to Nick with wide eyes. "That *does* sound like a bad idea."

"You're not going in there without backup," Hagan declared. "Not happening."

"I've got backup," Nick said with a jerk of his head toward Julian and Kelly.

Hagan rubbed his palm over his mouth, resting his elbow on the counter. It hit his fork and sent the utensil flying, but he didn't even try to catch it. "Partner to partner, how safe can you be doing this?"

Nick shrugged and grinned crookedly. "Just as safe as we were at lunch yesterday."

Kelly couldn't seem to stop pacing while Nick was on the phone. He'd told them he was making a call, then stepped out onto the deck and closed the door behind him. They couldn't hear what he was saying, didn't know who he was talking to, and Kelly couldn't even see him to try to read his lips.

Kelly knew enough about Nick's past to know this was a hugely stupid risk for him to take. Any interaction he had with the Irish mob here in Boston made him wide-open after the history he had with them.

They'd been drinking one night in Jacksonville while stationed at Camp Lejeune, playing pool and throwing darts, blowing off steam, when Nick had let slip why he'd joined the Marines. "It was that or keep running jobs for the Irish mob," he'd said with a signature O'Flaherty grin before he'd downed his beer and then gone to hustle a sailor in a game of pool.

Kelly had always felt there was more to the story, though.

Hagan had put up a few more weak arguments before he'd taken JD to the psychologist for his interview. None of them could give Nick a viable alternative, though. Without the map that was said to be hidden on the star brooch, there was no way to find the treasure for Julian. And without any idea of the whereabouts of the robbers, JD was still in danger as well, and so was Cameron.

Nick stepped back into the salon, looking grim.

"What happened?" Kelly demanded.

"We've got a meet tonight."

"That was fast," Julian said. "Jesus, what sort of in do you have with them?"

"A personal one," Nick growled. His tone made it clear that neither Julian nor Kelly were supposed to inquire further.

"Where's the meet?" Kelly asked instead.

"Liberty Hotel, six tonight. We're supposed to book two rooms, and reserve a spot for dinner."

"Liberty Hotel. Isn't that the place you wanted to take me? The old jail they turned into a hotel?"

Nick nodded. "Looks like we'll get to see it after all." He walked past Julian and Kelly, heading belowdecks without another word.

"Great," Kelly said.

Julian took a step closer, lowering his voice. "Is there a missing piece of information I need to know here?"

Kelly sucked in a deep breath and hesitated, eyes darting between Julian and the stairwell.

"I understand your loyalty to him, but I'm not used to working blind," Julian said, voice gentle and persuasive.

"Nick grew up here," Kelly said quietly. "During the time when teenagers either got out, or got initiated. You understand?"

Julian nodded curtly.

"Nick chose the Marines at seventeen to avoid the mob. That's all I know."

Julian nodded again, then smiled sadly. "Rather like choosing the RAF to avoid the IRA." The phone in the pocket of his jeans began to vibrate, and he scrambled to grab for it. "This is Cross."

Kelly was close enough to hear the murmur of the voice on the phone, but he couldn't make out what it was saying.

"I want to speak to him," Cross demanded. "I want to know he's alive before I give you anything."

Kelly mouthed the word, "Kidnappers?"

Julian nodded.

Kelly darted for the stairs, sliding down the railing with his hands and feet like he'd been taught twenty years ago when he'd joined the Navy. "Nick!" he hissed.

Nick poked his head out of the bathroom. Half his face was covered in shaving cream, and he was wearing no shirt, just his jeans and a towel resting on his shoulder. He held his razor in his hand like a weapon.

"Kidnappers on Julian's phone."

Nick tossed his razor over his shoulder and hustled after Kelly up the steps. He went to the banquette in the pilothouse and ripped one of the cushions off, then rummaged inside the bench. Kelly hadn't even known those benches were hollow.

Nick came out with a contraption that looked like one of the original mobile phones that had come in bags. He dropped it on the table and opened it up. Inside was an array of listening and GPS devices. Nick gestured for Julian to come closer, and as Julian spoke on the phone to his kidnapped boyfriend, Nick plugged the device into his phone. They had to contort to do it, and Julian wound up with shaving cream all over his shoulder.

He gave Nick one of the dirtiest looks Kelly had ever seen a man make, but Nick merely shrugged and turned the tracking device on. He rolled his finger through the air, telling Julian to stall and draw out the conversation. Then he handed him his towel almost sheepishly.

Julian wiped at his shoulder, still glowering.

Nick pulled Kelly to the side, dropping his voice to an almost inaudible whisper. "What did they want?"

"He just demanded to talk to his boyfriend before he'd give them information."

"They want an update on his progress. Means they're getting nervous. Fuck."

"They're going to kill this kid if he doesn't find that treasure," Kelly said.

Nick was watching Julian over Kelly's shoulder. His jaw jumped as he gritted his teeth. "God help them if they do."

Kelly glanced behind him. Julian's eyes were hard as obsidian and his shoulders were rigid. He was obviously back on the phone with the kidnappers. Kelly took Nick's elbow and pulled him toward the salon, then they stepped out on the deck and pulled the door closed.

"Are you going to be able to handle this meeting tonight? Because he's compromised as hell and I haven't been in a firefight in over a year."

Nick slid his hand up Kelly's arm, his expression softening. "I'd take a rusty you over anyone to have my back."

Kelly tried not to smile, but he couldn't help himself. He swiped his finger through the drying shaving cream on Nick's cheek. "You should have left it scruffy. I like it like that."

Nick smirked and then pursed his lips as he nodded. "I'll remember that. But tonight, we have to dress to the nines. Did you bring a suit?"

"Yeah, I've got one. Why?"

"Because the man we're going to see won't speak to scruffy cops in jeans and leather jackets."

A flutter of nerves went through Kelly's stomach, though he wasn't sure why. They'd faced dangerous men before. Something about the tension in Nick was bleeding into him.

"But hey," Nick said, putting on that bright-side mask he'd always worn in the Corps. He smiled, and somehow he forced the warmth to reach his eyes. Kelly'd always wondered how in the hell Nick did that. "At least we'll get that romantic night we were planning, right?"

Kelly snorted. "Whackadoo."

The door from the salon opened and Julian stepped out, still fussing with the shaving cream on his shirt.

"For Christ's sake, it's a cotton T-shirt!" Nick said. "I'll let you borrow one of mine!"

Julian huffed at him.

"What'd they say?" Kelly asked.

"Cameron is still safe. He swore he was unharmed, and I tend to believe him, though it was obvious someone was closely monitoring his words. He chose them with great care. They wanted to know where I was, and what progress I had made. I told them I'd been forced to enlist assistance. I got the distinct feeling they already knew that."

"You think they're following you?" Nick asked.

"If they were, I'd know it."

"They're keeping tabs somehow," Nick insisted.

"Maybe they heard about the robbery," Kelly suggested. "Knew it was either Julian or the other crew."

"Perhaps," Julian whispered.

"What role did you play in that?" Nick asked him.

"In what?"

"The robbery. The murders," Nick said, his voice hard. "Was any of that you?"

"No, Detective. I was merely tailing them. And doing so from quite a distance. I never saw them, other than the van they drove. I got there and the scene was already as you found it."

"You were tailing them?" Nick shouted. "Why didn't you say that before? Where'd they come from? Are they based somewhere in Boston?"

Julian remained irritatingly calm in the face of Nick's outburst. Kelly was impressed.

"They came from the airport. I followed their trail. I'm not concealing information from you, Detective. I want them stopped as badly as you do. More so than you, I would wager."

Nick pointed his finger at Julian, wagging it threateningly. He calmed quickly though, acknowledging the logic in Julian's explanation. "I'm going to go finish shaving," he said through his teeth as he left them.

Julian watched him go, then turned back to Kelly with a sigh. "He seems tense."

Kelly nodded.

"He struck me as the sane one when I met him before. Relaxed. Well-adjusted. He's not anymore."

Kelly pressed his lips into a thin line, nodding in agreement. "You said you were in the military?"

"Briefly, yes."

"The team was called back last year. Whatever work they had them doing, it fucked them all up a little."

"Why?" Julian asked. His concern seemed genuine.

Kelly's stomach roiled and he looked away, into the yacht to see if Nick was anywhere near. "He won't say."

Kelly excused himself before Julian could ask more questions. He almost barreled into Nick as he came back out onto the deck.

Nick had already finished getting dressed. He'd forgone the suit today, instead staying in the jeans he'd been wearing and putting on a plain black T-shirt. His favorite leather jacket was over his arm, and his badge was on a chain around his neck. He was also wearing a shoulder holster with a gun on each side, rather than the one he usually kept on his hip.

"What are you doing?" Kelly asked.

"Going to work." He held up his phone. "The trace didn't get their location, call wasn't long enough."

Julian sighed shakily and nodded.

"It did give us a region, though," Nick added.

"Really?" Julian blurted. "Where are they holding him?"

Nick's expression hardened, and he met Julian's eyes. "They're in Boston."

It took a few moments for Julian to get his temper and nerves under control; Kelly could actually see the emotions playing across his face. "I suppose that makes sense. They knew Boston was going to be in play in the end." He stood there a moment, and Nick and Kelly were both silent, letting him work through it. "Excuse me," he finally whispered, and he stepped past them into the salon.

"He's handling that well," Kelly said. "If they had you tied up somewhere and I found out you were in the same city, I'd be ripping things apart."

Nick hummed and nodded as he watched Julian disappear down the steps.

Kelly studied his profile a moment before jabbing him with an elbow. "Hey. What's wrong?"

"Something . . ." Nick shook his head and met Kelly's eyes again with a weak smile. He slid his phone into his back pocket, then pulled Kelly closer to kiss him. "Stick with Cross, will you? See if you two can make some headway with this treasure shit."

"You're the history buff, babe, I'm not sure I'd know where to start."

Nick nodded as if he understood that he was basically asking Kelly to sit on his hands all day. He looked annoyed with himself. "See what you can come up with anyway. Please? Don't let Cross out of your sight."

"You don't trust him?"

"Nope."

"You got it."

Nick gave him another kiss, lingering over this one, then headed off for the dock and the parking lot beyond. Julian joined Kelly soon after, wearing a shirt he'd pilfered from Nick's closet. Kelly and Julian stood together on the deck, watching Nick walk off.

"Care to take an unsupervised field trip?" Julian asked after a few moments.

"If I say no, are you going to ditch me the first time I take a piss?"

"Yes."

Kelly nodded dejectedly. "Let me put some shoes on."

Nick left his Range Rover for Kelly and Julian, knowing that as soon as he was out of sight, both men would be off. He trusted Kelly to take care of himself, though; he didn't need his hand held. And hell, maybe they'd drum something up.

He left a note on his windshield for Kelly, then went to the storage unit where he kept his motorcycle. He liked to ride the bike when he was running down leads anyway. It was easier to find parking, even with the police plates.

He headed for the station first, checking in on the requests they'd put in for JD's identity. A report had come in on the other robberies they'd searched for. Nick sat to read over it, then noticed a message on his desk from Boston College. One of the professors had responded to their inquiries, saying he recognized JD.

Nick tossed the robbery files aside and reached for his phone instead. When he called the number that had been left, a woman answered.

"This is Detective Nicholas O'Flaherty, I'm looking for a Professor Kris Singleton."

"This is Kris," the woman said. Nick had been expecting a man, but he shrugged it off. He liked her voice; it was smooth and a little hoarse.

"Professor, do you have a moment to speak to me in regard to the photos my officers were circulating yesterday?"

"Oh! Yes, of course, Detective. What can I tell you?"

"You recognized the man in the photo?" Nick asked.

"Yes."

"Is he a professor at Boston College? An employee?"

"Oh, no no. He's a writer."

Nick frowned and scrambled for his notepad. "A writer?"

"I teach one of his books for a course. I recognized him from the photo on the back jacket. My students ask me every year if I can convince him to come and guest lecture."

Nick smiled. He could see why college kids would want to sit and stare at JD for an hour. "Okay. What course is it you teach? Literature of some sort?"

"Archaeology and anthropology. I'm afraid I've misspoken, Detective; I recognized him from a book he wrote, but writing is not his profession. See, I teach a course on pop culture, and we discuss the differences between reality and fiction in the field of archaeology."

"I see."

"Expectation of the job versus the realities?"

"Right, telling them they're not Indiana Jones," Nick said.

"Exactly. But I try not to skew the course, so I offer readings from archaeologists and other scientists who . . . quite frankly are more like adventurers. Hiram Bingham III, Roy Chapman Andrews, Lonnie Thompson and Ellen Mosley-Thompson, and Mark Moffett, to name a few."

"Okay. Scientists who are also kind of badasses, I follow."

"I'm impressed, Detective, that you would know those names. They're rather obscure bits of history."

"I knew the first two," Nick admitted.

She laughed. "Fair enough. He's arguably one of those. His books are full of . . . treasure hunts and gunfights. Entertaining reading, but not the way it's done. Not really."

Nick's stomach turned with this new piece of information. "What's his name?"

"Hunt. Casey Hunt."

Kelly could see the parking lot from the flybridge, so he knew Nick had left the Range Rover. After going through all the drawers in the house, though, he couldn't find a spare set of keys.

"We'll either call a cab or hot-wire it," Julian finally told him when he reached the end of his patience. He swept out of the yacht and onto the dock without giving Kelly a chance to argue. Kelly had to jog to catch up with him.

"You know, you lose something without the long black coat. Little air of mystery is gone," Kelly told him as they headed for the parking lot. Julian gave his khakis and borrowed T-shirt an offended grunt. Kelly shrugged. "It's true."

Kelly's steps slowed when they came to the car and he saw a white note beneath the windshield wiper, fluttering in the breeze. He plucked it off and unfolded it.

Keys are in the wheel well. Please don't hot-wire her. O.

Julian read it over Kelly's shoulder. "He knows you well," he commented before making his way to the passenger door.

Kelly grinned and knelt to search for the keys. Of course Nick knew him well. That was part of the attraction. "Where are we headed?" he asked as soon as he had the Range Rover running.

"The bookstore." Julian held up Nick's badge, the one he clipped on his belt when he wore a suit. "I want to look around."

Kelly whistled and shook his head, putting the car in drive. "You're going to be in so much trouble," he sang.

"It'll be fine. He won't know if you don't tell him."

"Fat chance."

"I just need to get the accent down."

Kelly spent most of the drive critiquing Julian's imitation of Nick's accent. He'd heard some Boston accents that were damn near unrecognizable. Others, like Nick's, were softer or had faded due to being away from home for so long. Nick's grew heavier when he was drunk or ranting about something, usually baseball but also anything that required the word "fuckers" said with it.

Sometimes Kelly tried to rile him just to hear the original accent, but Nick was usually unflappable. He had to resort to saying "Go Yankees" to really get Nick worked up.

"You might get by with that one," Kelly advised after Julian's last attempt. "Just . . . don't say much. And don't use Nick's name; they all know him around here, and you definitely don't pass as a six-foot-one redhead."

When they reached the bookstore, Kelly parked on the street, trusting the police plates on Nick's vehicle to keep him from getting towed. Glass still littered the sidewalk, although it had mostly been swept into a pile. The shattered windows were boarded with plywood. Police tape sealed off the door, with a red tag attached near the doorknob that warned whoever entered about chain of custody. They were supposed to sign the little tag.

"Can you do his signature?" Julian asked. "There's no one here to see it isn't him."

Kelly grudgingly signed Nick's name on the red slip. "You're taking all the blame for this," he told Julian. "And I'm telling him you stole that badge."

"Understood." Julian pulled a knife from somewhere inside his jacket and slit the tape along the edge. When he tried the door, though, it was locked. He pulled a lockpick set out of another pocket, and knelt to work on it.

"How many pockets do you have in that thing?" Kelly asked.

Julian chuckled grimly. "You have no idea." The door popped open, and Julian replaced his tools and stepped inside.

It was dim and dusty, and the smell of old paper and leather was overwhelming. Kelly headed to the car and rummaged through the back for a flashlight. He found a heavy Maglite, along with other supplies that might come in handy in the next few days if this led to a treasure hunt like he expected. He rejoined Julian, and clicked the flashlight on.

It played over the mess that was left of the shop. "Jesus. Why'd they tear it apart?"

"I suspect they didn't actually find what they were looking for and this was either anger or desperation. Perhaps even a brawl. At this point, with little to no success, the rats may be turning on each other." Julian made his way carefully to the display case that seemed to have taken the brunt of the attack.

"How many of them are there?"

"Two to five. I'm not sure of their exact number," Julian answered, but he was distracted by the case. "Bring that torch here."

"Torch," Kelly echoed. "Oh, I miss the English."

"I'm not English, I'm Irish."

"Same thing," Kelly teased. He stepped over a pile of scattered books and shone the light on the display case.

Julian placed his palm over what looked like a handprint in the dust. Then he swept his hand through the air, curling his fingers into a fist as he did so, hovering over another hinted outline of a print.

The action seemed to mimic perfectly what someone had done to the display case.

"They wiped it down?" Kelly asked.

"I'm not sure. It could be a grab for whatever sat here. This case is extremely old, look." Julian tapped his fingers on the corner. "Dark walnut with cabriole legs and dovetail joints. I believe this itself is a Colonial era piece."

"Is that important?"

Julian fingered the wood like he was looking for something, but he shrugged. "I'm not sure. It's possible it was part of a collection of items, all from the same era. I don't know." He straightened with a sigh and glanced around the shop. "Whoever destroyed the rest of this store, though, left this case intact. I wager they knew it was antique and couldn't bring themselves to touch it."

"Murderers with a respect for history. Huh. I wonder what led them here," Kelly said as he began to explore the narrow, dusty aisles. "How far ahead of you were they in all this?"

"Too far. Much too far."

Nick sat at his desk, hunched over files and notes and several books he'd had one of the summer interns go find for him at a nearby bookstore. He didn't realize he was no longer alone until someone tapped him on the shoulder.

"You chasing down a lead?" Hagan asked him.

"Uh . . ." Nick's eyes darted to JD, who was beside Hagan, craning his head to see the books on Nick's desk. "Yeah. Yeah, I am."

Hagan threw himself into his chair and clunked his boots on the desk. "What you got?"

Nick glanced at JD again and gestured for him to sit. After a few seconds of trying to decide how best to word it, he simply said, "We found out who you are."

JD's eyes widened and he sat forward, a smile playing across his lips. "You're serious?"

Nick nodded.

"You don't look happy," JD said, dread creeping into his voice. "Oh God, I'm someone horrible, aren't I?"

Nick picked up one of the books he'd sent for. "You actually seem like a pretty interesting character," he said, and he set it down in front of JD.

JD eyed the book, then Nick from beneath lowered brows. "I don't understand."

Nick picked it up again and turned it over. On the back cover was a photo of JD wearing aviators and a canvas military-style jacket, standing on a mountain with Machu Picchu in the background.

"That's me!" JD he grabbed the book, pointing at the photo and then turning it over to see the title. "I'm an archaeologist?"

"The professor I spoke with probably wouldn't agree. She basically said you're a hack."

JD burst out laughing, then covered his mouth and nodded. "I can deal with being a hack. Oh my God."

Nick raised his head in time to catch sight of Kelly and Julian entering the squad room. He raised his hand and waved them over when the desk sergeant tried to stop them.

"Casey Hunt." JD set the book down gently, his fingers resting on the cover. "It doesn't sound familiar."

"What's going on?" Kelly asked as they approached.

"We got an ID on him," Nick answered.

"Yeah?" Nick could see the hesitation in Kelly's eyes. He obviously knew the chances of JD being a good guy were slim. "That's good, right?"

Nick didn't answer. He knocked his knuckles against the desk instead.

"I'm apparently . . . a lot braver than I feel," JD commented as he paged through the book. He looked a little crestfallen, even though they'd just had a major breakthrough.

"You okay?" Nick asked.

"Yeah. I was just hoping learning my name would . . . throw a latch or something, you know? Make me remember. It doesn't even feel right, though. Hell, JD feels more like my name than Casey."

Kelly sat on the edge of the desk, glancing at Nick again. "It takes three days to develop a new habit. We've been calling you JD for three days, so . . ."

"Yeah, I guess," JD murmured. "Can you keep calling me that? Just for a while, I mean."

"Whatever you want," Nick said quietly. He pointed at Julian and Kelly. "Can I see you two for a minute?"

They followed along without question, heading for one of the interrogation rooms. Julian glanced around the box uneasily as soon as the door closed behind them.

"Ever been in one of these?" Nick asked him in amusement. He leaned against the wall and crossed his arms out of habit. It was always his first position when questioning a suspect.

Julian rolled his eyes, but he refused to sit at the table.

"What are you two doing here?" Nick asked them.

"We found something," Julian answered.

Nick's eyebrows rose. "At the bookstore?"

Kelly had been kicking at the legs of the table, which were bolted down, but he pulled up short. "How'd you know we went to the bookstore?"

"It's the only lead you had, and neither of you strikes me as the type who'd look shit up on the internet or in a book. Did you get anything?"

"Not really," Julian admitted. "Looking over the scene, though, I felt as if they missed something. They went for the case first, where they thought it would be, then they ransacked the place when it wasn't there."

Nick nodded. "Crime scene analysts came back with a blow-by-blow. They said the shopkeeper surprised one man coming out of the store. Guy opened fire, killing the owner. And judging by the trajectory, he's the one who clipped JD. Meaning JD was walking away from the bookstore, toward the street. The others were in the street, likely by their van waiting. They opened fire on their own guy after *he* shot the owner, blew him away, took out the windows, left everyone for dead. Left the books the guy took. As soon as there was bloodshed, they bailed. Complete mission failure."

"This is the first murder to take place," Julian pointed out. "Perhaps they killed him to take the heat for it. Or perhaps he turned on them."

Nick shrugged.

"Wait a minute, if the first shots clipped JD, that means he was standing between the store and the van," Kelly pointed out. "What was he doing there? Why would they let him get that close instead of diverting him? And why do you look so pissy when you just broke his identity, what's wrong?"

Nick sighed heavily. "He's a professional treasure hunter. He has a degree from Columbia University, works out of a museum in New York. He's got a reputation for going into dangerous areas and getting out unscathed with local shiny things. He's also been accused of selling items on the black market, but there's no proof."

"Oh," Kelly said, and his shoulders slumped.

"And you're right. They wouldn't have let him get between them and the store," Nick continued. "Not unless he was one of theirs to begin with."

"That's a shame," Julian said. "I was beginning to like him. His sketch of Cameron notwithstanding."

"What I want to know," Nick said heatedly, "is if there was only one man inside, and his shit was still in his bag when they left him there, who the fuck has those missing artifacts now?"

Kelly and Julian both fell silent, frowning at Nick. Nick had been asking himself that all morning. The thieves hadn't gotten away with anything, the evidence suggested as much. But there were still two things missing. So where the hell were they? And why hadn't they been where they were supposed to be?

"Well," Julian finally said, taking a deep breath. "I suppose you should go ask your amnesiac that question."

"What's wrong?" JD asked Nick as soon as he saw him.

Kelly was right on Nick's heels, trying to calm him, trying to keep from blowing up. That had always been his job, and he was good at it on the rare occasions when he had to do it. Nick rarely even came close to losing his temper, but when it happened it was seriously impressive. And scary, for anyone who didn't know him. Kelly got in front of him and put both hands on his chest.

"Breathe and think, O," he ordered.

Nick lowered his head, and his eyes glinted when he met Kelly's. "I'm calm. Let me do my job."

Kelly knew when he'd been beat; he stepped aside and held his hands up. Nick grabbed his jacket off the back of his chair, pulling it up on two wheels and then toppling it over as the leather dragged it down. It clattered to the ground, and both Hagan and JD stood in alarm.

"What happened?" Hagan demanded.

"Order up an unmarked, we're going for a ride," Nick said. He took JD by the elbow and led him toward the door.

Kelly hurried to right the chair Nick had left in his wake, then shrugged in response to Hagan's questioning look and jogged after his lover. He caught up to them in the stairwell.

"What's going on, what happened?" JD kept asking.

"New evidence," Nick snarled. "Need you to walk us through something."

JD's eyes were still wide and confused, but he was smart enough to stay quiet. Even Kelly kept his mouth shut until they were in the parking lot.

"Nick," he finally demanded, and he grabbed at Nick's elbow. He turned him until they were facing each other, trying to make Nick look into his eyes and realize he was spiraling out of control. Kelly didn't want to divert the spiral, because he was of the opinion that JD needed to see what he was messing around with if he was faking. But he didn't want to be left behind, either. "Where are we going, and what do you want us to do?"

Nick's eyes darted over Kelly's face, then to Julian, who was silently following along. "You two follow us in my car."

Kelly nodded and let him go.

Hagan held up the keys to the unmarked sedan he'd requisitioned, and Kelly stood aside and watched Nick shove JD into the backseat and slam the door.

Julian clucked his tongue, then sauntered over to the Range Rover. But Kelly remained rooted to the spot for another few seconds. Nick hated being lied to, despised it with more passion than anything, even the New York Yankees. God help JD if he was trying to play Nick with a lie. God help them all.

Once on the road, Kelly had a hard time keeping up with Hagan until Julian casually flicked on the flashing dashboard light. They shared a look, both of them trying not to grin and failing.

"I could get used to this," Julian drawled.

"Hell yeah."

When they reached the bookstore again, Nick was already out of the car and standing in the middle of the street. They'd parked their vehicle with its lights flashing across the narrow lane to block traffic, and Nick was waving to Kelly, telling him where to park the Range Rover.

Kelly angled it, glancing around uneasily. He kept having to remind himself that Nick was a real cop on a real case and everything he did was with the appropriate authority. Kelly hoped it was, at least.

He got out of the Range Rover, his hand going to the butt of the gun under his jacket out of habit. He rarely wore a weapon on his hip anymore, but he was getting used to the feeling of having it there again.

Nick strode toward them and pointed to a chalk marking on the ground. "Shooter right here," he said to Kelly. "Stand there. Bullet holes in the building put the shooter facing this way. Don't move."

"All righty," Kelly muttered.

Hagan and JD joined them as Nick was positioning Kelly. "Getting a little bossy, there, O," Hagan observed. "It's a damn miracle you ever get laid."

Nick didn't respond to the attempt at banter. He beckoned JD with two fingers, walking midway into the street and pointing to another mark on the ground. "Stand here. Face the car."

JD nodded, standing where he'd been told. He kept staring up at Nick with wide blue eyes, like a puppy being scolded. Kelly and Hagan shared a concerned glance.

"This is the staff sergeant coming out," Kelly told Hagan quietly. "I'm used to it."

Hagan looked him up and down, narrowing his eyes. "You come like a fire hose when he gives you an order, don't you?"

"Only if he tells me to," Kelly countered with a smirk.

Hagan rolled his eyes. Nick called him from where he was standing on the sidewalk in front of the shop door, and Hagan strolled over to join him. They were far enough away that Kelly had to strain to hear what they were saying. Nick was telling Hagan he was the owner who'd been gunned down walking into the store. Then Julian obliged Nick's request to stand in the doorway, where the thief had been shot dead and fallen across the threshold.

When they were all standing where the evidence indicated they should have been, Nick walked through the scene, studying them, a frown firmly on his face.

"How do you know where the van was?" Kelly called to him.

"Window glass," Nick answered as he circled JD. "Had JD's blood on it. Bullet clipped him, carried onto the van." He stepped back, looking first at Kelly, then at Julian. Hagan stood to the side, out of the line of fire. But Julian and Kelly were directly across from one another, and JD formed a direct line of fire between the two.

Nick put his hands on his hips, prowling back and forth, chewing on his lip. "Fuck," he finally grunted.

Julian raised his hand as if he were holding a gun, and Kelly did the same, firing an imaginary bullet at him.

"No way of knowing what was fired first," Hagan called. "But if you ask me, this looks like an assassination. Whoever was standing where the Doc is, he took out his own man in cold blood."

Nick had a hand over his mouth, still circling JD, studying him, his feet, the way he was positioned versus the rest of them.

"You're making me really nervous right now," JD finally told him.

Nick stopped in front of him. He waited a beat, and behind them Julian raised his hand again as if aiming a weapon at them. "Turn around," Nick ordered JD.

When JD did, he flinched at the sight of Julian aiming at him. He took a step back and knocked into Nick, who didn't give an inch of ground. He held on to JD instead, keeping him from panicking or bolting.

Kelly abandoned his position and jogged over to them. "Hey. That shit's uncalled for, man. Not cool," he shouted. He moved to help free JD from Nick's grasp, but the stunned look of terror on JD's face stopped him. "You okay?"

"I remember . . . running." JD took a shallow, shaky breath. "I was running away from the store. Away from him."

"From him?" Nick asked, pointing at Julian.

"Wasn't me!" Julian called in a bored voice.

"No, from the man who was shot. I ran out of the store. I *was* in there." He put both hands to his head and closed his eyes. "Oh God. I really was in there."

When Nick finally met Kelly's eyes, he looked weary and almost sick. Kelly realized the hard-ass hissy fit he'd just thrown had all been part of a show he was putting on for JD, hoping to jog something loose. It had worked. It had been brutal and perhaps a little immoral, but it had worked.

"I'm sorry," Nick offered. He gave JD's shoulder a squeeze, then released him. "Let's go inside. See if anything rings that bell again."

JD nodded and headed woodenly toward the store.

Kelly stepped in front of Nick, glaring at him briefly. "You either believe him or you don't," he whispered. "If you do, you can't pull shit like this. He's already been through enough trauma, and he trusts you. Only you. You got to live up to that, babe."

Nick nodded, his jaw jumping. "If he has to hate me to keep him safe, I can live with that."

Kelly was left standing there, mulling that over as Nick sidestepped him and followed the others into the store. That was Nick's major vice, though, wasn't it? He'd rather have someone hate him than get hurt.

Two of Nick's four sisters resented him and his distant relationship with his parents because they had no idea he'd been the only thing standing between them and a childhood of being knocked around by their father. And to Kelly's everlasting annoyance, Nick refused to set them straight. He would rather they hate him and continue in their safe little bubble than learn the truth.

It took Kelly a while to get his temper in check before he could join the others in the shop. They were gathered around the display cabinet, scrutinizing it as if it might somehow provide them with doughnuts.

"I'm telling you, if this is authentic, it has a panel," JD was saying.

"What's going on?" Kelly asked. Glass crunched beneath his feet as he approached them.

"I was right about this cabinet," Julian answered. "It's Colonial era."

"Pieces from this era, of this style, often had hidden drawers or panels, places where papers could be hidden from the authorities," JD told them.

"Why?" Kelly asked.

"The Stamp Act, maybe? Every piece of paper the colonists touched had to be affixed with a stamp. It was very costly."

Nick snorted derisively. "They didn't hide their papers because of the Stamp Act. They hid them because they were planning a rebellion. The Stamp Act was one of the Intolerable Acts; it was a series of bullshit handed down from the crown, created a rift that made the atmosphere one of secrecy and paranoia. That professor was right, you are a hack."

"Shut up!" JD griped. "You watch too much History Channel."

"I'm sorry, the Stamp Act? What the fuck are we talking about?" Kelly demanded.

Hagan gave the bottom of the case a nudge with his boot. "The hack believes something could be hidden in the display case."

"We just need to . . . find it," JD said, and he reached his fingers out to touch.

Nick grabbed his wrist, making a hissing sound. "Active crime scene," he grunted, and he extracted a pair of latex gloves from his pocket.

"Sorry," JD said as he tugged them on. He ran his fingers gingerly over the wood. "It's in remarkably good condition. I'm not seeing any obvious spots."

Julian sighed heavily and shoved his hip against the case, rattling it down to its legs.

"Watch it!" JD shouted, and Nick and Hagan both jerked like they were going for their guns.

The decorative panel on the far right of the case rattled loose and fell. Julian caught it deftly, as if he'd just pulled it from thin air. He was smirking when he glanced up at them. "I sell antiques," he quipped.

JD and Nick both glared at him, but Kelly moved forward and peered into the hidden compartment.

"What's in there?" Nick demanded.

Kelly raised one eyebrow. "Guess."

"What are they doing in there?" Hagan asked. "How'd they get there? Unless the owner knew he was going to be robbed, what the fuck?"

"I put them there," JD said, realization dawning. He nodded excitedly and placed his hand on the case, where the outline remained in the dust. He swept across it as if grabbing up the two items, and his motion followed the dust trail perfectly. "That's the only thing that makes sense. I was subverting them. That's why I ran. Has to be." He glanced around at them all, the hope renewed in his eyes and his half smile.

"It gels," Hagan said to Nick. "He comes in under duress, they tell him to find this shit, but he's able to hide it and claim it's not here. Other guy starts tearing shit up, JD bolts like any sane man would, dead guy comes running out of the place shooting at JD. Then the killing starts."

Nick was nodding, his eyes unfocused. Then an idea must have hit him; the color drained from his face. "That's why they came after you again, at the pub," he said to JD. "They didn't know you hid this stuff because you went down in the street and they had to get out before they could check either body. They thought you still had it."

"Why kill him, though?" Kelly asked. "Why not try to grab him and get the items back?"

"So I don't get there first," JD said, his eyes on Nick. Nick nodded grimly, eyes darting between JD and Kelly.

"We *have* to get there first," Julian said.

Kelly straightened, shaking his shoulders out and clapping his hands together to rattle everyone from the suddenly heavy silence. "Well, let's get on it! We've got until our meeting tonight to look over these letters and figure this shit out, so let's work it out, bitches."

Nick chuckled, but held his finger up before Kelly could reach for the papers inside the case. "Crime scene."

Kelly's shoulders slumped and he rolled his eyes. Nick got out his phone to call the techs in. "Use your badge to have sex in a parked car but won't let me National Treasure a piece of evidence," Kelly muttered as he walked away.

"Parked car?" Julian asked as he followed Kelly out.

"He's more fun when he's off duty."

CHAPTER 7

Kelly's plan to spend the rest of the day going over the bundle of letters they'd found in the display case backfired spectacularly, because Nick apparently had shit to do that didn't involve trying to decipher Colonial-era penmanship and he refused to help.

He also refused to let Kelly do it, so Kelly was left with nothing to do but watch Nick fill out paperwork. He was so bored he could have cried.

Nick assigned the letters to Julian and Hagan instead, along with the contemporary diary that had been recovered at the scene. Nick and Kelly were sitting at Nick's desk as Nick finished the report on their visit to the crime scene, and Kelly was still glaring at his lover.

Nick finally looked up, blinking at Kelly when he met his eyes.

Nick put his pen down and glanced around the squad room. He gestured for Kelly to come with him, and he stood, heading for the stairwell. Once in private, Nick trailed his fingers down Kelly's cheek with a soft smile. "You're pissed at me."

"Irritated, yes."

Nick's smile was gentle, almost amused. "What'd I do?"

"You're being a little more cavalier than I'm used to seeing you, it's throwing me off."

"I'm sorry," Nick offered. He sounded sincere. "The letters are important, you're right. But I want Cross off the streets, you with me? If he's combing through letters, he's not shooting up my city looking for Cameron."

"Yeah, makes sense," Kelly grudgingly acknowledged. "What about me, though? Why am I sitting and watching you do paperwork?"

Nick narrowed his eyes. "One, because it was you and not me who cut the tape at the scene and I needed you to give me the details."

Kelly flushed and scrunched his nose. "Oh yeah."

"Two . . . I need you to come somewhere with me."

"To do what?"

"We need to buy JD a suit that'll get him past security for the meeting tonight. And I don't feel like living through a *Pretty Woman* scene today, so I want you with me."

Kelly laughed before he could stop himself. "Wait so, Hagan and Cross are delving into historical mysteries, and we're going *shopping*?"

Nick nodded, though he looked thoroughly disgusted with himself. Kelly grabbed Nick's face and kissed him. "I love you, you know that?"

"I know. I know I'm lucky," Nick rumbled.

Kelly kissed him again. "Does this count as a fight?"

Nick hummed deeply. "It does if you want to rack up makeup sex for next time."

"We'll count it as a fight then."

Nick kissed him again, holding him tighter.

"Can I get a new suit too?" Kelly asked against his lips.

Nick bit him. "As long as I get to pick it out."

The task didn't take them particularly long. The suit they wound up getting JD wasn't perfectly tailored or anything, but it was close enough to pass Nick's rather critical inspection. He also got JD a few more items of clothing, because he'd been borrowing jeans from Nick and shirts from Kelly, and neither fit him particularly well. JD kept promising to repay him, but Nick shrugged it off in the way only Nick could.

JD certainly looked more comfortable leaving the store in clothes that fit him well.

Nick dropped Kelly and JD off at the marina and told them to spiff up like they were getting a chance to walk the high-dollar street corner, then left them. They were supposed to take a cab to meet up with Nick and Julian at the hotel that evening.

A few hours later, Kelly and JD were climbing out of a cab and gawking at the odd building that was the Liberty Hotel. It was made of brick, and laid out in the cross shape of an old prison, which Kelly knew it had once been. A huge decorative window graced the front entrance, and a smiling doorman greeted them as he held the door for them. Kelly craned his neck to take in the impressive lobby.

"Jesus, this is cool," JD said. He was doing the same thing as Kelly, and they probably looked like chickens in the rain, staring at the wonders above them. The brick was all exposed, and so were the remains of the bars from the cells. The catwalks still encircled the lobby, where giant iron chandeliers displayed twinkling lights high overhead.

Kelly grinned. Of course Nick loved this place. It had everything Nick was drawn to: a dark history, a story of regeneration and retribution, luxurious surroundings, and alcohol. His breath caught when he saw the escalator that would take them to the main lobby floor and realized the man standing there watching him was his boyfriend.

Nick was wearing a sharp three-piece suit with a thin, green silk tie and matching handkerchief in his lapel pocket. It had likely been tailored, because it fit him perfectly. Kelly had never seen it on him before, but god*damn*. Nick was watching Kelly with a small smile, one hand in a pocket.

Kelly whistled when he walked up to him. "Don't you look fancy."

Nick stepped into him and kissed him on the corner of the mouth, right where he knew it would send shivers through Kelly's body. "Not so bad yourself," he whispered into Kelly's ear.

It took Kelly a few seconds to realize Julian was with Nick, and that he and JD were waiting for them to stop flirting long enough to get on with things. They both looked a little amused, though.

"Sorry," Kelly offered.

Nick snorted. "I'm not."

Though Nick was trying to keep an easy smile on his face, Kelly could feel the tension in Nick's body. It was making him nervous again. He supposed anyone meeting with a famous mob boss would be tense, but especially someone like Nick, who had childhood ties to the organization and a job that was inherently opposed to everything the mob stood for.

He was a white knight, stepping into the shadows.

"Come on, he's upstairs waiting for us," Nick said.

A man was indeed waiting for them in the lobby when they reached the top of the escalator. He was attractive, with dark hair and kind eyes that seemed at odds with his job. He was dressed in a soft-gray suit, his sky-blue tie the only anomaly. Nick slowed when he saw him, coming to a stop a few yards in front of him.

They stood opposite one another, silent, their expressions stern. Kelly glanced uneasily at Julian and JD. This was going to go so wrong. He could feel it, they were going to destroy this beautiful hotel lobby in a firefight.

The man took a step forward, and Nick moved to meet him. Instead of violence, though, they embraced. The stranger patted Nick on the back and held a fistful of his hair as Nick hugged him. They broke apart and both men were smiling, although Kelly recognized the wistful glint in Nick's eyes. This was a bittersweet reunion, at best.

"Damn, you look good, Nicky," the man said, and he brushed at Nick's shoulders, grinning.

"No one calls me that anymore." Nick turned and waved a hand at Kelly, keeping his other hand on the man's shoulder. "Mikey, this is Kelly Abbott."

"The boyfriend?" Mikey asked with a raised eyebrow.

Kelly didn't know how to answer that. He knew enough about mob and gang culture to know that having a "boyfriend" usually got a man killed. Mikey stepped forward to shake his hand, though.

"Word went around town a few years ago Detective O'Flaherty liked to play for the other team," Mikey said with a sideways grin at Nick. "First thing Paddy did was lay down the law. No one touches him or his flavor of the month."

"Is that right?" Nick's tone sent a chill up Kelly's spine.

Mikey nodded, still grinning at Kelly. "This one's more than just a taste, though, huh?"

Nick met Kelly's eyes, his expression guarded and a little frightened. He obviously hadn't realized the mob had been keeping such close tabs on him, or that Kelly might have been in any kind of danger in the first place.

"These the two need the meeting?" Mikey asked with a nod at Julian and JD.

"Sort of," Nick said. He introduced them, but he seemed a little thrown off his game now. Kelly was too. He stayed quiet, trusting Nick to lead them into the fray.

Mikey escorted them around the lobby, toward a hallway marking the ballroom and elevators to the jail hotel rooms. They piled into the elevator, with Mikey putting his back against the wall. He might have greeted Nick warmly, but the man wasn't letting his guard down with them.

They rode to the second floor, which consisted of a private gallery bar that had once been the catwalk ringing the prison. When they filed out, Mikey took Nick by the arm and stopped him.

"You know what you're doing here, Nicky? Boston police detective asking Paddy for favors? Oh, son."

Nick gave him a curt nod. "I got no other options. Friend of mine is in trouble."

"Life or death trouble?"

"That's the one."

A hint of sadness passed over Mikey's dark eyes, and he nodded slowly. He walked by them, leading them past the hostess toward a point in the middle of the catwalk where chairs and sofas had been set up in an isolated lounge.

Two large men stood in their path, both dressed impeccably in tailored suits. They refused to let the group pass.

"It seems the sister organization in Boston is far better dressed than the ones in New York," Julian commented. He sounded like he approved.

A man sitting on a sofa behind the bodyguards stood and greeted them with a crooked smile. Something about it struck Kelly deep in his gut, like it was familiar to him. "You dress like a thug, you get treated like a thug," the man told them. He pulled at his bow tie and raised a glass to them. "Nicholas, join me a moment, won't you?"

Nick stepped forward and held his hands up so Mikey could pat him down. Then the bodyguards let him by, leaving Kelly and the others unable to get to him if anything went wrong. Kelly shifted from foot to foot, not liking the way any of this felt.

The man they called Paddy handed Nick a glass of champagne. "To celebrate your safe return from war."

Nick hesitated only briefly before touching the tip of his crystal glass to Paddy's and taking a sip. Kelly was fascinated and confused by the ritual. It seemed almost like Paddy was taunting Nick for coming to him for help, forcing him to consort with the very criminal element he had sworn an oath to protect the city against.

Nick set his glass on the table after a small sip, and Paddy did the same. "Good then. Shall we take this upstairs?"

The bodyguards backed the four of them against the railing as their boss walked by. They fell into step behind Paddy, and Kelly and the others followed, with Mikey bringing up the rear. They were instructed to wait for the next elevator, then left without escort in the vestibule.

"What the hell?" Kelly asked as soon as they were alone. "Why not just have us meet them in the room?"

Nick cleared his throat, looking a little sick. "A lobby full of people just saw a Boston police detective having a drink with a mob boss. Did you see the tourist with the camera on the floor above us?"

Kelly shook his head.

"Added security," Julian commented. "One hint at corruption and it could bring the police force to its knees. I like it."

Nick scowled at Julian. "Try not to keep reminding me that you're not a good person, okay?"

"I will do my very best."

"I'm so nervous," JD announced. "I might throw up on this suit."

Kelly shook his head. "You throw up, I throw up. Nobody wants that in an elevator."

JD laughed shakily.

"It'll be fine," Nick said. "Just keep your mouth shut unless they ask you a direct question. Don't try to play them, just answer honestly."

Kelly stood beside Nick, staring at his profile, waiting until he got tired of feeling Kelly's eyes on him so he'd look at him. Nick's jaw jumped and he swallowed heavily, but he never turned, never met Kelly's eyes.

"What's this going to do to you, babe?" Kelly finally asked him. "What does it mean, owing Paddy a favor?"

Nick licked his lips, a nervous habit he'd nearly broken himself of over the years but which had returned full force when he'd come home the last time. "It'll be fine."

"O'Flaherty," Julian said softly. "I understand what you're doing. I can assure you, the next time you call I will answer. No matter the reason."

Nick glanced over his shoulder, but never actually at Julian. He returned his eyes to the elevator doors. "I do hope you mean that."

The elevator opened up before they could say more. Nick's face could have been cut from marble when Kelly finally saw it.

Kelly had always wondered about those tales Nick had told of barely escaping the grasp of the mob, if Nick had simply been a young man exaggerating about a rough past because it gave him that added air of authority among the other Marines, or if he'd been serious.

The look in his eyes now, of stark fear and resignation barely covered by steely determination, told Kelly he hadn't been exaggerating all those years ago.

Nick would go to the ends of the earth, carve out little pieces of his soul, to keep a promise. Kelly could see him carving away right now, preparing another piece to throw into the fire.

"Hey," Kelly whispered. "Whatever this costs you, I'm here to pay it with you. Got it?"

Nick's green eyes shone bright in the lights of the elevator. He leaned closer and kissed Kelly, his hand gentle on Kelly's cheek, his fingers trailing down Kelly's neck when he pulled away.

The elevator lurched to a stop, and Mikey was standing there waiting for them when the doors opened up. He had seen the last bit of their kiss, and he was pursing his lips and frowning. "Got to tell you, Nicky, I'm good with it and all, but it's still weird. You want to keep your face pretty, you might want to keep your hands inside the ride until you reach the exits."

Nick huffed a laugh, and they followed Mikey down the hall. Mikey turned to Kelly and patted him on the arm. "This guy taught me how to kiss when we were kids," he whispered. "Landed Mary Katherine McDowell on that lesson."

Kelly laughed despite the nerves roiling through him. "How's that work?"

"I'll show you later," Nick promised with an almost playful smile.

"Hey Nicky, does that make me gay by proxy?" Mikey asked.

"Yeah, Mikey," Nick answered, deadpan. "Yeah it does."

"Fuck." They reached the room and Mikey turned his back to the door. He met Nick's eyes, his expression sobering. "You know you're even with him right now," he said softly. "Still time to head back."

Nick didn't respond, merely returned Mikey's stare.

Mikey sighed heavily. "If you hadn't left, *you'd* be in that room right now, and I'd be screening *your* visitors. You know that, right?"

Kelly could barely restrain the shock, or his questions. He looked between the two men, wide-eyed. How the fuck would Nick have ended up in that position when his childhood friend was still basically a bodyguard?

Nick nodded curtly. "That's why I had to leave."

Mikey mimicked the nod, eyes melancholy and brow furrowed. Then he shook off the dark mood and gave the rest of them a grin that struck a little false. He pointed to Nick. "Most stand-up guy I ever known."

Pure devastation flashed in Nick's eyes as Mikey spoke. Kelly wanted to reach out to him, to comfort him somehow. But he didn't think even he could make this better for Nick.

Mikey patted each of them down, being pretty thorough about it, and then he knocked on the suite door. It was opened by one of the bodyguards from before, who allowed them into the suite.

Kelly couldn't stop himself from gawking. He could see more and more why Nick had wanted to bring him here for a little romance. Hints of the brick from the original jail structure showed along the outer wall, but the majority of the wall consisted of an enormous decorative window, just like the one that had greeted them at the front entrance.

The room had been rearranged, with more seating being brought in to accommodate everyone. Paddy sat near the window, smoking a cigar. He gestured for them to join him.

One of the bodyguards stopped them, though, stepping in front of Nick when he moved forward. Nick didn't back away, merely side-eyed the larger man, jaw tightening. Kelly cursed internally and slid a little so he was in front of JD if things went south.

"Need to check you over one more time," the bodyguard told Nick. There was something in his voice, though, a taunt perhaps. Enjoyment. Kelly got the feeling that Mikey's attitude in regards to Nick's sexual orientation was perhaps the outlier in this organization. Keep your hands inside the ride, indeed.

"Be gentle with that one," Paddy warned, and he sounded amused.

The bodyguard sniffed, then grabbed Nick's arm and turned him, shoving him against the wall. Nick hit hard, slamming his face and chest. The man kicked Nick's feet apart, then pressed his hand against the back of Nick's head and rammed Nick's cheek into the plaster again. Kelly jerked to move, but Julian's hand on his elbow stopped him. If they started a fight here, they'd all leave the hotel in body bags.

Nick's face was turned away from them, so Kelly couldn't see his eyes, couldn't gauge his expression. Kelly gritted his teeth, preparing to watch this guy manhandle his lover and unable to do anything about it.

"Watch the suit, huh?" Nick said, and his voice was deceptively calm.

The bodyguard laughed. As soon as he took a step back and gave Nick enough room, Nick brought his elbow hard into the man's temple, then spun and kicked him, grabbing for the holster under the man's jacket and pulling the gun away as he stumbled back from the kick. It was all dizzyingly fast, even for Kelly, who had seen the move plenty of times before.

With a few rapid flicks of his fingers, Nick had pulled the slide off the Glock and dropped the magazine to the floor. He stepped on the magazine, then dropped the gun and tossed the slide toward Mikey, who caught it with a grin as wide as a cartoon cat.

The bodyguard got to his feet again, glaring at Nick and flexing his shoulders. His nose was bloody.

Paddy cackled gleefully. "Told you to be gentle with that one. Now get the fuck on that door, both of you," he added, waving at the bodyguards. "Fucking useless bastards."

They grudgingly took up their posts on the door, but not before the bloody one pointed at Nick and murmured a threat under his breath. Nick watched him, only turning back to face Paddy once he was between JD and the bodyguard.

Paddy stood and came closer, opening his arms for a hug that Nick returned stiffly. The mob boss pulled him close like he was embracing a son, though, patting him on the back and then on his head like a proud father might before pulling him over to the couches. "Been a while, Nicky."

"No one calls him that anymore, boss," Mikey informed him with a cheeky grin.

Paddy gave Nick's cheek an affectionate tap, then sat. He gestured for all of them to take seats. Kelly was confused again. Nick had been so tense, so worried, but this was a warmer reception than Nick received at his own home when he visited.

Paddy propped one leg on his other knee and reclined, arms on the back of the sofa. He surveyed the four of them. Julian had remained standing, his arms crossed. Mikey stood beside him, hands in his pockets, looking at ease. JD and Kelly flanked Nick on the sofa. They waited silently while Paddy looked them over.

"So," he finally said. "You need my help again."

"I wouldn't be here if I didn't," Nick said, words coated in ice.

Paddy laughed. He pointed at Nick while glancing at Kelly. "So fucking stubborn. He ever told you this story?"

Kelly shook his head, then remembered Nick's warning about being respectful. "No, sir."

Paddy grunted. "First time I saw these two chuckleheads, they were sixteen, walking down the street from baseball practice. That one had a black eye." He pointed at Nick again. "Looked so much like my son, Patrick Jr. Lost him to a goddamn drunk driver the year before. Saw Nicky and thought he was a ghost. I stopped my car, called to him, asked him how he got that shiner. And this fucking kid, he looks me straight in the eye. You know how many people look me straight in the eye, even back then?"

Kelly shrugged uncomfortably.

"No fucking one." He looked back at Nick almost sadly. "Didn't take a fucking genius to figure out his old man was knocking him around, so I asked him, big kid like you, why don't you knock back? He meets my eyes again and he says, 'Cause I got people more important than me at home to take care of, Paddy.' He fucking knew who I was. Wasn't afraid of me."

Kelly glanced at Nick, his heart aching. "With a father like his, why should he be afraid of anyone?" he asked softly.

"You damn right," Paddy snarled. "Damn right. I told him I'd help him out. I'd protect his sisters if he'd protect me. He was good on his word, and I was good on mine. Even gave him a ride to the airport and paid for his fucking ticket to go to Parris Island when it was time. I had pride in my heart for this boy just like he was my own son."

Kelly's eyes widened. He'd never heard any of this. Nick was stone-faced, though, not reacting at all to the information being revealed, or to the almost kind words the notorious criminal was saying about him.

"He came back home and went to work for the other guy," Paddy said with a sigh. "Always were the good egg no matter how hard I tried to boil you. So you come to me asking for help, I'm giving it to you. No questions asked."

Nick swallowed hard. "Mikey told you what we're looking for?"

"He did." Paddy gave Mikey a nod.

Kelly didn't like the fact that Mikey was moving around behind him, but he was trying not to be tense or appear nervous. He had to trust Julian to watch their backs for them, which was admittedly a little hard to do.

"You have a lead for us?" Nick asked, growing impatient.

"Better."

Mikey set a reinforced suitcase on the table between them, and Paddy leaned over to put in a code, then prop the lid open. He turned it to display the contents to them with a flourish.

On the cushioned interior of black felt sat a sparkling piece of jewelry. Roughly four inches wide, with bright-blue enamel that was covered in diamonds, emeralds, and rubies. Kelly recognized it as the star brooch from Julian's photo.

"Jesus Christ," Julian blurted.

Nick lowered his head, rubbing his hands over his face. He'd just been shown stolen goods and was powerless to do anything about it. It had to be killing his sense of duty. Kelly put his hand on Nick's knee.

"A replica, of course, of the one stolen and smuggled into Boston a century ago," Paddy said cheekily. "I keep it to . . . honor our Irish roots."

"Right," Nick grunted. He sat forward, looking but not touching.

"What exactly is it you need from this?" Mikey asked.

Nick gave him a wary glance. "It's supposed to point to a location."

"Like a treasure map?" Mikey asked.

Nick nodded.

JD slid off the sofa to his knees, his fingers gripping the table. "May I touch it?" he asked. It was the first thing he'd said since the elevator. He'd obviously forgotten he was scared.

Paddy merely chuckled. He waved for JD to go ahead.

They crowded around it, scowling at the priceless piece like it was a Rubik's Cube instead of a treasure that had gone missing over a hundred years ago. The emeralds were stunningly green, and they made up a clover in the center of the field of diamonds. Brilliant red rubies formed an X behind it. But there was nothing else. Just precious gems. No message, no sign. Nothing that would point in any way to a location or clue.

"I don't understand," Julian said. He was leaning over the back of the couch, breathing down their necks. "They said it would be there."

Nick massaged the bridge of his nose. "Is it possible these people wanted you to locate *this* instead of something more?" he asked.

"Good luck to them, if that's the case," Julian said with a salute toward Paddy.

"Why did they think it would be here?" Kelly asked.

"The man responsible for the design was a descendant of the soldier who hid the stolen goods," Julian explained. "There were several accounts, private accounts, that the clues to its whereabouts were passed along."

JD tore his attention away from the star to turn it to Paddy. "Do you have a loupe?"

Paddy rubbed his finger across the tip of his nose, nodding. He gestured for one of the men at the door to retrieve it.

Nick still had his head down, his thumbs massaging his temples. "This treasure hunt is just as pointless as the one we send those kids on every summer."

Kelly patted his knee, trying to offer some sort of comfort. Nick had just sold his soul to get a look at this thing, all for nothing. The memory of Nick's notes for that treasure hunt flashed through Kelly's mind. Then it hit him.

"Oh my God, it's a pigpen cipher!" he blurted.

Nick raised his head, blinking rapidly at Kelly then glancing at the star in JD's hand.

"Look it," Kelly said, reaching to take it from JD. He drew his finger across the rubies, then pointed at each tip of the clover so they could envision it. It formed a perfect piece to a pigpen cipher, with the shapes of the clover creating the message.

"Motherfucker," Nick breathed.

"What does it mean?" Julian demanded.

"Pigpen ciphers are usually dots, but this is shapes," Nick told him. "Three circles and an arch. I know arches are supposed to represent power, monarchy, manliness . . . sometimes the warrior class. But this one's on its head, I have no idea what that means. And circles, I don't know."

"You said there were more pieces stolen when this was?" Kelly asked. "I bet together, they form a complete cipher."

Nick nodded toward Paddy. "Any ideas?"

"The other pieces, I can't help you with," Paddy told them. "You can imagine that stealing the Irish Crown Jewels brought enough attention; keeping them together as a collection would have been . . ."

"Stupid," Nick provided.

Paddy gave them that crooked grin again, and again it made Kelly uneasy.

"Where the other pieces ended up, I don't know. You could speak to our . . . brethren in New York. Chicago. But even I can't get a cop through their doors for a treasure hunt, kiddo."

Nick's jaw tightened and he nodded.

"Maybe there's more etched in the stones," JD said. He pointed to the jeweler's loupe Nosebleed was bringing them. They were all silent as JD examined the stones for markings. After a few minutes, he sighed and set the star brooch and the loupe down on the cushion. "Nothing."

"Where does that leave us?" Julian asked.

"With a very expensive . . . copy," Nick answered, voice gone soft with defeat. His eyes were locked on Paddy's.

"Well," Paddy said, and he clapped his hands together. "It seems our meeting has come to an end." He climbed to his feet, and they all stood with him. He reached for Nick's hand, shaking it warmly, and a moment later he pulled Nick into another hug. For an infamous mob boss, he sure did seem fond of the police.

This time, Nick returned the embrace a bit more sincerely. "Thank you," Nick said, almost inaudible.

Paddy tapped Nick's cheek with the tips of his fingers. "Don't be a stranger, kiddo."

"Don't hold your breath, old man."

Paddy barked a laugh. "This make us even?"

"I got one more left," Nick told him. "Mark it in your damn book so your boys know it."

Paddy was still chuckling when the door closed behind them.

"One more?" Mikey asked Nick as he led them to the elevator. Nick was silent, but Kelly wished like hell Mikey would press him for details so Kelly wouldn't have to later. Mikey stopped him in the middle of the hall, standing in front of him with his hand on Nick's chest. "You telling me Paddy owed you a solid? Owed you *two* solids?"

A slow, crooked smile spread across Nick's face. It was his only response.

"Jesus fucking Christ, you fucking fucker," Mikey said affectionately, and he stepped aside so they could continue on to the elevator. Kelly punched the button. Mikey pulled Nick into a hug, squeezing him tightly. "You be careful out there, huh? You left Boston to save your fucking life and then spent every fucking day trying to die."

"Watch your fucking mouth." Nick patted him on the back of the head, and then they released each other. "You get in trouble, you know who to call."

"Anybody but you."

"That's right," Nick drawled, and stepped into the elevator with the others. Mikey stood there grinning, his hands in his suit pockets as the doors closed.

"How the bleeding hell do you acquire not one, but *two* favors from the Irish mob?" Julian demanded on the way down.

Nick remained silent. For one, he kind of enjoyed frustrating Julian. And two, you acquired favors from the Irish mob by keeping your damn mouth shut about how you did it.

They reached the bottom floor and Nick led the way to Alibi, the restaurant situated amidst the remains of the old jail cells on the bottom floor. As in the lobby, the walls were brick and the iron bars were still set into the windows and doors where the cells had once stood. The room was littered with little pods of comfortable chairs and love seats, and the tables were just big enough to set a few glasses and a plate of appetizers on.

They took up residence in a corner, where the lights faced away from them and no one would look their way.

"That's funny," JD said as soon as he sat down. "Alibi."

They all stared at him.

"You can't tell me that's not funny. I don't care," he insisted. "Irony."

Nick finally chuckled.

"I lied," JD blurted, and though he kept his voice at a whisper, it was obvious he had been desperate to say the words.

Nick looked up from his menu, eyes pinning JD before he could speak again. JD met his stare and flinched. He was astute enough to see the distrust in Nick's expression. He looked wounded, but he continued. "The star," he said quickly. "It did have something on it."

"What do you mean?" Kelly asked.

"The diamonds inside the clover, there were symbols etched on them."

Nick sat back, a mixture of relief and irritation flowing through him. "You didn't want them to know."

"No, I figured the less people who know about this, the better. Especially people who steal priceless treasures and hoard them in suitcases."

"Fair enough." Nick cleared his throat. "Do me a favor and never Google your real name, okay?"

"What? Why?"

"No reason." Nick raised his hand for a waitress. "I need a fucking drink."

When the first round came, JD took one of the napkins from beneath his glass and drew the cross and clover on it. Inside each leaf of the clover, he wrote the symbols he'd seen.

Kelly had his phone out, frowning at the screen.

Nick leaned toward him. They were sharing a love seat, so he scooted closer, sliding his hand between Kelly's thighs so it would look like they were merely lovebirds on a date rather than a group of men who'd just met the most notorious criminal in Boston and were now here drinking so Paddy and his boys could slip out the back of the hotel without being seen. "What are you doing?"

"Looking up what circles mean."

Nick tightened his grip, squeezing his thigh and pulling him closer. He whispered in his ear. "No beginning. No end." Kelly tried to turn his head, but Nick nudged his cheek with his nose, refusing to let him move just yet. He closed his eyes and rested his forehead against Kelly's temple. "Like a wedding ring. Represents eternity."

Kelly finally leaned away and turned to meet Nick's eyes. Nick couldn't tell what color his eyes were tonight in the low light of the restaurant. He thought they might be gray.

Nick kissed him before Kelly could speak. "I love you," he whispered. His words came out almost desperate and he wasn't entirely sure why. Kelly had just seen a part of him he'd hoped no one would ever see. He didn't know what Kelly would do with that.

"Do you two need to go to your room?" Julian asked with a long-suffering sigh.

"Soon," Kelly answered, his voice hoarse and serious. He gave Nick a barely perceptible nod and they both sat up straighter. Kelly cleared his throat. "This says the circles can represent anything from eternity to fidelity to the meeting of the spirit and matter."

"Spirit and matter?" Julian repeated. "Why?"

"The solid line encircling the inner part that's made of nothing," Kelly summarized as he read what he'd found on his phone. He clicked it off and put it away.

"The sideways arch?" JD asked.

"It's probably just an arch," Nick guessed. "They had to work in the confines of their task, which was to make it look like a clover. Instead of a straight line, though, they chose to curve it to make it an arch. What numbers did we end up with?"

JD handed him the napkin. He had drawn the star, with circles representing each gem. He'd shaded in the pieces that were red or green, and copied the writing on the diamonds. They weren't numbers after all, but more symbols.

"You're sure this is right?" Nick asked.

JD nodded, looking a little perturbed that Nick would question his memory.

"Seriously, you're giving me a bitchface for doubting the memory of someone who can't remember his own name?"

JD tried to maintain his frown, but he finally snorted and gave Nick a sheepish smile. "It's correct. I promise."

"This isn't a pigpen cipher," Nick said. "There aren't enough letters."

"How many are represented?" Julian asked.

"Just eight. You have the four symbols in the cross that are represented by the emeralds, then he has four more here within the diamonds."

"So eight symbols. With no point of reference as to what they mean," Kelly concluded. "Great."

Nick was still shaking his head, examining the napkin. He was at a complete loss. "I . . . I don't know what to do with this. I don't know where we go from here with this."

"Hold on," Julian said with a wave of his hand. "You're not giving up, are you? This is information the others don't have, information they won't get unless they intend to go to the bloody mob for it. Not many people have the stones to do what you just did. We're finally a step ahead. And we have *him* now; they don't."

JD was nodding his head with Julian's words. "I don't remember any of the important things, but I sure as hell remember this stuff," JD told them. "We can do this. We can get there ahead of them."

Nick narrowed his eyes and cocked his head at JD. "You're very eager to get to this treasure."

JD sighed heavily. "You still suspect me? My motives? That's fine, Detective, because I do too. I don't remember why I was there with people who would rob and kill. I don't know why I hid those things from the people I was supposed to be working with. Maybe I was a hostage like his boyfriend. Maybe I was there of my own free will and I decided to cheat them out of something I found. I don't know. But you know what, Nick, I know there's at least one person out there who *does* know the answers to those questions. And that person is looking for this same treasure. *That's* who I want to find, *that's* why I'm eager. If you want to arrest me and put me in a cell, you go ahead and do it, but one thing I know for damn sure is that I'm your best shot at this, and no matter what my motivation was for being there, I'm here right now for the three of you. Because you're the only people in the world I know well enough to care about right now."

Nick and the others stared at him, stunned by his outburst. It was the first hint of real heat Nick had seen from him.

JD stood and straightened his suit, closing his eyes. "Am I under arrest, or can I go to the room and get some sleep now?"

Nick was torn between respecting the man for standing up to him and being upset with himself for not hiding his suspicions better. He nodded, and JD turned away without another word.

Julian tossed back what was left of his drink and stood. "I'll try to calm him. Keep an eye on him. Good night," he added with a nod to them both.

Nick sat forward and held his head in his hands, groaning softly. Kelly's fingers were tentative on his back, at first. Then he placed his palm on Nick's spine and left it there.

"Your instincts are telling you to trust him. He'll be here in the morning."

"Only people he knows well enough to care about. Jesus Christ, just stab me in the heart already."

Kelly chuckled. "He sounded a little like you there. All self-righteous logic and sass. Let's go to bed, huh?"

Nick looked back at him, and Kelly gave him an exaggerated leer.

"You know what, fuck it," Nick growled. He held up his hand for the waitress, ordering another round of drinks.

"What are you doing? I thought we were going to bed."

"No, we're not. I'm having drinks with my boyfriend at one of my favorite places in the city." Nick sat back and slipped his hand over Kelly's thigh again. He squeezed and pulled Kelly closer, sliding him on the leather love seat.

Kelly laughed and ran his teeth across his lower lip. "Does that make this a date?"

"It'd be our first real one if it is."

"First date includes stolen treasure and the mob. How romantic. And fitting." Kelly leaned closer, smirking. He kissed Nick before Nick could come up with any clever responses. Kelly's hand found its way into the pocket of Nick's tailored suit pants.

"Don't," Nick warned. He knew he'd jump on the chance to vent his frustration, and he didn't want to be banned from this bar for indecency.

Kelly grinned against the kiss. "Why, Detective? You don't mind making me come all over my sweatpants in the car."

"You didn't pay a thousand dollars for your sweatpants," Nick gritted out as Kelly's fingers brushed against his thigh. "I could hire a high-class hooker cheaper than I could replace this suit."

"Are you offering to pay me?" Kelly asked, eyes sparkling.

Nick growled in the back of his throat and fished Kelly's hand out of his pocket. "No, but I will fuck you into oblivion as soon as we get to the room."

"Oh yeah?"

"Yeah, just keep your hands out of my pants."

Kelly laughed. The sound was like a balm on Nick's fraying nerves. He squeezed Kelly's thigh tighter, keeping his fingers between Kelly's knees as they drank and talked for the next hour. Nick would have given anything to have left as soon as Kelly's lips had touched his, to take him upstairs and just take him as many times as they could handle.

But they were here for a reason. He had to be seen tonight.

"How do you earn a favor from the mob?" Kelly asked after his seventh or eighth drink.

Nick almost spit his alcohol all over the table. He had to struggle to swallow, and he set his drink down before he could spill it. He leaned closer to Kelly, his voice full of gravel. "You keep your fucking mouth shut in public, that's how."

Kelly blinked at him, then nodded obediently. He stared into Nick's eyes for another few seconds, and then a smile spread over his lips. "That actually made me shiver. Can you do that again?"

Nick's lips twitched.

"No seriously, that was the hottest you've ever been. Will you threaten me when you're fucking me later? Or better yet, will you just fuck me right here?"

Nick laughed, and he stood to straighten his suit. He picked up his glass and finished off his drink, then held his hand down for Kelly. Kelly wavered when Nick pulled him off the couch.

"Oh, this is going to be fun," Nick hissed in his ear as he guided him between the chairs and the table.

Kelly slowed enough that Nick pressed into him from behind. "I'm not going to make it to the room."

"You're not that drunk."

"No, but I am that horny. This place is dark, I bet no one will notice."

Nick shoved him ahead, ushering him out of the bar. It took every ounce of willpower Nick had to not pull Kelly close and grind against him on the escalator. Kelly obviously didn't give a shit about decorum, because he stepped into Nick's space and tugged at his belt.

"Control yourself," Nick ground out, trying to keep calm. The entire lobby could see people on the escalator. He didn't want to give anyone a show. Actually, he did. But he wouldn't.

"Where's the fun in that?" Kelly challenged. He stuck his tongue between his teeth, grinning, then he hopped off the escalator when they reached the top, pulling Nick by his belt.

Nick finally pried Kelly's fingers off the belt and held Kelly's hand instead.

"I like this," Kelly said as they strolled across the lobby, fingers twined. "Holding your hand. Walking around. You in that suit, Jesus Christ."

Nick pulled him closer, bringing his hand up to kiss it. "I'll remember that."

They got to the elevator without incident, and without public indecency, but as soon as the elevator doors closed, Kelly grabbed Nick and shoved him against the wall. His hand worked at Nick's belt and the buttons of his vest, and he kicked Nick's feet apart so he could slip himself between Nick's thighs and press their groins together.

Nick grasped at Kelly's hips, holding on to him so he wouldn't fall on his ass as his shoes slid against the marble floor. Kelly kissed him messily, his movements just sloppy enough to turn Nick on even more. He fucking loved when Kelly got like this. It went rough and messy and loud.

He grunted a warning that he was about to move them, and Kelly moaned in response, wrapping his arms around Nick's neck. Nick spun them, pressing Kelly against the array of buttons.

Kelly grabbed two handfuls of Nick's hair and yanked.

"Fuck," Nick hissed. He rubbed his hardened cock against Kelly's. "You couldn't have waited five more fucking minutes to start this?"

"I'm sorry," Kelly gasped. "I am, but I couldn't fucking help it. You went all fucking badass evil mastermind on me with the Irish mob. Then you were talking about beginnings and ends and eternity and rings and that fucking tone of voice you use when you get all hard and drunk. God! This is your fault!"

The elevator dinged, and Nick slammed his palm against the emergency stop button. The lights flickered and the elevator shuddered to a stop. He pressed closer.

Kelly blinked up at the emergency lights. "You're really going to fuck me in the elevator, aren't you?"

"No," Nick hissed. Although he did want to. Badly. "Not enough lube to go half as hard at you as I want to. I'm going to take you back to our room. I'm going to bend you over the end of our fucking bed, and I'm going to fill you so full of me you'll be screaming in a Boston accent. Make you forget everything you saw and heard tonight."

Kelly licked his lips slowly. "Promise?"

Nick closed his eyes, taking a deep breath before hitting the button again. The doors slid open, and Nick escorted Kelly out with a hand on his lower back. Thankfully there was no one there to see their disheveled suits or flushed faces. He'd had his share of exhibitionist moments, and most had been well worth it. He didn't want that with Kelly, though. He wanted Kelly all to himself.

"You're such a fucking white knight when you start drinking." Kelly flopped against the wall beside their door, nestling into the corner of the part that jutted out around the doors. "Your alcohol tolerance sucks for you, but it's awesome for me."

Nick blocked him in and bent to kiss his neck. "Just means I get to take advantage of you."

"I love it when you do that."

"I know you do," Nick purred against Kelly's ear. Kelly shivered all over, and Nick held him tighter so he could feel it.

Kelly rested his head against the wall, clumsy fingers working at Nick's belt. "Eternity rings and manly soldiers. You Irish really know how to seduce a guy."

Nick hummed against Kelly's neck as he kissed and nipped. His entire body thrummed with bourbon and electricity. Kelly's hands on him were kicking him into overdrive.

Kelly's words finally sank through the haze, though, and Nick lifted his head.

Kelly spread his hands over Nick's stomach, bunching his fingers against Nick's vest as he worked the buttons loose. "What? What's wrong? If you don't have the room key I'm going to kill you. Or give you a sloppy blowjob in a hallway, whatever." He gave Nick's dress shirt a yank, and buttons went flying.

"Motherfucker," Nick hissed as Kelly laughed raucously. Nick fought past the allure of Kelly's hands on him and asked, "What did you say before?"

"I said if you don't open the door and fuck me, I'm dropping to my knees right here in the hallway." To emphasize his point, he pulled the zipper on Nick's pants and popped the button free. "Actually I like that plan, key or not."

The image tore through Nick, almost wiping his mind clean of any other thought. He even reached up to grab Kelly's hair, his fist tightening in preparation of holding on while he thrust into Kelly's mouth later. But he shook his head, fighting the niggling feeling that he was missing something. "Before that," he said, and his voice was hoarse. "What'd you say?"

"Uh, about the Irish?" Kelly asked. "White knights? Circles and arches and eternity and warriors? I don't know, I talked a lot tonight, you shouldn't let me do that when I'm drunk."

Nick grabbed Kelly's face with both hands. "Eternity. Spirit meeting matter. Archways. Warriors." They stared at each other for a few seconds, and then Nick made a sound like an animal in pain as he backed away from Kelly and slapped himself in the forehead. "God! Why the fuck couldn't I have figured that out an hour from now?" he shouted.

"What, figured what out?"

"It's a cemetery," Nick hissed. "The star points us to a cemetery."

Nick zipped up his pants and stalked off, heading toward JD's and Julian's room.

"Hey," Kelly called after him. "Does this mean I'm not getting fucked, because I don't like this new plan at all!"

Nick stopped in the middle of the hall and turned. Kelly was standing in front of their door, his hair mussed, his suit awry, his cock obviously hard, his hands out like he couldn't believe Nick had just walked away. But he was still smiling. Kelly was always smiling.

Nick glanced at the door of the other men's room, then back to Kelly. Kelly deserved better than being abandoned for a treasure hunt. When it came right down to it, if Nick had a choice to make, he'd always choose Kelly. "Fuck it, it can wait 'til morning."

He fished the key out of his pocket and headed back to his lover. Kelly's grin widened and he began to unbutton his own shirt in anticipation. Nick grabbed him around the waist, kissing him, then lifting him to his toes to deepen the kiss. Kelly's hands were once again in his hair.

"You trying to sweep me off my feet?" Kelly asked, a little breathless.

Nick grinned. "No. But I am going to take you up on that sloppy blowjob you offered."

Kelly cackled as Nick dragged him inside. "Who says romance is dead?"

Nick attacked his clothes, dropping the expensive material here and there. They both kicked clumsily out of their shoes, and Kelly wasn't even out of his briefs before Nick tossed him onto the bed. Kelly stretched out, pushing his briefs down as he scooted closer to the middle of the king-sized bed. Though he'd seen Kelly's hard body a thousand times before, he still nearly stumbled over his own feet when his eyes raked over the ornate six-shooter tattoo spanning from the juncture of Kelly's thigh to his lower ribs and highlighting the muscle beneath it.

Nick tossed his last piece of clothing away and stood at the side of the bed, admiring his lover. Kelly'd had that six-shooter ever since Nick had known him, and Nick had always loved it and not quite known why.

"I thought I was going to get on my knees and let you fuck my mouth like a cheap whore," Kelly drawled. "I mean, since you can't afford a high-dollar escort with your pants." There was a sparkle in his eyes. He knew *exactly* what he did to Nick when he started talking like that. When he laid that tight body out for Nick to gaze upon.

"You were, but plans change," Nick growled. He dug in his overnight bag and pulled out two things, showing them to Kelly for him to choose which would come first: a tube of lubricant, or the little red flip camera they kept for . . . special occasions.

"Camera," Kelly gasped. "Oh God, yeah. The camera."

Nick crawled onto the bed, wrapping Kelly's hips in his arms and pulling him closer. He handed him the flip cam, and Kelly scrambled to turn it on so he could catch the first touch of Nick's tongue to his cock.

Ten minutes later, Nick was on his back, Kelly straddling his chest and fucking his mouth as he filmed it. He wasn't going easy; he was far too drunk for that. But the rougher he was with Nick, the harder he pulled Nick's hair, the deeper he thrust even after Nick nearly gagged on him, the more he bruised Nick's lips, the more turned on Nick became.

Kelly arched over him, gritting his teeth and shouting Nick's name. He cried out again and met Nick's eyes, fist clenched in his hair. "If I came all over your face, you'd take it out on my ass, wouldn't you?"

Nick dug his fingers into Kelly's hips, nodding.

Kelly turned the video camera to face him, and gave it a sly smile. "Not usually recommended, but this is going to be worth it."

CHAPTER 8

Kelly groaned when the light lanced through his eyelids. He buried his face in the mattress, burrowing under his pillow. Someone picked the pillow up and tapped his shoulder.

"No!" Kelly griped. "Fuck PT, dude."

"Get dressed, babe, it's almost six."

Kelly sat up too fast, and his head swam. His stomach churned briefly, but he got it under control. He was surprised to find not just Nick in the room, sitting on the end of the bed, but also Julian and JD loitering near the doorway. "Jesus, how long did I sleep?"

"What happened to your neck?" JD blurted.

Kelly gingerly touched his neck. "Something about . . . holding on to the headboard. I can't remember. Jesus, what was in those drinks?"

Nick chuckled darkly. He pulled a boot on and stood to stamp his foot against the ground. Then he sat again and laced it up.

"How'd you come up with cemetery?" Julian asked Nick.

"Call it divine inspiration."

"Yeah, I'm betting God was invoked a lot last night," JD said under his breath.

"Shhh," Kelly begged. He put a hand to his head. "What are we doing, why are we up? Oh my God in Heaven."

"There are two main cemeteries we need to look at," Nick explained. "If we start early, we won't have to split up to cover the ground."

"I think we've proven we work better as a hive mind than we do solo," JD added.

"Indeed," Nick agreed cheekily.

Kelly was groaning when he rolled out of bed. He had to hold his head to make sure it stayed attached. "Let me shower and throw up," he muttered. He wobbled toward the bathroom, not even self-conscious about being bare-assed naked. Especially odd since he was pretty sure there was a bite mark on his ass. If they didn't want to see him post-fuck, though, they shouldn't have been in his room at six in the morning.

Julian merely rolled his eyes as Kelly walked by, but JD tried his best not to look. Kelly patted him on the shoulder, then slid the pocket door to the bathroom closed and promptly threw up everything he'd had to drink the night before.

"Charming," he heard Julian comment after a few seconds of gagging with his head in the toilet.

It was going to be a long day.

Rather than piling into the Range Rover and driving to the cemetery, Nick suggested they walk it. It was a glorious day, full of sunshine and birds singing and a nice cool breeze.

Kelly had to stop occasionally, apparently to make sure he didn't hurl again, and Nick did his best not to laugh at his lover's misery. He distinctly remembered trying to discourage the last two rounds. He slipped his arm around Kelly's shoulders, patting him in the same way he'd done a hundred times before when they were suffering through a morning after.

The fact that they'd started fucking after almost fifteen years of knowing each other hadn't changed many of their habits.

"I hate you," Kelly groaned.

"Poor Boo Boo."

"I hate your high tolerance," Kelly groused. "I hate that I can't drink you under the table or knock you out with normal drugs 'cause your stupid body is immune to chemicals. I hate that when I try I wind up in a ditch in Mexico."

"There there," Nick cooed.

"I hate you so much." Kelly's hand in his back pocket as they walked told a different story, though.

They headed for Boston Commons, which was a nice easy stroll from the Liberty, and from there Nick explained that the city had created a red brick line through the old town that led tourists along the Freedom Trail. It was a nice easy walk that took people from historic spot to historic spot, all related to the American Revolution. They picked up the red trail and followed it toward the Granary Burying Ground.

The morning sun hadn't yet risen over the buildings around them, casting the cemetery in a gloomy haze. Nick led the way through the gate, glancing around at the crooked headstones with their macabre carvings. It was an odd little lot. It included the graves of Revolutionary heroes, including Sam Adams and Paul Revere. In the center was a massive monument dedicated to Ben Franklin's family. The buildings that had cropped up around the old burial ground had come so close to the boundaries that their brick walls incorporated headstones into them. Many of the headstones that had once been here had been removed and used as sidewalks, and there were estimates that hundreds of bodies still remained beneath the ground, unmarked and lost to history.

What remained was a mixture of veneration of the past and compromise toward the future. Nick had always felt a little uneasy when he'd visited this place.

"The headstones are . . . irreverent, to say the least," JD commented. He was kneeling in front of one. Many of them had skulls grinning impishly, with wings behind them. Nick has seen a few with dancing skeletons, capering around as death chased after them.

"So?" Julian asked. "What now? Is the treasure supposed to be buried here?"

"It couldn't possibly be," JD answered. "Not if the stories surrounding its theft are true."

"There's another marker here somewhere," Nick added.

"Are you fucking telling me we came out here before the fucking sun for another *clue* to where this treasure is and not the treasure itself?" Kelly asked. He had Nick's aviators on despite the lack of light.

"It makes sense; if he was leaving clues behind for someone to follow to this treasure, he would have done it on permanent fixtures. Or, things they would have considered permanent then. Graveyards, churches, buildings of importance he had to trust wouldn't be torn down."

"So, you believe we're looking for a gravestone," Julian said.

Nick nodded. "The date of death would be 1775."

"Why?" Julian asked.

"A clue carved on a tombstone would have been left as soon as it could be commissioned, when they still had access to the city," Nick explained. "Had to be that year because they evacuated shortly after."

"What else?" Julian asked.

Nick shrugged and dug in the pocket of his jeans for the napkin JD had left on the table last night. "No clue. That's where JD's diamonds come in."

JD took a deep breath to steady himself and stepped closer to take the napkin. Nick touched his arm gently.

"I'm sorry," Nick offered.

JD held his gaze for a few seconds, then nodded and gave him a weak smile. "I tried putting myself in your shoes last night, when I went to bed. I get it. I wouldn't trust me either."

Nick cocked his head, raising both eyebrows in surprise. "I do trust you. I'm sorry for making you feel like I didn't. And I made you a promise. I intend to keep it. Let's do this."

JD squared his shoulders. "Right."

Kelly groaned off in the distance. Nick glanced around for him and found him sitting on the steps that led down to the sidewalk, resting his head against an iron fence. He was pretty hungover, but the last historic graveyard Kelly had been in had almost killed him. Nick couldn't help the shiver that ran up his spine with the memory.

"Hey, babe, you alright?"

"I hate you!" Kelly called back.

"Okay, well . . . keep lookout for us then," Nick said, his voice shaking with laughter.

He turned, and Julian fell in step beside him. The man was actually smiling. "One night, Detective, you and I will sit and have a drink just so I can say I survived it."

Nick laughed. "It's a date."

They split off, each of them wandering the crooked lanes of the graveyard, examining each headstone for any sort of clue. They didn't know what they were searching for, though, and it was a large graveyard.

Nick kept glancing back to the steps, where JD now sat beside Kelly, his head bent over the napkin. Kelly was still leaning against the iron gate.

"What if it's a grid?" JD called.

"Oh my God," Kelly grunted. He covered the ear JD had just shouted into. "Dude."

"Sorry," JD offered with a wince.

"A grid," Nick repeated, drawing closer to them.

JD nodded and stood. "If you turn it on its point, with the X forming a cross-like grid instead, then the symbols start to make a little bit of sense. Look."

Nick stood at JD's shoulder, eyes going from the napkin to the graveyard. JD was right. One of the symbols that had looked like a less-than symbol now appeared to represent the obelisk monument of the Franklin family in the center of the burial ground. Another, which Nick had assumed was an infinity mark, appeared to represent a barrel-vaulted tomb near the edge of the ground.

"Nice," he said with a pat on JD's back.

JD was grinning, looking pleased with himself. "It's a legit map. I mean, we have to take into account that I freehand drew it from memory, so it might be iffy on exact locations. But still."

"What are we looking for, then?" Kelly asked. He still sounded miserable, but he was up and peeking over JD's shoulder.

"Is there an X on it?" Julian asked, his voice laced with sarcasm. "An X would make this easy."

"No. But there is a cross," JD told him.

"It's a cemetery," Julian grunted. "There are crosses everywhere."

"The treasure he buried was a cross," Nick pointed out. "What better to mark it with?"

"Are you thinking the treasure itself is buried here?" Kelly asked again. "'Cause I don't have my grave-desecrating boots on."

"No, this is just another hint. The treasure would have to be northwest, somewhere along Battle Road," Nick guessed.

Julian pulled up short. "How do you know that? And why the fuck are we here rather than there?"

"The wagon was intercepted on the road to Concord and Lexington," Nick told him. "It had to be hidden before it reached the checkpoint at Boston. See, at the time, Boston was a peninsula; there was only one way in by land. The British troops occupied the city, but the Colonial troops controlled the countryside. They had a gentleman's agreement to allow passage to and from the city as long the traveler was unarmed. A stolen wagon full of gold being driven like hell by British soldiers wasn't going to be making the cut. They would have had to have hidden it between Lexington and here."

Julian frowned. "Fair enough."

JD was watching Nick, his blue eyes unreadable.

"What?" Nick asked.

"You know a hell of a lot more about this than you let on."

Nick's only response was an unapologetic shrug.

"Where's the cross on the goddamned napkin? Let's get this shit over with," Kelly mumbled.

JD held it up, positioning the two main landmarks appropriately. Nick pointed to the cross on the napkin, and they all turned toward the spot in the graveyard it indicated.

Julian glanced toward the sidewalk as Nick and the others moved forward. "I'll hold down the fort," he offered. "I'm not very good at this stuff anyway."

Nick stopped and looked back at him. Julian cocked his head almost imperceptibly, and Nick's eyes strayed toward the perimeter. A city cab sat idling on the other side of the street, just out of sight unless you stood near the cemetery gate to see beyond the buildings on either side.

Nick nodded. Julian had picked up on their tail before Nick had. That was a little spooky, but Nick tried to shrug it off and trust the man to have his six as he headed for the indicated section of the graveyard.

JD and Kelly were wandering around the graves, bending occasionally to examine a headstone or wipe at the words to better read them.

"I think I got something," Kelly said quietly. Nick came up behind where he was kneeling. The carvings on the marker had been nearly obscured by hundreds of years of weathering, which was odd since most of them had held up reasonably well. But the date was still clearly visible. There was no date of birth, merely the date of death: April 19, 1775.

"That's weird," JD whispered.

"That's the day of the Battles of Lexington and Concord," Nick told them.

"Could it be a soldier who was killed there?" Kelly asked.

"It's not a body," JD said. "The marker was placed here as a clue to the location of the stolen loot."

"Would explain why there's no date of birth, and why the carving isn't as deep: it was done in a hurry or on the sly," Nick added. "This must have been the only way the soldiers could tell what they'd done, leaving a monument to the theft, a map pointing the way."

Kelly fished his phone out of his pocket, then took a picture of the gravestone.

"What are you doing?" Nick asked.

"Being awesome, how about you?" Kelly drawled. He pulled up the shot he'd just taken in his photo app and began to play with the contrast, adding to the shadows, brightening the lighter bits. Soon he had a representation of what the marker probably read. He stood and showed it to Nick.

Nick grinned and nodded. "Being awesome indeed."

"What's it say?" JD asked, and they crowded around the phone.

"Russell B. North," Kelly read. "Is that significant?"

"Not to me," Nick admitted.

"North," JD said with a wave of his hand. "And the Battles of Lexington and Concord. The Old North Bridge. It was where the first shot of the war was fired."

"How would he have gotten back there to leave something?" Nick argued.

"He obviously stuck around Boston long enough to commission a fucking headstone be carved. That would have been what, at least a week? A few days? Time for him to range out of Boston while it was being done. A single man traveling out of the city with no weapons would have had free passage, you said so yourself. Maybe the treasure itself was hidden there."

Kelly and Nick shared a look, and Kelly nodded. "Sounds good to me."

"Okay. Let's roll."

They rejoined Julian as he loitered near the entrance. "Find it?"

"We think so. How are our friends?" Nick asked. He carefully positioned himself between the cab and JD, just in case.

Julian grunted. "Nosy."

"Should we deter them?" Kelly asked.

Nick stared at the cab for a few moments. He wanted their tail to know they'd been spotted. "No," he finally growled. "We'll lose them on Battle Road. If they can keep up, they're welcome to come and get us."

Kelly had commandeered Nick's spare set of sunglasses in the car and was nursing a cup of the strongest coffee he'd been able to buy on the walk back to the hotel. He was slumped in the front seat, trying not to watch the scenery pass by.

He felt a million times better than he had when he'd woken, but he'd much rather be in bed on Nick's boat being cuddled than here right now.

"Doing okay?" Nick asked him. He'd stopped sounding amused, and his voice was laced with more concern every time he asked.

"Yeah, I'm fine," Kelly grunted. "Don't look at me. Stop looking at me."

"Forgive my ignorance of this particular war, but what is the importance of this bridge we're going to see?" Julian asked.

"The North Bridge was part of the Battle of Concord," Nick answered. "Four-hundred minutemen and Colonial militia against just under a hundred British regulars. It was the first battle of the war, the opening bell that told the British the Americans were going to put up real resistance."

"I see," Julian said.

Nick handed his phone to Kelly. "Call Hagan for me, will you? I told him we might have to go off grid last night, but he'll call out the cavalry if I don't check in."

Kelly pushed Nick's aviators down his nose and flipped through Nick's recently dialed numbers. He paused when he saw that Nick had called Ty Grady several nights ago. He glanced at Nick in surprise. Nick hadn't spoken to Ty about anything that didn't have to do with work since they'd come home from Scotland.

"You talked to Ty?" Kelly asked.

Nick glanced at him, then again before returning his attention to the road. "Yeah, he called to check up on us. I called him back, he pegged JD's accent for us. Why?"

Kelly shrugged. "If you two are on speaking terms again, he'd be a good one to call in for this shit, you know?"

"Are we talking about Tyler?" Julian asked, leaning forward to put his face between the two of them from the backseat. "Please do call him, I have missed being handcuffed to every possible surface whenever I speak."

Nick glanced at him in the rearview mirror, smiling slightly. Then he tapped Kelly's knee and shook his head. "We got this. Call Hagan."

"Okay." Kelly found Hagan's number and dialed, then handed the phone to Nick. He watched him, though, his hangover forgotten. Ty and Nick had known each other since they were both seventeen years old. To think that their friendship was crumbling, or worse, coming to an end, made Kelly immeasurably sad. It was like losing a family member.

"Hagan. Yeah, I'm sorry, I should have checked in last night. I know." Nick glanced at Kelly and rolled his eyes. "We got distracted. Anyway listen, we're on our way to Concord."

Kelly returned his attention to the passing scenery as Nick filled Hagan in. He shifted around, trying to get comfortable. He wasn't sure what Nick had done to him last night, but he hoped he would do it again when Kelly could remember the specifics of how he'd gotten so fucking sore. It was probably fun.

It was about a thirty-minute drive to the bridge, and Kelly was surprised when they arrived to find a visitor's center, loads of tourists, and stone monuments commemorating the battle.

"It's a national park?" Kelly asked when he joined Nick at the bumper of the Range Rover. He'd expected a little parking lot next to a creek with a bridge over it. But there were monuments and walkways and visitor centers and tour bus parking. He couldn't even see the river, much less the bridge.

Nick leaned against it, his arms crossed. "And it's the first Sunday of summer."

Julian was pacing, eyeing the crowds like they might be filled with hidden assassins gunning for him. Kelly would have been amused by it, but he had to acknowledge that it might actually be true.

"What's our plan?" JD asked them.

Nick pursed his lips, his expression mostly hidden behind his sunglasses. He lowered his head. Kelly glanced from him to JD with a wince, then looked over to Julian, who simply shrugged.

"Do we have a plan?" JD asked, sounding a little more agitated.

"You're the treasure hunter," Nick told him.

"Look, I'm not a hound dog who'll point on command, all right? I don't remember any of my fucking training."

"Let's do a recon of the bridge," Kelly suggested. "If he carved a message in it, it's got to be somewhere accessible, but hidden enough to escape notice all these years. Can't be too many places like that on a bridge in the middle of all these tourists."

"We'll split up along the scenic paths," Nick agreed. "Approach it from each side. Kels, you and Cross circle around the north end, JD and I will take the south. We'll meet you at the bridge's head."

"Right." Kelly patted Julian on the shoulder and they headed off together as Nick and JD went the other way.

"Can I ask you a personal question?" Julian asked almost as soon as they were out of earshot of the others.

"I guess, sure."

"Does it bother you that he orders you around like he does?"

Kelly's head jerked up. "No," he answered. "If we were making breakfast or going to a movie, he'd be asking for opinions left and right. This is a tactical situation, though, and he's reverting to his training. If he hadn't, I'd be worried about him."

Julian arched an eyebrow as they walked along the paved path.

Kelly just shrugged. "People see Nick in all kinds of ways." He smiled fondly. "He's so much more than you see on the surface, though."

"If you say so." Julian returned his attention to the crowd as they meandered along the path, trying to blend with the tourists.

Kelly briefly let his mind wander to Nick before he did the same. He didn't care if he was the only one who saw through all Nick's layers. He knew the man who'd hold the hand of a dying enemy, who would let a kid tie a piece of yarn around his wrist for luck and still be wearing it five years later, who would lay his head in Kelly's lap and sigh as if he'd just dropped a huge weight from his shoulders. He was the man who would never, ever make a promise unless he intended to keep it or bleed trying.

"There's the bridge," Julian said, pulling Kelly out of his reverie.

Ahead of them was a large stone monument, rising over the bank of the river. A concrete path led around it toward an arched wooden bridge.

"It's wood," Kelly blurted.

He and Julian shared an uneasy glance. "There are covered bridges in the area that are over two hundred years old, right?" Julian asked. "It could have survived, being an important landmark."

"I guess . . ."

They loitered near the monument until Nick and JD came into sight. JD was talking animatedly, and Nick had his head down as he walked. Kelly could tell he was staying aware of his surroundings by the tension in his shoulders, but he also looked irritated.

"What's wrong?" Kelly asked as soon as they approached.

Nick just looked away and shook his head.

"The bridge is a reproduction," JD told them. "It's been rebuilt three times since the Battle of Concord."

Kelly swiped his hand over his mouth. "Well fuck."

"Perhaps it wasn't on the bridge itself; perhaps it was carved somewhere near," Julian tried. "The bank of this river is littered with large boulders."

"Yeah." JD nodded, eyes sparkling. "I was telling Nick, we passed a sign for something called Egg Rock, apparently it's a big deal. The city even carved a memorial into it. It can't be the only one."

"What are we supposed to do, inspect every rock on the riverbank?" Nick snapped.

"We can try the area around the bridge, at least." Julian sounded almost desperate. He took a step toward Nick, one hand up. "We've come all this way."

Nick met Kelly's eyes briefly. He seemed at his wit's end with this. Kelly knew it was frustrating for Nick to fail, especially when lives hung in the balance. But it wasn't *his* boyfriend who was being held prisoner, and Julian was asking for nothing but a little more patience. So they headed for the bridge as a brisk wind plucked at their jackets and ruffled Kelly's hair.

Nick stepped onto the wooden bridge and peered over the edge. It was made entirely of wood, but the ends were built into rock walls. Spring had brought a lot of rain, and the river was swollen with it. To see the faces of the stones, they would have to get wet. He gestured to Julian. "You two check the other end."

Julian and JD headed across the bridge, their footsteps echoing on the planks. It was a peaceful day, filled with the sounds of birds chirping, groups of chattering tourists, and the babbling of the water as it flowed beneath them. Kelly was kind of enjoying this.

"Who's going in the water?" Nick asked Kelly.

Kelly held up his fist. Nick mimicked him, and they counted off. Kelly threw paper, then laughed as he covered Nick's fist with his hand. "Always the rock."

"Which makes me wonder why you throw scissors half the time."

Kelly grinned impishly. "Depends on the punishment. Sometimes I like to lose."

Nick narrowed his eyes. "Next time I'm taking vacation days and we're never wearing pants."

"Deal."

"Help me out here," Nick grumbled as he shrugged out of his leather coat. Kelly took it and slung it over the railing.

Nick swung around the end of the bridge and edged his way down the steep bank. The ground was mushy and oversaturated; Nick's boots made deep furrows in the mud, and he reached up to grip the wooden boards of the bridge. Kelly laid himself out and slipped his arm under the railing, his hand hanging down so Nick could grab for it if he started to slip further.

Nick held on to the bridge as he examined the wall of rocks. Every couple minutes he would bend and wipe away dirt or pull moss from one of the rocks, his movements growing jerkier and more frustrated the longer he searched. Finally he was low enough that the water was lapping at his boots.

"See anything?" Kelly asked after a few moments.

Nick glared up at him, his eyes flashing. He gave a single jerk of his head in answer. Kelly heard footsteps on the bridge, then felt them in his chest. He twisted to see JD and Julian walking back toward them. JD was wet up to his chest.

"You can see the original pilings," JD called down to Nick. "You got to get wet, Detective."

"I don't get paid enough for this," Nick griped. He grasped Kelly's hand and slid further down like he was surfing a wave. Then he was in the water. He moved beneath the bridge, his fingers slipping out of Kelly's grasp and finally moving out of Kelly's sight.

JD and Julian both leaned over the railing, trying to see him. Kelly stayed where he was, though, his hand still hanging down. Nick was moving upstream, so if he lost his footing and the water took him, he could at least try to make a grab for Kelly's hand as he went by.

"Fucking morons," Nick shouted after several more minutes of silent searching. "Who writes a goddamn message on a wooden bridge?"

"Oh boy," Kelly muttered. He pushed to his knees and headed to the end of the bridge, stepping out onto the rocks so he could see where Nick was. He was standing in waist-deep water, one hand gripping the piling of the bridge, one hand on a rock in front of him.

"In the middle of a fucking war, where bridges were *literally being burned*!" Nick shouted.

Kelly beckoned with his fingers. "Come out of the water, bud."

"He had to know wood wouldn't stick around!" Nick shouted. "Fucking idiot."

"There there," Kelly said.

"This shit was gone by the time they put that message in the diamonds," Nick railed. "What was the point? It's a fucking dead end!"

"Babe, come on, get out of the water," Kelly tried again.

"We have a problem," Julian said.

Kelly glanced up at him, then followed the direction of Julian's gaze. A couple was strolling toward them. The woman had a mop of wavy auburn hair, almost the same color as Nick's, and she was quite striking. High cheekbones, full lips that curved into a smirk. Kelly looked her up and down out of habit. The man was considerably less attractive, with a hard edge to his eyes and a scar that went from one of his heavy eyebrows to his rather square chin. They definitely didn't look like they fit as a couple.

Julian positioned himself in front of JD.

Kelly watched their approach, the gun on his belt feeling heavier as they came closer. He gave Nick a quick look over his shoulder, but Nick was gone. The water flowed peacefully over the spot where he'd been. Kelly stood, making certain his jacket covered his gun. He didn't have time to get back up to the bridge, but at least this way they were offering two separate targets.

"Good afternoon, gents," the man called in a genial Irish accent.

"Hello, Dr. Hunt," the woman added with a kind smile. "I hear you're having a rough few days."

JD took a tiny step sideways so he could see them over Julian's shoulder. He was smart enough to stay behind Julian, though.

"Where's the detective?" the woman asked.

Kelly and Julian shared a glance, then Kelly looked over his shoulder into the water.

"Oh my," the woman cooed. "I do hope he can swim. My name is Alex Kincade. And I understand we're all searching for the same thing."

"Somehow I doubt that," Kelly challenged.

"Doubt all you like, it's true. The Golden and Rosy Cross. You're quite the resourceful little group; we'd like to combine forces."

Kelly grinned when he saw movement behind the pair. "Good luck with that."

"Hands up," Nick said as he stepped behind them, his gun out. He was dripping from head to toe, his curly hair plastered to his head. "On your knees, both of you. You're under arrest."

Nick only had one pair of handcuffs on him. He pestered Julian until the man rolled his eyes and provided a handful of white zip ties from one of the pockets of his jacket.

"Where do you keep all that stuff?" Kelly asked.

"Doc, help me," Nick grunted. He yanked the woman's hands behind her back and tightened the zip tie. "You have the right to remain silent," he said against her ear. "Professor Singleton."

"Wait, you know her?" Kelly blurted. He had the man restrained and on his knees. Both suspects were staying quiet.

"She's the one I spoke to on the phone. Told me who JD was."

"JD," she said, her voice like smooth honey. It was even nicer in person than it had been on the phone. "Like John Doe. That's cute."

"You teach pop culture archaeology huh? Nice cover."

"I try," she said with a shrug.

JD stalked toward her, and Nick put a hand out to keep him from getting close enough for her to hurt him. "How do you know who I am?" JD demanded.

"You really don't remember anything?" she asked.

"Answer the question," Nick growled. He poked her hard in the back.

Alex cleared her throat. "If you're going to court me, Detective, I like roses. Red ones."

"How do you know who I am!"

"We were colleagues, Casey," Alex said with a hint of injury in her tone. "We find lost works of art and liberate them from their prisons."

"Wow," Kelly drawled. "That's the fanciest 'I steal things' I've ever heard."

Nick hummed in agreement.

The woman laughed. "I imagine you think it's along the same lines as Mr. Cross's 'I deal antiques' in reference to cold-blooded murder."

Julian's eyes widened. "You know me?"

"I know of you. I was warned you'd be out here."

Nick recognized the signs of Julian coiling to attack, but there was no way he could get to him in time to keep it from happening. He wrapped an arm around Alex and turned her, instead, putting himself between her and Julian. Kelly intercepted Julian as he launched himself at them, wrapping him up and trying to talk him into being calm.

"They have him!" Julian snarled. Kelly had his hands full trying to restrain him.

JD edged away from them, a hint of a wild animal in his eyes, which were darting from Julian to Nick and back.

"It's them, they took him!" Julian railed.

They were drawing way too much notice from the crowds of tourists. Nick tucked his sopping wet shirt in under the badge on his belt so it would be visible.

"We didn't take anyone," Alex insisted. She looked over her shoulder, and Nick turned a little so he could see Julian. Kelly had him in a headlock, but he was trying not to hurt him so they were both struggling. "Good Lord," Alex said quietly. "You have a leash for him, right?"

Nick tightened the zip tie, and Alex winced. "What was your endgame here, huh?" he asked. "You followed us hoping we'd lead you to the treasure?"

"Pretty much, yeah. When the clues led you here, though, I realized you were as stuck as we are. This isn't the right place."

Nick's brow furrowed, and he glanced again at the others. Alex's Irish henchman was standing calmly aside, his hands tied behind his back, watching. He hadn't tried to make a run for it. Julian was on his knees, head hanging, chest heaving. Kelly stood over him, a hand on his back, murmuring words to calm him.

Nick wiped his wrist over his forehead to stop the water from dripping in his eyes. As soon as he'd heard Julian give his warning on the bridge, he'd sunk below the ripples and let the current take him downstream, then doubled back to get the drop on their unexpected company.

"Okay," he said almost to himself. "Okay. Hold on."

Julian glared at him, seething.

Nick turned Alex again, making her stumble as he forced her to face the others. "Tell us a story, Professor," he growled. "From the beginning."

Alex cleared her throat. "You seem like a CliffsNotes crowd."

Kelly stood and shook out his shoulders. He helped Julian to his feet. JD came closer.

"Okay, let's start with the basics. Do you know who the Rosicrucians were?"

"Secret society precursor to the Masons," Kelly grunted.

"They were esoteric, focused their efforts on nature, healing, and chemistry," Nick added.

"Impressive. They are rumored to have made incredible breakthroughs, including gaining mastery in alchemy and, most famously, creating the philosopher's stone."

"Like Harry Potter?" Kelly asked.

"No," Alex said, her voice cold. "Not like Harry Potter."

"Get to the point a little faster," Nick urged.

"The point is, those are myths and legends, but the reality behind them is true. The Rosicrucians made valuable advances with their equations and formulas. They could cure illnesses in the Middle Ages we could only *hope* to fight against today. There are even contemporary sources that imply they were able to cure cancer."

"The Rosicrucians had a cure for cancer?" JD asked. He'd pulled to his true height as Alex spoke, a look of recognition dawning on his face. He winced and smacked his forehead. "They wrote the formulas on gold scrolls to keep them from being destroyed."

"Exactly," Alex said. "He hasn't lost all that knowledge up there after all."

"Golden scrolls?" Nick repeated.

"When the Masons rose to power, they sought to protect that knowledge. They were at war with the Catholic Church, who was in the midst of a power grab. The Pope decreed everything the Rosicrucians had discovered was magic, of the devil, all that crap. The burgeoning Masonic powers couldn't risk the Church obtaining the scrolls and melting them down. All that knowledge, lost . . ."

"I get it," Kelly said suddenly. "The cross is made of layers of gold. It's wrapped in the scrolls, isn't it?"

"Yes, it is." Alex was solemn. "They knew the Church would never desecrate a cross. The scrolls would be safe until . . . well, I guess until more enlightened minds could discover them."

"Enlightened minds like yourself?" Nick asked.

Alex rolled her eyes. "Don't pretend you're after that treasure for altruistic reasons. Please. Dr. Hunt and I were hired by Alco Pharmaceuticals. We're supposed to find the ancient formulas."

Julian scoffed at her. "A pharmaceutical company hired treasure hunters?"

"Cancer is big money," Alex stated almost sadly.

Nick loosened his hold on her arm. "Why'd you pretend to be a professor at Boston College to give me an ID? Why not just come in and claim JD?"

Alex met JD's eyes. "Because he ran out on us. One night we figured out that the trail led us to Massachusetts, and we finished a bottle of wine in celebration. The next morning, he was gone. I thought he was after the treasure for a rival company, so I had to follow him quietly."

JD met Nick's eyes. He was breathing hard, realization sweeping over his face. "Oh my God," he whispered.

"JD . . ."

"It's all true then," JD cried. "I *am* a bad guy! I'm a murderer and a thief and . . . and maybe a kidnapper! And I betrayed people who were supposed to be my friends and colleagues! You even said you trusted me! Jesus!"

He ran both hands through his hair and turned away to pace.

"How did he get murderer and thief from what I just said?" Alex asked Nick.

"It's a long story."

"Will you untie us now?"

Nick took his knife from his belt and sliced through the zip tie. Kelly followed his lead and released the man, whose name ended up being Colin.

Alex rubbed at her wrists, eyes on Julian. "The man who hired us told us you'd be out there too. He said you were dangerous and motivated. That's why we bring Colin along everywhere."

Colin gave a silent nod.

"We didn't know anyone had been kidnapped," Alex said. "Who is it?"

"My husband," Julian said through gritted teeth. "I was told to give them the location of the cross and they wouldn't harm him."

"Your husband?" Nick blurted. Julian nodded. "Congratulations," Nick offered lamely.

"You haven't found the cross?" Alex asked.

"I haven't been looking for it. I've been looking for *them*. Who are they?"

Alex's eyes went wide. "I don't know. We were told rival companies were after the cross and we'd have to move fast."

Kelly stepped forward, close to Nick, and he lowered his voice when he spoke. "So we have *three* parties in play here? Alex's group, JD's group, and Julian?"

"That's what I'm taking away from all this," Nick answered. He reached to his belt, pulling his handcuffs from their holster. "One thing I do know . . ."

Kelly nodded. "Evidence is saying you have to arrest him, huh?"

Nick sighed. JD turned and halted his pacing when he saw Nick watching him. The look in his eyes was one of both resignation and betrayal. "You're really going to arrest me now?"

Nick held up the handcuffs and moved closer to him. "Turn around," he said softly.

JD lowered his head and turned his back to Nick, his shoulders slumping. Nick took one wrist in his hand, but before he could put the handcuffs on him, JD jerked his elbow. He landed a blow on Nick's side, and Nick's knees buckled. JD whirled and grabbed Nick's gun from its holster as Nick went to the ground, and his hands were trembling. He backed away, the gun pointing from one person to the next.

"I'm sorry," he said to Nick. "I'm sorry I hurt you. But I can't let you arrest me, not yet. I have to find them and find out the truth first."

Nick braced a hand on the concrete walkway, gasping and wincing as his blazing eyes tracked JD, who was still backing away from them all.

JD's eyes darted around the hordes of tourists, and then he pointed the gun in the air, aiming it in the general direction of the river. The blast of the shot echoed off the rolling hills and stone monuments and created instant panic: tour groups screamed and scattered, families with children flattened to the ground, kayakers on the river dove out of their vessels into the water for safety.

JD met Nick's eyes one last time as he moved away. "I'm sorry. I'll turn myself in after, I promise!" he called, and then he bolted into the crowd.

CHAPTER 9

Kelly loitered near the park ranger's office, listening as Nick gave a report to someone on the phone. From the tone of his voice, he wasn't enjoying the conversation. When he was done, he emerged from the office and gave everyone a grim smile.

"How'd it go?" Julian asked.

Nick laughed bitterly. "Well. I brought a suspect to a public place while I was supposed to be on guard duty, lost control of my department-issued sidearm, and then allowed the suspect to abscond with it into a crowd. Oh, and fire it. Apparently it hit a goose downriver."

They all stared at him, wide-eyed and waiting for him to continue.

"Let's just say it didn't go too well."

"Have you been shelved?" Kelly asked.

"No. I've been given forty-eight hours to fix it."

Alex had been keeping her distance, but she was edging closer. "You know the only way to find where he's going is to find the treasure, right?"

Nick narrowed his eyes at her. "Thank you for at least being transparent in your motives."

Alex shrugged. "What do you say, Detective? You want to work together in this?"

"No," Nick growled. He headed for the door, and Kelly fell into step beside him.

They reached the door, and Kelly glanced back to find Julian hadn't moved. He tugged on Nick's damp shirt, and Nick turned as well.

"You jumping ship?" Kelly asked Julian.

Julian smiled softly. "I have to find Cameron."

"Good luck to you," Nick told him. "You have my number if you need it."

"And you will have mine."

Nick turned and left the office without another word. Kelly gave Julian a small wave before following his lover out.

"We going after the treasure?" Kelly asked as Nick stalked toward his Range Rover.

"No," Nick said through gritted teeth. "We are going after my fugitive."

He opened up the back of the SUV and rummaged around for a duffel bag he kept there. Kelly leaned against the car as Nick pulled out a fresh pair of clothing and began to change, right there in the middle of the parking lot.

Kelly pursed his lips, leering when Nick took his shirt off.

"You're staring like a pervert," Nick said without looking over at him.

"So is everyone else in the parking lot," Kelly shot back. "You should put on dry boxers too. You know. For your health."

Nick glanced around the lot, then glared at Kelly.

"Come on, Irish. You did everything right, here. You were careful and he still burned you. No way to see it coming."

"Maybe. Don't have to bend over and enjoy getting played, though."

Once Nick had gotten dry clothes on, they climbed into the Range Rover, but Nick didn't start the car.

"You okay?" Kelly asked him.

"I just . . . if this was a dead end, what was the point? The plaque we saw on the way there said the original bridge had been dismantled in 1793. Why the hell would you create a clue in 1831 that led to something you knew was gone?"

Kelly nodded, resting his head on the seat. "Maybe we had the clue wrong?" Nick's green eyes sparkled. "Maybe it didn't lead us here. I mean, why should it? The treasure was stolen at a tavern between here and Boston. The British were retreating to Boston. They wouldn't have come back here with the treasure; it'd be hidden between the original theft and the city. So why put a clue that brings you *past* the treasure? It was a long way by horseback, why all the wasted mileage?"

Nick was nodding as Kelly spoke, his eyes going unfocused.

"What was the whole name on the gravestone?" Kelly asked.

"Russell," Nick answered. "Russell B. North."

"We took North as the clue, but what if it's just the direction we were supposed to head in? Or nothing at all?" Kelly mused. "Is the name Russell important? Is it a town or something?"

Nick sighed heavily and shook his head. "I don't know. Get your phone out, look it up. I'm going to call Hagan, see if he's come up with anything in those letters."

Kelly did a few searches on his phone, trying to combine the words Russell and Revolutionary War with Lexington and Concord. He got results for several soldiers and historians, but one result popped up over and over. "Think I got something," he told Nick.

Nick had his phone to his ear, but he raised both eyebrows at Kelly. He put the phone on speaker and lowered it to his lap. He was apparently on hold.

"The Jason Russell house?" Kelly said. "This says it was the bloodiest part of the Battles of Lexington and Concord."

"Where is it?"

"It was in a town called Menotomy. Where is that?"

"That's what the town of Arlington used to be called," Nick said as he stuck the keys in the ignition. "It's not far from here."

Nick pulled out of the parking lot, sliding his sunglasses on. Kelly grinned at him, kicking his feet up onto the dashboard. "I know I always used to make fun of you and Owen for being history nerds, but I got to say, it's kind of doing it for me right now."

Nick glanced at him, and the sun flashed in his aviators.

Kelly nodded, still smiling widely. "The way you just pull facts out of your head like it's magic? It's hot."

Nick chuckled and returned his attention to the road.

"O'Flaherty?" Hagan's voice came from the phone on Nick's lap. Nick picked it up and held it against the steering wheel.

"Hey, what you got for me?"

"What do you mean?" Hagan asked.

"The letters you were supposed to be reading over. Have you found anything?"

"Bro, you took the letters with you."

Nick looked down sharply, then at Kelly. "We didn't take anything," Nick told Hagan.

"Your buddy Cross came in before you left, told me you wanted him and JD to skim over the letters last night for a lead. Said you'd decided they would catch more than I could."

"Fuck!" Nick shouted.

"Did I get played by a CIA hit man?" Hagan asked dejectedly.

"Fuck, fuck, fuck! That's why Cross ditched us, and that's why he wasn't interested in finding anything on the bridge. He has the right location already."

Kelly leaned forward and flipped the flashing lights on. "We better get there first then, huh?"

Nick gunned the engine, and the Range Rover roared to life as he gave Hagan their destination. Kelly settled back to enjoy the ride.

Nick wasn't trying to hide the Range Rover. It was a distinctive car, especially since everybody and their brother had seen him driving it. He wanted the other players in this to know he was there, that he and Kelly weren't the stupid grunts they'd assumed.

So he parked it right on the street in front of the swinging white sign that denoted the Jason Russell House. "Site of the bloodiest fighting between the Minutemen and the Redcoats on the first day of the American Revolution," it claimed.

Kelly gave him a questioning glance, then got out of the car. Between them they only had two guns, and they each carried a knife. Nick had a feeling his badge wasn't going to be a lot of help to them when this all went down.

"What's our play?" Kelly asked.

Nick clucked his tongue. "JD and his accomplices in handcuffs. Help Cross retrieve Cameron and then kick his *fucking* ass. And the location of any possible treasure in the hands of the appropriate authorities."

"Who are the appropriate authorities in this case?"

"I don't know. Not me," Nick growled, and they started off across the lush lawn toward the large yellow house.

"What do you know about this site?" Kelly asked.

"Nothing, why?"

Kelly did a double take as they walked. "Nothing? Seriously? I thought you knew everything."

"Only thing I know is this is the path the British took when they retreated to Boston. Obviously something important happened and now it's a museum."

"Smart-ass."

Nick stepped up to the door and tried the handle. It was locked. The sign had indicated the place was open from mid-April to October.

"Maybe they mean *late* mid-April," Kelly said.

Nick used his badge to knock on the window. They could hear someone moving inside, and finally a woman with a white bonnet and a Revolutionary-era costume came bustling up to the door.

"I'm sorry, dear, we're closed for the day," she said through the window.

Nick held the badge up for her to see through the glass. "We'll only need a minute," he told her.

She took a deep stuttering breath and glanced furtively over her shoulder. "If you'll come back tomorrow," she said, her voice shaky.

Nick cocked his head, looking behind her into the ancient home. The stairs still sported bullet holes from the fighting over two-hundred years ago, and everything had been restored to its original state. Like most homes built in Massachusetts during the early days, the front faced south. The afternoon light streamed through the western windows, and Nick could see a shadow moving on the floorboards in front of the stairwell.

He gave the woman a nod and a smile. "Tomorrow it is then," he said kindly. "Thank you, ma'am." He turned away from the door and pulled Kelly with him.

"Someone had a gun on her," Kelly whispered.

Nick hummed and pointed toward the car, slipping Kelly his gun while their backs were turned to the house. "I want you to go around back, get in the house quiet."

"Got it."

Kelly headed around the corner of the house, disappearing within seconds. Nick took out his phone and dialed Hagan. It was still ringing when the door creaked open behind him. He turned, holding the phone away from his ear.

A man stood with the woman in the bonnet, his arm around her neck and a knife to her cheek. "Put that mobile down," he ordered. His was another Irish accent. "Get inside."

Nick dropped his phone to the ground without ending the call and put his hands behind his head, walking toward the door obediently.

"You're a cop?" the man spat. "Son of a bitch." He slammed the door behind Nick, and shoved the woman at him, forcing them both through a doorway. "Get in there!"

Nick caught her and put an arm around her shoulders. "You okay?" he asked as they moved into the other room.

She nodded jerkily. Nick walked her over to a nearby chair and she sat, then he turned and stood in front of her. Only then did he get a good look at the other players in the room. There was one more man with a gun, and a third hunched against the wall near the fireplace. It took a moment for Nick to recognize him. Cameron Jacobs.

"Cam?" he blurted. "Are you okay?"

"Detective O'Flaherty?" Cameron made to stand, but he winced away from one of his captors when the man made a move toward him. He had a few bruises around his face and arms, and his lip was cracked and bloody. He'd obviously been kept under control through physical means.

"Hey!" Nick shouted. "Touch him again and you deal with me."

"You want to get hard, motherfucker? Come on!" the man challenged. His accent sounded like home to Nick. It almost made him laugh. Some Southie thug with a gun coming at him like he'd last a minute hand-to-hand with Nick.

"Sit the fuck down!" the other kidnapper shouted at Nick. Nick remained standing, meeting the man's eyes without flinching. The guy moved closer, putting the muzzle of his gun against Nick's cheek. "I said sit your arse down."

Nick cocked his head, lips twitching. "Make me."

Before the man could react, Kelly whistled behind him. When he turned, Nick grabbed the gun, hitting a pressure point in the man's arm that would immediately incapacitate his fingers. Kelly hit him with a roundhouse punch that threw him back into Nick, and Nick picked him up and slammed him to his back. The floor shook beneath him, artifacts around the room rattled. Nick kicked the heel of his boot into the man's head to put him down. The museum curator screamed, covering her face with her bonnet.

Nick turned his stolen gun on the other man, but he had grabbed Cameron and was using him as a shield.

"Oh, son," Nick drawled. "That wasn't your smartest move."

A dark shadow passed in the corner of Nick's vision.

"You might want to let him go," Nick warned.

"Fuck you! Put your guns down or he gets one in the skull!"

The door creaked open behind Nick, and Kelly turned to cover their new guests as Nick kept his gun on the Southie kid.

"Looks like we're having a party." It was the smooth honey tones of Alex. "Are we invited?" She moved around the corner, a gun pointed at Nick.

"Drop your weapon," Kelly ordered.

"You first. Ladies can't be too careful these days."

"All of you drop your weapons!" the Southie kid shouted.

"Cam, stay calm," Nick called across the room. There were way too many guns in play now. Nick moved just enough to put his shoulder to Kelly's, both of them facing opposite directions in the middle of the two forces.

"Cameron?" Julian called. He stepped out into the open. Nick couldn't see him, but he could tell where he was from his heavy footsteps on the old floorboards. He felt Kelly tense against him.

"Julian!" Cameron cried. He tensed, but the gun at his cheek dug deeper.

"Don't fucking move!" Southie shouted.

The man on the floor groaned, and Nick turned, preparing to deliver another swift kick to the man's temple.

"Don't," a new voice said urgently. "He's got information we need."

Nick's head jerked up. JD was standing behind Southie, obviously having snuck in from the kitchen. He had Nick's gun in his hand, but he wasn't pointing it anywhere. Yet.

"JD," Nick said in warning.

"Hunt!" Alex called.

Kelly hummed under his breath, and the sound vibrated through Nick's entire body. They pressed closer together, their first instinct when they were hemmed in. "There are way too many people here."

"Everyone stay calm," Nick said in a loud, clear voice. "We can all leave here with what we want. No one has to get hurt."

"He keeps that gun pointed at my husband, and someone will indeed be hurt," Julian snarled.

"Tell him to put his gun down," Southie shouted, nodding his head at Nick. "Or I blow his head off!"

Nick felt Julian move, and Kelly tensed beside him but couldn't take his attention off Alex and her gun. Nick glanced back in time to see Julian with the barrel of his gun aimed at Kelly.

He sounded apologetic, but deadly serious. "Drop your gun, O'Flaherty."

The man on the floor groaned again and raised his head, shaking off the stupor. He rolled to his stomach and began to crawl toward his compatriot. His hand went to his belt, where a backup weapon was likely hidden. Nick transferred his aim to the man. "Stop!"

In rapid succession, Southie turned his gun from Cameron's head to Nick, and JD raised his gun and put it to the back of Southie's head.

"Don't!" JD ordered.

No one moved.

"Everyone have a gun on them now?" Alex called. "Is this what boys do for fun?"

Nick grunted, afraid to move with so many nervous and inexperienced personalities involved. Not to mention Julian, who would definitely blow out the brains of an ally to save his husband.

"Okay," Nick said slowly. "No one move, let's talk this one out, huh? Bottom line, Cross is here for Cam and the rest of you are here for treasure. I think we can accommodate everyone."

"What are you here for, cop?" the man on the ground asked.

"I heard they had doughnuts," Nick said through his teeth.

"Treasure?" the woman in the bonnet asked. She was nearly screaming. "What are you talking about?"

"The Continental payroll," Nick said to her. "Know about it?"

"Of course," she said, wiping a hand over her face. "You're in the wrong town! The Continental payroll was stolen from Buckman Tavern in Lexington!"

"It would have been brought this way," JD said, speaking to the entire room. "I remembered why we had to break into that bookstore. I remembered everything, Nick."

Nick glanced up at him briefly, afraid to take his eyes off the kidnapper on the floor for too long.

"They took me from my hotel room," JD continued. "Alex, I'm sorry, I didn't leave you guys. Two men came in with guns and said I was dead if I didn't come with them."

If Alex responded, she did so silently, because Nick heard nothing from behind him. JD's blue eyes pleaded with Nick. "I'm not a bad person, Nick. I swear. I remember. Please."

Nick tried not to examine the melancholy feeling settling in his chest. "I believe you," he finally whispered. "Tell us what happened."

"There were three of them," JD said as he poked his gun at Southie's head. "Two Irish guys, and this one. They had Cam with them, had him tied up. I kept promising him I'd try to get us out of there and he kept saying his husband would find us, that he was some sort of spy."

Cameron closed his eyes, swallowing hard.

"They had Julian after the Crown Jewels lead, so they put me on studying the contemporary writings, trying to pinpoint when and where the wagon of treasure had been spotted. I knew about the letters in the bookstore because I'd requested to read them a couple months back. I had the digital copies, but I needed to see the original ones. So much in that time period was done in secret, the originals could have had messages concealed in them. That's why we went to the store, that's why they robbed it. I hid the letters to slow them down until *someone* figured out we needed help or we could get away."

Nick couldn't take his eyes off JD as he spoke. His voice was shaky, his eyes were sincere. Every bone in Nick's body told him JD was telling the truth.

"How'd you figure out it was here?" Kelly asked without turning around.

"When I started remembering things, I remembered a diary entry about this place. How a wagon was seen being guarded by the redcoats. It was the last sighting. And then the name on the headstone, Russell. As soon as I remembered everything, I knew it had to be here."

"We did the same," Julian offered. "As soon as I told her what I knew, she directed us here."

Nick growled softly. "Yeah, we need to talk about the stealing evidence thing."

"I'd rather talk about the gun to my head thing," Kelly said wryly.

"Where is it?" the man on the ground asked. "We'll let him go without hurting him if you tell us."

Julian growled.

"How did you get here?" JD asked him.

"I called them," Julian answered.

"Great, so no one actually knows *where* we're looking?" Kelly asked.

"There's no treasure here!" the curator cried. "This museum commemorates a battle!"

"What happened here?" Nick asked her. "What's the story? Give us the tour."

"Are . . . are you serious?"

Nick nodded, still not looking away from the man on the ground.

The woman glanced around at all the hardware being wielded, at all the people filling a little house that must have seen so much violence in its history, if the bullet holes still in the walls were any indication. She took a deep breath.

"After their defeat at Lexington and Concord, the redcoats were retreating to Boston. Along Battle Road there were many skirmishes, and the retreating forces were ordered to clear out any houses they came across to prevent snipers from attacking. Jason Russell, the man who lived here, evacuated his family, but then returned to his home. Nearby, along the stone wall you probably saw when you came in, the minutemen had set up an ambush. They concentrated on the main body of the redcoats coming through, but were outflanked and retreated to this home."

She took a deep, shuddering breath. It was obvious that giving her lecture was helping to calm her a little. Nick's mind was whirring, trying to fit the puzzle together as she gave them more pieces.

"Jason Russell was an old man, and he arrived at his home just as the minutemen were retreating. He was gunned down just outside his door and then stabbed by bayonets eleven times. The British soldiers massacred everyone else in the house, save for eight minutemen who were able to barricade themselves in the basement. When Jason

Russell's widow returned to her home, she found her husband and the rest of the dead, numbering twelve men total, laid out in rows in the kitchen. She is said to have claimed the blood on the kitchen floor rose to her ankles. Jason Russell and the dead Continental soldiers were buried in a mass grave, no coffins and no services. It took over seventy years for a monument to be erected over the grave."

She fell silent, swallowing repeatedly, blinking rapidly as she fought off tears.

"That's it?" the Irishman on the ground asked.

"That is . . . it. Yes. There is no treasure."

"What about the basement?" Alex suggested.

"We're looking for redcoat treasure; the basement was barricaded by minutemen," JD countered.

Nick slowly lowered his gun, his eyes unfocusing.

"Nick?" Kelly whispered.

Nick didn't answer.

"Irish?"

Nick winced and lowered his head. "Fuck," he whispered.

Kelly lowered his weapon as well, meeting Nick's eyes with a dawning dread. "You know where the treasure is, don't you?"

"I know where the treasure is," Nick confirmed. He looked at the woman apologetically. "Can you tell us exactly how big that monument is?"

"Over the grave?"

Nick nodded. Someone in the room cursed under his breath.

"It . . . it's rather large. It's a granite obelisk. Maybe twelve feet tall?"

Nick nodded, lowering his gun further. "That's that," he said.

"They buried the treasure with minutemen?" JD asked. "They knew the grave wouldn't be desecrated by Colonials, so the treasure would stay hidden. And when the war was lost, going back to the shiny new America and digging up national heroes was not an option for any persona non grata like an Irish redcoat."

Nick glanced sideways at Kelly. Kelly slowly lowered his gun, his body relaxing against Nick's. Alex had stowed her weapon as well, and she looked crestfallen. She seemed to really be in it to find missing pieces of history, not merely for profit.

Julian had transferred his aim back to Southie, who was still holding Cameron and pointing his gun at Nick.

"That's it," Nick said softly. "Game's over. Time to give up the gun."

"Fuck you, we didn't come this close to let a piece of fucking rock get in the way. We'll come back tonight with a Cat. Knock that bitch over, dig up our treasure, and get our payday."

Kelly looked over his shoulder, his brow furrowed. He didn't dare turn around though, not when he knew there was still a gun pointed at Nick.

"We're leaving, and we're taking this fucker with us as insurance," Southie snarled with a jab at Cameron's cheek.

"Over my dead body," Julian growled. "No. Make that over *your* dead body."

Nick felt the mood in the room shift almost instantly. It was an instinct honed over many years of gunfights and negotiations, the ability to tell when a situation had just turned hopeless.

The man on the ground went for his belt, where a gun had indeed been hidden beneath his shirt. Nick shoved his shoulder into Kelly, sending them both to the floor. Southie fired at them, holding Cameron in front of him as a human shield. Cameron knocked his elbow into Southie's chin, and Southie stumbled back, falling into JD as the gun went off again.

Nick sat up and fired a single shot, taking the Irishman through the back of the hand as he attempted to pull the trigger. His gun went flying and he screamed, holding his bloody hand to his chest.

Julian also took one shot, but he wasn't aiming to maim. Southie took the bullet right between the eyes as he was trying to scramble to his feet. His body made a solid thud when it hit the floorboards.

And just like that, it was over. Nick slowly got to his feet, gun still in hand. Alex had taken cover on the stairs, and as soon as she raised her head, Nick gestured to her to get out of the house. She darted forward, not for the door, but for the museum curator with her bonnet in hand. Alex pulled her to her feet and propelled her toward the door, running after her and shielding the woman's body with her own.

Julian pulled something from his pocket and tossed it into the center of the room. Nick stared at it, not registering what it was.

"Flashbang!" Kelly shouted, and he grabbed Nick and pulled him down. They both covered their ears and squeezed their eyes tight as the flash grenade went off.

The high-pitched whine in Nick's ears was one he knew all too well, and even with his eyes closed and his face buried against Kelly's chest, the flash had caused stars behind his eyes. He sat up dazedly, trying to shake off the cobwebs.

Julian and Cameron were both gone.

"Motherfucker," Nick muttered. A groan from the other side of the room drew his attention, and Nick struggled to his feet. He bent over Kelly first, patting his cheek. "Okay?"

"I hate those things," Kelly shouted. He put a finger in his ear and wiggled it.

Nick nodded, straightening. He stumbled through the smoke across the room and found JD on his back, blood flowing freely from a wound in his torso. Nick stared at him for a few seconds, his mind chugging to catch up.

"Corpsman up!" he finally called, his voice so hoarse that Kelly's abused ears didn't hear it. "Doc! Man down!"

Kelly fumbled his way over, falling to his knees at JD's side. Nick patted his pockets for his phone before remembering he'd dropped it outside before all the shooting had started. When he looked down at his hand, he realized there was blood spreading across his shirt. He pulled his jacket away, confused about where it was coming from. When he pulled his shirt up, he found the wound.

"Go call an ambulance, Irish," Kelly said to him. He was working on JD, trying to stop the blood.

"Kels," Nick whispered.

"Go call!" Kelly shouted without looking up.

Nick nodded. When he turned to go after his phone, though, a man was standing there, gun drawn, badge out. Nick stopped in his tracks, blinking at him.

"Son of a bitch, Nick!" Hagan shouted.

Nick winced, and his head pounded. He took a step back, his foot hit something on the floor, and he sat down hard. Kelly's hand groped for him, his fingers finally threading through Nick's as Nick lay back and put a hand over his eyes to block out all the brightness.

"You're hit!" Kelly shouted at him.

"It's not bad," Nick muttered. "Not bad."

"Stay with me, bud," he could hear Kelly saying. "Don't let go."

Nick turned his head. Kelly was sitting between JD and Nick. He was holding his shirt to JD's wound with one hand, and pressed Nick's palm to his own wound with the other. Nick cried out.

"Don't let go, okay?" Kelly whispered to him, applying more pressure to the wound.

"Never," Nick managed to say. "I love you."

Kelly leaned over and kissed him gently. The warmth of his lips was painful on Nick's.

"Is he okay?" Nick asked, head rolling in JD's direction.

"He'll be fine if we get an ambulance to him soon."

Nick closed his eyes. The pain from the pressure against his wound was gone. Everything was gone except Kelly's hand on his.

"So will you, bud," Kelly added, and his voice was far away, echoing off the recesses of Nick's memories. "You'll be okay. Don't let go."

CHAPTER 10

Kelly stood off to the side, his hands stuffed in his pockets so he wouldn't be tempted to jump in and help. The bullet that had hit Nick had punched clean through the muscle over his ribs, right above another bullet graze he'd received recently, and along with the massive Y-shaped incision from his recent surgery, Nick's torso was going to be more scar than skin after this. Knowing Nick, he'd turn those scars into some sort of tattoo eventually.

The wound probably wasn't too serious, but the loss of blood meant they were loading him onto a stretcher and preparing to put him into one of the ambulances standing by.

JD hadn't fared quite as well. The kidnapper with the Boston accent had shot him as they'd struggled, and while the bullet had gone all the way through, it had clipped some vital pieces on its way out. They'd loaded him into an ambulance and taken him off with a police escort before Kelly and Nick had even gotten out of the building.

Alex Kincade, who really was who she'd said she was this time, was cooperating with all the questioning she'd been submitted to so far. She'd been legally contracted to find the whereabouts of the treasure. Kelly felt sort of sorry for the fact that she was out of a job now. Her colleague, Colin, had showed up five minutes after it'd all gone down with a tray of coffees. They obviously hadn't been expecting trouble.

Hagan was grilling the Irish kidnapper in the back of his unmarked car. Kelly thought Hagan was telling the man he'd only send someone into the house to find the fingers Nick had shot off if he talked, but Kelly was trying hard not to listen since he was pretty sure that wasn't legal.

Julian Cross and Cameron Jacobs were in the wind. Kelly had a feeling they wouldn't be seeing either man again.

Soon enough, Nick was being wheeled over to the ambulance, and Kelly jogged over to take his hand as they negotiated the curb.

Nick shook his head, obviously knowing Kelly was trying to come up with something nice and cheerful to distract him with.

"When we were in New Orleans and I took that bullet," Kelly said, like he was starting a bedtime story. "All I remember is you leaning over me and asking me what to do."

Nick snorted and squeezed his eyes tight. The stretcher jostled him and he winced. "That was Digger, Kels."

"Was it?" Kelly laughed. "All I remember is you. And the only thing I could think to tell you was don't let go. Don't let go of me. That's all I could say."

Nick opened his eyes, meeting Kelly's as his grip on Kelly's fingers turned almost painful. "You never said that, Doc."

Kelly blinked. "I didn't?"

"You couldn't say anything. You tried."

Kelly waited a beat, brow furrowed. "I always thought I got it out because . . . you held on to me the whole time." He glanced up as they neared the ambulance. When he looked back down, Nick's eyes were on him, that same smitten, indulgent gaze Kelly had grown accustomed to over the past year. His hand tightened in Nick's. "I thought I said it. You never let go of me."

"I couldn't," Nick gasped. Kelly didn't know if he was in pain or if the memory of Kelly's near-death experience in New Orleans was overwhelming him. "I couldn't let go of you, Kels."

Kelly struggled to swallow, nodding and holding back the urge to cry. He squeezed Nick's hand harder. "Neither will I."

He had to, though, to let the EMTs load Nick into the ambulance. Kelly followed them to the hospital in the Range Rover, his mind tossing and turning over the events of the day.

Had they really just tracked down a centuries old treasure? Was it possible the Continental payroll was more than merely gold bars, that it was really a missing Masonic treasure trove? His mind was reeling with the possibilities, but all he really wanted was to get to Nick. He'd go over the implications of the past few days later, when he knew Nick was okay.

When he finally found Nick in the hospital, he was already sitting up and bitching because they'd cut his shirt off him.

"It had a bullet hole in it," the nurse argued.

"It was a graze!" Nick shouted.

She rolled her eyes as she left the room, nodding to Kelly when she passed.

"You're running out of spare clothes, babe," Kelly said with a relieved grin. If Nick could bitch about his clothes, he was doing just fine, despite his so-called "graze" actually being a through-and-through. They had an IV in him, probably with pain medication in there, and they were giving him a transfusion for the blood he'd lost.

"I want to go home," Nick grunted.

Kelly strolled into the room, nodding to placate him. "Soon. Get a little more blood in you first, huh?"

Nick didn't say anything. He reached out when Kelly got close, grabbed a handful of his hair, and pulled him into a ruthless kiss. He left Kelly panting when their lips parted, and Nick closed his eyes, sighing as if he'd been holding his breath until he could get Kelly into his hands.

Kelly took him by both shoulders and forced him to recline. "Faster you get this over with, faster we'll go home. Promise."

Nick nodded, his eyes staying closed.

Kelly sat on the edge of his bed, reading the medications labels, trying to just be a worried lover rather than a worried SARC for once. He leaned over Nick and pressed his forehead to Nick's, closing his eyes. He didn't know how long they stayed that way, but when a PA came in to check Nick's stitches and vitals, it was dark outside.

Despite the doctor's advice, Nick demanded that he be allowed to go home, claiming Kelly was perfectly capable of keeping an eye on him overnight. They had no choice but to let him check himself out, and Kelly knew Nick too well to argue against it.

Kelly helped him to his feet, and Nick hugged him close, pressing his face against Kelly's cheek. "Take me home," he whispered.

Kelly nodded jerkily. He wrapped his arm around Nick's waist, letting him rest some weight on him as he helped him over to the wheelchair.

Once Nick was in the passenger seat of the Range Rover, Kelly hopped behind the wheel. Nick was silent on the drive home, keeping his eyes shut as Kelly struggled with the GPS. He finally got it to work and headed for the route home, glancing at Nick worriedly.

"Hey," he said. He reached over the console and touched Nick's thigh. "You should be proud of yourself. You found a two-hundred-year-old missing treasure today."

Nick chuckled softly, the sound sending a chill up Kelly's spine. He opened his eyes and sighed. "No, I didn't."

"What are you talking about?" Kelly took his eyes off the road long enough to look at Nick. "You were faking it?"

"Yep." Nick closed his eyes and sighed again. "No idea where that treasure is. I know where it's not, though."

"Where?"

"It's not under that monument. Redcoats didn't dig that grave; they never stopped to bury the rebel dead. It's not there."

Kelly stared at him for so long he almost ran off the road. "Huh."

"What?"

"You had me going. I didn't know you could still fake something and fool me." Nick was staring at him again. "What?"

"I love you."

Kelly grinned lopsidedly, biting his lip and nodding. "Yeah, you do."

They were silent for most of the ride home. Nick actually dozed for a little while, until they got into the older part of the city where the streets were smaller and confusing and Kelly almost killed them by not realizing that a Boston turn signal was just a blaring horn rather than a blinking light.

He breathed a sigh of relief when he got them to the marina in one piece. "From now on, you do the driving."

Nick nodded. He was gripping the handle above his head so tight his knuckles were white. "Deal."

Kelly helped him ease out of the car. It was a long walk down the docks to the *Fiddler's Green*, and Kelly could have kissed the boat when he finally saw it. Nick was shucking his hospital gown and jeans before they'd even closed the doors to the salon behind them.

"Shower. Bed," Nick grunted.

He disappeared down the steps, and Kelly trailed along in his path, picking up the things he'd discarded. A badge here, a gun there. He was on his way to the steps when he noticed a card on the galley counter that certainly hadn't been there when he and JD had left the boat the day before.

He picked it up, frowning at the precise handwriting. "Detective O'Flaherty and Doc Abbott."

"What the fuck?" Kelly glanced around the yacht out of habit. He didn't feel anything out of place, didn't have that sense that someone was with him or that he was being watched. The envelope wasn't sealed, so Kelly pulled the card out and cocked his head at it. It was a simple sheet of creamy white stationery, and the only things written on it were an international phone number and the letter J.

"What are you doing?" Nick asked. He had poked his head above the railing and was scowling at Kelly.

Kelly held the letter up. "He wasn't kidding. He left us a 'get out of jail free' card."

Nick stared at the card with Julian's number on it, then nodded. "Save that shit for the next time Grady calls us," he drawled. "Come help me shower."

Kelly left the card on the table, along with Nick's badge and sidearm, and followed after him, stripping as he went.

Two hours later, they were curled together in bed, Nick's head resting on Kelly's chest and his arm wrapped around him as he snored. Kelly stared at the ceiling, frowning. They'd showered and Kelly had checked Nick's stitches. Nick had even taken a few of the painkillers the hospital had given him, which meant he thought everything was over.

Nothing felt over.

Nick's phone rang from beneath the pillow, where he apparently stuffed it all the time. It made the pillow vibrate. How that didn't set him straight off into a flashback every time it rang, Kelly didn't know.

Nick woke with a gasp and dug the phone out, answering it before he even had his eyes open. "O'Flaherty."

Kelly was so close to Nick's face that he could hear the voice on the other end. "JD's out of surgery, he's awake and he's remembering more and more," Hagan was saying. "He'll only talk to you, though."

"Okay," Nick said on a sigh. "Be right there."

He hung up, and they stared at each other for a few seconds, both of them silent, both of them frowning.

"I have to go," Nick finally mumbled. "Take his statement, wrap this up."

Kelly nodded, unsure of why this simple phone call, out of everything that had happened in the last few days, was the first thing to truly upset him. He tried not to let it show, but Nick could read him like book. He had been able to from the day they'd met.

Nick swallowed hard. "It's always going to be like this," he said slowly. "There's always going to be another case. Another call."

"I know. But you love everything about your job."

Nick bit his lip and dropped his eyes. His finger traced the pink scar on Kelly's chest, where a bullet meant for Nick's head had stopped just below Kelly's heart instead.

"It's not going to work," Nick finally said with a sigh.

The air left Kelly's lung so fast he had to gasp to reclaim it. His body tingled, and a shiver ran through him before he could manage a sad smile. He ran his fingers through Nick's hair. "Are you breaking up with me, babe? 'Cause that's what this feels like."

Nick quickly met his eyes. "I'm quitting," he declared. "I'll wrap up this case, then give them my resignation."

Kelly held his breath, his heart pounding out his relief like Morse code. He was uncertain of whether he wanted to encourage Nick to do it this time, or talk him out of it again. Then the melancholy feeling of that phone call settled into his chest, the same feeling he'd always suffered back in the day when he'd said good-bye to Nick on leave, the same hollow sense of something missing when he'd watched Nick escort a woman out of a bar, the same ache he woke up with when he was in bed alone in Colorado and knew Nick was so many miles away in Boston. The same feeling that had rushed through his body when he'd thought Nick might be choosing his badge over Kelly.

He didn't want to feel that every time Nick got a call and had to leave him behind.

He nodded, his entire body heavy with the decision. He'd talked Nick out of quitting before because he knew Nick loved his job, and he'd been curious to see if it would work, if *they* would work, with their lives continuing on the way they had been. They'd tried it, and it didn't work. It was the right decision this time, and Kelly could rest easy knowing Nick had chosen him over his former life and would have no regrets.

Nick kissed him. "Come with me."

Kelly grinned. "I'm going to be hearing that a lot in the next fifty years, aren't I?"

"I can guarantee it."

Nick took the wheel for their trip to the hospital. He trusted Kelly with his life in most situations, but driving in Boston was apparently not one of those situations because he would sooner fuck a rhinoceros than do that again. Even drugged up, he would get them to the hospital safer than Kelly would.

"So, I have an idea," Kelly announced on the way there. "Are you in an Abbott Idea kind of mood?"

"Well, I am drugged, so yeah, shoot."

Kelly chuckled. "Emma."

"Emma . . . Grady? Ty's cousin, Emma?"

"Yeah." Kelly was nodding. "She offered us both a job with her team, and as far as I know the offer still stands."

"You're talking about Emma *Grady*," Nick said again. "And the adventuring, treasure-hunting, monster-seeking, myth-believing crew of crazy people?"

"Yes."

"Okay?"

"They need a medic, a historian, and team leader. And if I'm not mistaken, we are a medic and a team leader. Plus, you're quite the fucking historian if I do say so myself. And I do."

"Kels, I'm not so sure about that shit," Nick said. "I mean . . ." He glanced at Kelly, who was sitting in the passenger seat watching him. Smiling. He was always smiling. Nick came to a stop at a red light and stared at Kelly, thinking about that smile.

"We said before that we didn't know what to do. Colorado or Boston? Cabin or boat?" Kelly said. He shrugged. "Why choose, though? If you're quitting, I can too."

"Kels, you love that camp. Those kids," Nick argued. Kelly had been orphaned at twelve, and while his experience in the foster system had been a good one, he had still devoted his post-military life to helping troubled kids—often orphaned or abandoned street kids who'd chosen the camp over juvenile hall—adjust and learn life skills. It had given Kelly purpose at a time when every member of Sidewinder had been drifting and listless.

"I could still volunteer here and there. We'll have down time, time to . . . Nicko, we can settle down when we're dead, babe," Kelly finally said. "I had fun this week. For the first time in years, this was really fucking fun. I want to do things like this with you, I want—"

"Okay," Nick whispered.

"What?"

"Okay," Nick said, his voice stronger. "We'll call her when we get home."

"Really?"

Nick smirked.

Kelly's smile burgeoned into a full-force beaming grin. He reached across the console and grabbed Nick's hand, kissing his palm. "Thank you."

Nick tried to repress an indulgent sigh, but he couldn't. He was so screwed. He'd give Kelly anything and everything.

They were both still grinning like idiots when they reached the hospital. Nick had to school his features into a more professional mask as they inquired into JD's room number and rode the elevator up.

When they found the room, Hagan was there, and so was Alex. She was sitting beside JD's bed, filling him in on the details he was still missing. They both looked up when Nick and Kelly entered.

"Hey," JD said with a tentative smile.

"How you feeling?" Nick asked him. He moved closer, giving Alex a nod in greeting.

"I'm okay," JD scooted up a little in the bed, wincing and holding to his side. "Alex says this isn't the first time I've been shot, so . . . hey, no big deal, right?"

Nick smiled and patted JD's arm, unable to quell the urge to continue trying to comfort the man. He noticed a stack of books on the table beside JD's bed. They were all his adventures, told by him.

"His story all checks out, O," Hagan offered. "He was taken from his hotel room in New York by a group that had been contracted by a company called Sanco Pharmaceuticals. Apparently it's not uncommon for these big companies to take unusual routes for miracle cures. First time one of them's ended in kidnapping and murder, though."

"Pharmaceutical companies after medieval scrolls," Kelly mused. "Sure, why not."

"I'm sorry I kicked you in your transplant scar," JD offered, looking at Nick with what could only be described as hope.

Nick cocked his head, frowning. "How'd you know it was there?"

"Saw it the night I was talking to your friend on the phone."

"Great. Thanks," Nick grunted. But he couldn't help but smile. JD—or Casey Hunt, he supposed he was going to have to start thinking of him as—was an interesting man. He was smart, quick-witted, capable, and observant. He'd handled the trauma he'd been subjected to better than most. Despite everything that had happened, Nick liked the guy.

"So, are you out of a job now?" Kelly asked.

"No, apparently I work out of a museum as a wandering acquisitions specialist," JD said with a laugh. "Alex was telling me about some of my seedier adventures. It seems I'm kind of a big deal. You should read my books. I know I'm going to have to."

Nick and Kelly both chuckled. Kelly waved a hand at Alex. "What about you? Are you a seedy adventurer too?"

"No," she said with a melancholy smile. "Not anymore, at least. I *am* out of a job. I worked full-time for Alco, hunting down new avenues of research. After all this, they don't want the scrutiny for why they have an archaeologist on staff."

"I'm sorry," Kelly offered.

Nick was scowling at Alex, though. She'd shown her true colors during the standoff at the Jason Russell house, shielding the museum guide with her body as she got the woman to safety. She'd shown Nick something, something he liked. He patted Kelly on the arm, and when Kelly turned, Nick jerked his head at Alex. It seemed to dawn on Kelly as well. His oddly colored eyes sparkled, and he grinned at Alex.

"Would you like to get a cup of coffee?" he asked her. "I have a proposition for you."

Alex gave him a wary sideways glance, but after examining the smiles on both their faces, she agreed and followed Kelly out of the room.

"What's that about?" JD asked.

"Kels has a thing for redheads," Nick quipped. "We're going to file these reports in the morning, work to start getting your name nice and clear, okay? You're going to have to answer for some things, including assaulting an officer of the law and discharging a firearm in a public area."

"I figured."

"Since I was the officer you assaulted, we can handle that one. National parks are federal territory, though."

JD blanched, but he nodded. "I'll . . . I'll take the punishment. I did it, I deserve it."

"I got a buddy with some favors owed him in the Bureau," Nick said. "I'll see what I can do for you."

"Yeah. Thanks, Nick."

Hagan cleared his throat loudly, shifting his weight from foot to foot.

JD chuckled. "And you, Alan. Thank you."

Nick gave Hagan a melancholy once-over. He would have to tell his partner that he was quitting for good this time. It wasn't going to be a mental health break like last time. There wasn't going to be any coming back once he tendered his resignation, once he gave up his badge. His stomach turned at the thought. God, was he really ready to do that? He pushed it aside to worry about later, to talk to Kelly about it further, and turned back to JD.

"I know what you did," JD said with a smile.

"Oh yeah?" Nick asked. "What's that?"

"There's no treasure under that monument. Not in a grave dug by minutemen."

Nick laughed. "I guess you still have some work to do then if you want to find yourself a Golden and Rosy Cross. Huh?"

"I guess I do. You could have just put me in a cell, let me rot there," JD said quickly. "You didn't have to believe me. But you did.

You took me in. You trusted me. You saved my life. I can't thank all of you enough."

"Well, you can try," Hagan commented. They all laughed. "Next book you write."

"I'll try to remember that." JD tapped his temple and smirked.

"And hey, when you get out of here you can take us to dinner," Nick offered. "Drinks on you."

"That's the least I can do," JD agreed. He was smiling, though there was a hint of sadness to it. "And . . . Nick. You and the Doc don't work out . . ." He smiled almost shyly, pointing to himself. "My books claim I'm amazing in bed."

Nick laughed. He patted JD's arm again. "I wouldn't hold my breath for that if I was you. I'm going to go before Kelly does something I'll regret."

Nick said good-bye to JD, told Hagan he'd see him in the morning, and then left to find his wayward boyfriend. Kelly had probably already recruited Alex, called Emma, signed them up for a trip to Siberia, and gotten on his phone to buy subzero gear.

Nick smiled at the thought, but the smile rapidly turned into a worried scowl, and he quickened his pace. The probability that Kelly was already through half those steps was extremely high.

Well, either way, Nick knew he'd be going along for the ride.

Dear Reader,

Thank you for reading Abigail Roux's *Cross & Crown*!

We know your time is precious and you have many, many entertainment options, so it means a lot that you've chosen to spend your time reading. We really hope you enjoyed it.

We'd be honored if you'd consider posting a review—good or bad—on sites like **Amazon, Barnes & Noble, Kobo, Goodreads, Twitter, Facebook, Tumblr,** and your blog or website. We'd also be honored if you told your friends and family about this book. Word of mouth is a book's lifeblood!

For more information on upcoming releases, author interviews, blog tours, contests, giveaways, and more, please sign up for our weekly, spam-free newsletter and visit us around the web:

Newsletter: tinyurl.com/RiptideSignup
Twitter: twitter.com/RiptideBooks
Facebook: facebook.com/RiptidePublishing
Goodreads: tinyurl.com/RiptideOnGoodreads
Tumblr: riptidepublishing.tumblr.com

Thank you so much for Reading the Rainbow!

RiptidePublishing.com

ALSO BY
ABIGAIL ROUX

ABOUT THE AUTHOR

Abigail Roux was born and raised in North Carolina. A past volleyball star who specializes in sarcasm and painful historical accuracy, she currently spends her time coaching high school volleyball and investigating the mysteries of single motherhood. Any spare time is spent living and dying with every Atlanta Braves and Carolina Panthers game of the year. Abigail has a daughter, Little Roux, who is the light of her life, a boxer, four rescued cats who play an ongoing live-action variation of *Call of Duty* throughout the house, one evil Ragdoll, a certifiable extended family down the road, and a cast of thousands in her head.

To learn more about Abigail, please visit abigailroux.com.

Enjoyed this book? Visit RiptidePublishing.com to find more romantic suspense!

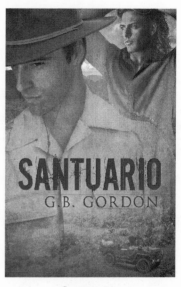

Catch a Ghost
ISBN: 978-1-62649-039-0

Santuario
ISBN: 978-1-937551-65-0

Earn Bonus Bucks!

Earn 1 Bonus Buck for each dollar you spend. Find out how at RiptidePublishing.com/news/bonus-bucks.

Win Free Ebooks for a Year!

Pre-order coming soon titles directly through our site and you'll receive one entry into a drawing to win free books for a year! Get the details at RiptidePublishing.com/contests.

RIPTIDE
PUBLISHING